SMOKY ESCAPE

KNOXVILLE FBI - BOOK THREE

LIZ BRADFORD

Stand on the Rock Publishing LLC

Lizbradfordwrites@gmail.com

Lizbradfordwrites.com

Print ISBN: 978-1-960692-00-9

Cover Design by Alyssa at Alyssa Carlin Designs http://www.alyssacarlindesign.com/

Comprehensive Edit by Teresa Crupmton at AuthorSpark, Inc. authorspark.org

Copy Edit by Sharyn Kopf https://sharynkopf.wordpress.com/

Letter to the Reader

Dear Reader,

I imagine you're as excited about reading this story as I was about writing it. If you've read the first two books in this series (and if you haven't, stop what you're doing and read those first as this is a continuing story), I bet you already love Gio and Morgan. And oh, you are about to love them even more.

However, I must warn you, the content in this book is not easy. You already know much of what Morgan's life looks like, and it doesn't get easier in the first half of this book. I have done my best to handle the realities of the trafficking world with care and as tastefully as possible, but it is, frankly, downright ugly.

Still, I am making a *huge* promise to you: stick with me through this story, feel free to skip areas that are too heavy, but read to the end. It's well worth it. Morgan will learn what true love—God's love—looks like by the end of the book, and you do *not* want to miss it!

My prayer for you, dear reader, is that as you read this book, you "may have strength to comprehend with all the saints what is the breadth and length and height and depth, and to know the love of Christ that surpasses knowledge, that you may be filled with all the fullness of God" (Romans 3:18-19).

Christ loves you so much He gave His life for you. He thinks you are worth dying for. And if you believe in your heart and confess with your mouth that Christ is Lord, you will be saved. If you don't know the saving power of Jesus, please reach out. Let's talk. You can visit my website at lizbradfordwrites.com/hope to find out more.

I truly hope you enjoy this story. I know I love it!

Happy reading!

Blessings,
Liz

To the one who needs to hear God loves you.
You are worth dying for.

Isaiah 43:1-3 (ESV)

...Fear not, for I have redeemed you;
I have called you by name, you are mine.
When you pass through the waters, I will be with you;
and through the rivers, they shall not overwhelm you;
when you walk through fire you shall not be burned,
and the flame shall not consume you.
For I am the Lord your God,
the Holy One of Israel, your Savior...

Romans 12:19 (ESV)

Beloved, never avenge yourselves, but leave it to the wrath of God, for it is written, "Vengeance is mine, I will repay, says the Lord."

1 Corinthians 13:4, 7-8a

Love is patient, love is kind ... it always protects, always trusts, always hopes, always perseveres. Love never fails.

Chapter One

HOMEMADE CHOCOLATE MUFFIN IN one hand and travel mug full of black coffee in the other, Gio Crespi left the Jacobs' farmhouse kitchen and headed to the living room where he'd left his keys and wallet on the piano. He wasn't ready to leave. He wanted to see Morgan again this morning, but it wasn't his place to stick around. He needed to get back to the office and question the suspect they had in custody. After a shower.

Once Morgan and Jacq had finally gone upstairs last night, Gio and his best friend, Dylan, had crashed on the downstairs couches. He didn't exactly smell like Irish Spring. It's a good thing that, despite being totally exhausted, his mind had woken him up as if his alarm had gone off, right at six-thirty.

Gio set the travel mug on the piano bench, snatched his wallet and shoved it into his back pocket. He frowned. Something was missing. His keys. Had he left them in the car like a dork? After last night's events it was possible, although unlikely.

"Bad word." Gripping the muffin gingerly with his teeth, he crouched and hunted for his keys on the floor.

From the couch, Dylan grunted. "You might as well just swear. You sound ridiculous saying *bad word* every time anyone else would drop a darn or such."

Gio sat back on his heels and removed the muffin from his mouth. "Shut up."

Dylan rolled onto his side. "And what *are* you doing?"

"My keys vanished. I'm sure I put them here with my wallet last night."

Dylan swung his feet to the floor and sat up. "They couldn't have gone far. They have teeth not legs. Maybe they ate their way behind the piano."

Gio rounded the side of the upright. No keys.

"Bupkis?"

Gio nodded and stood. "I guess I'll check the car."

"It's not like you to leave your keys in the car."

"Nope, that's your job."

Dylan grunted.

Gio grabbed his coffee and strode outside. This didn't make sense. He distinctly remembered clicking the key fob to lock the SUV as he and Morgan walked up the path last night.

He quickly descended the front steps and rounded the corner.

He expected to see his blue Kia Sorento right there beside Dylan's Dodge Charger. But it wasn't.

His stomach dropped. Where on earth had his car gone?

Had Dylan pulled some stupid prank? No, he hadn't had time for that. Plus, he was so focused on proposing to Jacq last night.

Spinning around, Gio made for the front door. The sinking feeling worsened, as possibilities of where his car was ran through his mind. He went inside.

Jacq stood in the hallway at the opposite end of the front entryway, her face pale and brow pulled taut.

In unison, they both asked, "What's wrong?"

Gio shook his head. "You first. I have a sneaky suspicion it's connected."

"Morgan is gone."

His stomach found the bottom of the pit it had been plummeting to. "And I know how."

Jacq tilted her head.

"My car is gone."

Jacq stepped backward as if the words had hit her like a giant gust of wind.

Gio stood there unable to move.

Dylan came into the room. "Gone?"

Gio and Jacq both nodded.

"But why?" Dylan opened his arm to Jacq. She slid under it and snuggled against his chest.

Gio thought he'd be ill. Why would Morgan leave? They could keep her safe. If her trafficker found out how she'd helped the FBI yesterday, there was a good chance he'd kill her. Jacq, her friend who'd been searching for her for years, was here giving Morgan all the support she could need. Why run?

God, what is going on? What do we do? Protect Morgan. "Whatever the reason," Gio said, "we need to find her and my car."

"LoJack?"

"Of course not."

"How many times have I—"

Gio put up a hand to stop his friend. "Don't start. I'm going to call the local LEOs and put in a BOLO."

Jacq gripped Gio's arm. "For Morgan?"

"Only my car. If the car is spotted, I'll request notification and label 'do not engage.' I don't want her to think she's in trouble."

Dylan let out a slow breath. "But she stole your car."

Gio said, "We're assuming a lot. Did anyone check the barn? What if she went for a walk or something?"

"Then where'd your car go?" Jacq's voice was tighter than a fully stretched rubber band.

Gio looked past Jacq and Dylan.

Bonnie Jacobs, their host, stood in the doorway, where Jacq had been a few moments ago. Her arms hugged her plump body. "Something is wrong."

Gio asked, "Have you seen Morgan this morning?"

She shook her head. "Oh dear. I heard someone up around four, but I assumed it was nothing more than a trip to the restroom. Did she leave?"

Gio half-shrugged and told her about his car.

"Well, let's look for her to be sure." Bonnie took charge like any mother of five children would and sent them all off in different directions.

As Gio walked toward the barn, he called Gabe, Bonnie's son and a Knoxville police officer. Gabe took charge of getting the BOLO out on Gio's car.

Morgan was not in the barn. Or in the house. Or anywhere they looked on the property.

Dylan slapped Gio on the back when they met up at the house. "Let's go to the office. Something will come up with the BOLO."

Gio spotted Jacq on the porch, saying goodbye to her three-year-old daughter. "How's Jacq?"

Dylan raised his eyebrows. "Glad that Bonnie offered to keep Harper today."

"Is Harper going to be all right with Jacq working after yesterday? The kid needs time to recover from being held hostage."

"Jacq was pretty torn about leaving Harper. She wanted to bring her, but Aliza's kids are coming over, and Harper is super excited to play with them. I told Jacq she could stay back and we'd keep her in the loop, but with Harper safe and happy, there was no convincing Jacq to not look for Morgan."

Gio let out a dry chuckle. It'd been a stupid question. Of course they had it figured out. Still, Gio knew Harper needed her mom. Heck, he'd been on the outside, part of the rescue, and he could use his mom right now too.

He glanced at his watch. She was probably still in bed. He'd have to call later.

"Let's get to the office." Dylan walked toward his car.

Gio followed, but his mind wandered in the other direction. What if they couldn't find Morgan? What if her trafficker found her first? What if she really was past saving from the trafficking life? He'd seen it before. The normal world can be too much for someone who has experienced so much trauma at another's hands.

Morgan leaned her head on Gio's steering wheel. She couldn't believe she'd stolen his car. But she hadn't had a choice, had she? She'd tried to sleep last night, but all she could see was Lily's face. Despite all the times she'd been jealous of her "wife-in-law," as Ronan sometimes referred to them, she still felt the need to watch out for the twenty-year-old girl.

Lily had been in Ronan's grip since she was eighteen. He'd wooed her, then worked her, even when she still lived at home on the other side of Knoxville. When Ronan convinced Lily to move in with him, she didn't know Rose and Morgan, or Daisy as Ronan had renamed her, already lived with him. Morgan had been drawn to Lily like a sister. Really, she felt that way about all the girls who lived in their house now, except maybe Celeste.

Celeste was one of the reasons Morgan was concerned about Lily. Celeste could be a bully. Probably because she was trying to find her place among Ronan's girls after her guy got himself arrested. But regardless, Morgan didn't like her.

She lifted her head and glanced over to her car, parked exactly where she'd left it last night when she helped save Jacqui from that lunatic.

Taking in a deep breath, she tried to draw in the courage she needed to step back into her "normal" life. She didn't want to do this, but if she didn't go home, the other girls, especially Lily, would suffer. She didn't want to make Ronan mad. This was her lot, and she had to suck it up and deal with it.

Her breath shook as she released it. Fingering the cash she'd stolen from Gio's wallet, she counted it. It was enough, barely, to keep her from getting a beating. She'd spent the last couple hours since she left the Jacobs' farm rehearsing the lines. Duke would owe her. Hopefully, he'd keep his word about covering for her. Before she'd found so much money in Gio's wallet, she had planned on calling Duke and asking for cash.

Why did an FBI agent have so much cash? In small denominations too. Maybe Gio wasn't as clean cut as he looked. Did he frequent strip clubs or something? She didn't want to know.

Yes, she did. Something about the man drew her in. She couldn't explain it, but the force between them was like the hottest electromagnet you could imagine. But he'd never want anything to do with her. And if he did go to strip clubs, she didn't want anything to do with him.

She scrounged around in his console and found an envelope and pen. Maybe she should write them a note.

Jacqui and Gio,

She scratched it out.

Gio, sorry I stole your car and money. I'm glad you found your car, but I needed the money. I have things I need to take care of. I can't explain it.

Jacqui, I'm sorry. I love you, friend. Don't look for me anymore. I'll find you again one day.

Morgan put the pen back where she found it, swiped her eyes with the heel of her hand, and propped the envelope between the steering wheel and the dashboard. After turning off the engine, she tucked the keys under the mat near the pedals, hoping Gio would find them there.

She slid out of the SUV and got into her own little coupe; well, not really hers. But whatever. She shook her head. At least the police had left it, and it didn't seem Ronan had found it.

After grabbing her keys from inside the console, she found her phone in her purse. She had three missed calls. One from the agency that connected the girls with tricks, one from Duke, and one from Lily. But no voicemails.

Lily didn't answer a call back.

But Duke did. "Daisy."

"You called?"

"Are you all right?"

"Well, yeah. I'm fine."

He cleared his throat. "I've heard a lot of crazy things went down last night. And apparently we had a delightful evening together."

How did he know she'd used him as an alibi?

He chuckled. "Don't worry. Ronan is none the wiser. I don't know what you think you were doing, but he won't suspect you had anything to do with Ezra's arrest."

Ezra? Ronan would be furious. Ezra worked under Ronan, and she wasn't sure how all of it got started, but some of the girls in the house belonged to Ezra. Still, Ronan took a large cut from them.

"Not that I'm suggesting you did. Nor am I going to ask."

"Really? You don't want to know why you're covering for me?"

"Nope. Because I want you to know ... I was going to wait, but ... I want you to leave Ronan."

Her mouth went dry. She waited for him to say more. He'd made it clear she shouldn't question him.

"I can give you a better life."

There it was. Did he want her to be his personal sex slave? Or was he just another pimp? She'd been around long enough to not fall for the "I love you" line.

"Daisy?"

"I'm not sure what to say."

"Don't say anything at all, but as soon as you're ready, say the word, and Ronan will be a blot in your past."

"May I ask what you said to Ronan?"

"That you couldn't talk, and if he questioned me again he'd have hell to pay. That was around nine last night. Didn't hear from him again, so you should have the freedom to cover your tail in any way necessary. Unless you don't want to go back to him now."

She pondered his offer. But why? Why would she go with Duke if she wouldn't even stay with Jacqui? Lily. She needed to get home.

"Thank you, Duke. But I have to go."

"That's fine. Even if you aren't ready to stay with me, I'd like to see you on Tuesday. At the hotel."

"Yes, sir." They said goodbye and hung up.

Morgan's gut twisted into an unrecognizable mess. She started the car and drove. Three choices. Jacqui? Duke? Ronan. She wished it really was a choice.

She drove toward Ronan.

At the FBI field office, Gio, with a quiet Dylan and Jacq beside him, pressed the elevator button. Seven a.m., and already this day was not turning out as planned.

Matt Olsen, one of their teammates, came up behind them. "What on earth? How do you get your car stolen?"

Gio turned and shrugged.

Matt was in his running shorts and shoes with two water bottles strapped to his hips. Based on the sweat glistening from his forehead, he needed a shower as badly as Gio.

"It's not like—"

Matt slapped his back. "Whatever. Just giving you a hard time. I'm here to help."

When the doors slid open, Jacq and Dylan entered the elevator, followed by Matt. As Gio stepped forward, his phone rang. He stopped. Was it something about Morgan?

Dylan reached out and held back the elevator door.

He answered. "Agent Crespi."

"Gabe here. I found your SUV." Gabe gave Gio the address, and they hung up.

Gio was equal parts relieved and frustrated. Gabe hadn't mentioned Morgan. Where was she if she wasn't with his car?

Dylan offered to take Gio.

"Please." He met Jacq's eyes. "I know you want to look for Morgan. But can you get Ezra up to an interrogation room? I think he may know something."

Jacq nodded. "But we can't let him know about Morgan."

"Agreed." There was too great a chance anything they said about her could get back to her pimp.

Matt nodded. "We'll take care of it."

"Thank you."

The elevator doors closed, and Gio and Dylan headed for the parking lot.

As they got in Dylan's car, he asked, "How do you want to handle this? Are we going to a crime scene?"

"No. I don't care that she took my car, especially since it was found so quickly."

"All right." Dylan turned on the car and drove across town.

When the GPS told them to turn down a familiar road, Gio's lungs tightened. Of course. "She went back to her car. We never pursued how she'd arrived at the bar and grill last night."

Dylan hit the steering wheel with the palm of his hand. "Why didn't we come here first?"

Gabe's squad car sat in the parking lot of a dentist's office next door to the bar and grill, where Scar had tried to kill Jacq less than twenty-four hours ago.

Gio asked, "You okay? And don't pull a Jacq and say 'if by okay …'"

Dylan let out a terse chuckle but didn't answer the question. Silently, he pulled up next to Gabe and got out.

Gio exited the car and strolled past Gabe to his SUV. He reached for the handle.

"Gio, did you want it dusted?"

Letting his hand hover over the handle, he glanced at Gabe and Dylan. "I don't see why."

Dylan stuffed his hands in his pockets. "We might be able to tag her in the system, so we get a call if she turns up somewhere."

Dylan had a point, but fingerprint dust would be a bear to get out of the light gray upholstery. "I'm not pressing charges, so there's no reason. Last thing she needs is to get associated with what went down over there last night." Gio gestured toward the abandoned restaurant.

With a shrug, Dylan turned and shuffled around the parking lot as if searching for clues.

Gio opened the door, and a piece of paper floated down from the steering wheel. He retrieved it and read. "Money?" What money did she steal?

No.

He pulled his wallet out of his pocket. In the search for his keys he hadn't even realized how thin it felt. Zero cash remained. Zero of the thousand dollars he'd saved up over the last six months. Zero.

He deflated like a balloon beaten by a crazy child. He'd have to contact the lady from marketplace and tell her he wouldn't be able to buy the bedroom set after all. Seemed as if all his plans for today had taken a flying nosedive off a cliff.

After balancing himself, he read the remainder of the note, even the part addressed to Jacq. *Don't look for me.*

This was going to stomp on Jacq's already injured heart. His didn't feel much better, and his skin was barely in the game. Then why did it hurt so much? But wasn't Morgan the very woman who had been on his heart for so many years?

"You don't look so good." Dylan appeared beside him.

Gio half-sat against the driver's seat and handed Dylan the note.

Dylan's eyes closed as he reached the end. "Think I can get away without showing this to Jacq?"

"Not if you value your future marriage. And I'm pretty certain Jacq's not going to acquiesce to Morgan's request."

"Are you?"

"Nope. Then again, she didn't ask me to not look for her."

Dylan smiled and shook his head.

Gio turned and slid into the seat and banged his knees on the lowered steering wheel. Oh, how he would love to actually share his car with a woman, even if it meant whacking his knees every day.

"Did she leave your keys?"

"Good question." He checked the obvious places: the visor, cupholders, console. Nothing. He shifted to check beneath the seat and his foot hit a lump under the mat. "Found them."

Gabe walked over. "Do you need anything from me?"

"I don't ... actually, would you mind checking with the dentist and see if they have surveillance video they'd be willing to share without a warrant? It would help in our unofficial search for Morgan."

"Can do. I'll also see what I can pull up in my arrest history. She recognized me as having arrested her in the past, so I'll find what I can."

"Thank you," Dylan said. "Jacq will appreciate it."

Gabe said farewell and left.

Gio mumbled under his breath, "So will I."

"I heard that."

"Whatever. Let's get back to the office." Gio closed the door and started the engine.

The vehicle had a slight hint of Morgan's perfume. Deep inside, a painful twinge pinched at his very being. What was going on with him? Why did the mysterious woman from his dreams suddenly have a name and a tantalizing scent? Why was she gone?

Lord, please protect Morgan. Wherever she is headed, bring her back.

Chapter Two

MORGAN WAS LATE. SHE didn't mean to be, but hopefully it was close enough that Ronan wouldn't lose it. According to Duke, Ezra had been arrested. This could be bad.

She eased the front door open. The plan was to run upstairs and be out of her dress as fast as possible and look like she'd been home and Ronan had missed her.

Holding the knob, she shut the door quietly behind her.

"You're late." Ronan was sitting on the stairs. Had he been waiting for her?

"I'm sorry. I—"

"Shut up. I don't want your excuses." He stood but still hadn't looked at her, as if he was distracted. "Where's the money?"

She pulled Gio's money out of her purse. "Duke's going to pay me later, but you know he's good for it." Ignoring the pain in her heart, she handed the wad of cash to Ronan.

He grabbed her chin and jerked her head side to side. "What happened to you?"

She'd practiced how to answer this question. "A trick wanted to play cat and mouse. I tripped and hit my head on the counter. His EMT friend patched me up."

"What's he gonna want now?"

She took Ronan's hand. "No worries. We're all squared up. I'd have a little more money but paying him for his services took time."

"Fine." He pulled his hand away. "Go shower and meet me in my room."

Beneath a fake smile, she gritted her teeth. He wanted her to spend an entire night entertaining other men and still expected her to perform for him too. But she played the part. "Absolutely." Despite her effort to make her voice sound chipper, it fell flat.

She skittered past him and up the stairs. Trying not to think about anything, she took a shower. After donning a skimpy night gown, she strolled downstairs to Ronan's master suite. The door was closed, so she knocked.

He opened the door and fingered the strap of her negligée. He laughed. Sliding his hand to her upper arm, he gripped it and dragged her across the room toward the bed.

Iris, Ezra's bottom girl, lay in Ronan's bed, naked. She looked high and as if Ronan had been rough with her.

Ronan let go of Morgan's arm, strode across to Iris and slapped her. "Get out."

"More?"

"Out."

Iris got to her feet and staggered through the doorway.

Morgan couldn't catch the question. "What was she doing in here?"

To her surprise, Ronan answered. "Ezra got himself arrested. That makes his girls mine. Get over here."

She obeyed.

He pushed her down onto the bed and climbed on top of her. He kissed her neck. "Listen, Daisy. Things are going to change around here."

She played along and ran her hands down his bare chest.

"You aren't to trust anyone but me. There's someone out there spilling our secrets, and secrets are supposed to stay in the family."

She plastered on a smile, hoping he wouldn't see the fear in her eyes. At least he didn't seem to know *she* was the one playing out of pocket.

He took her hands and pinned her arms above her head. "I need to know my girls are behaving themselves, so we're going to stick a little tighter now."

He released her arms and snatched something off the nightstand. A strip of rubber tubing.

"Of course, Ronan. You can trust me." She tried to wiggle free.

He gripped her left arm. "I sure hope so. But this will help." He tied the tube around her upper arm.

She tried to pull away. "No, Ronan, please."

He restrained her arm beneath his knee. "It has to be this way."

She'd done heroin before and managed to get clean. She never wanted to do it again. She had to fight. With her free hand, she pushed him.

He slapped her and gripped her hand. Stuffing it under himself, he sat firmly on her hips pinning her arm between their pelvic bones.

Pain shot through her arm.

He grabbed a bottle and syringe. Plunging the needle in he pulled the clear liquid into the syringe.

She tried to move, but his weight was too much for her to fight. "Ronan, please no."

He ignored her.

"No, please. At least not that much. Please." Her eyes blurred, but she couldn't even wipe the tears away.

After a prick to her skin, the cool liquid mixed with her blood. In the time she blinked, the drug took effect.

Ronan leaned close to her ear and snapped the tubing free from her arm. "You are mine, Daisy. Don't forget that." He got off of her and left the room.

She fought the euphoric feeling the drug caused in her brain and tried to cling to the pain of the slap, the squished arm, the heartache of leaving Jacq and the others.

"I'm sorry."

Gio. Jacqui. God.

Gio strode down the third-floor hallway of the FBI field office toward the interrogation room, his heart growing heavier by the moment. His stream of prayers for Morgan hadn't let up in the last twenty minutes. Where was she? Was she okay? He was pretty sure she wasn't, but he couldn't explain why.

He opened the door to the interrogation room and entered a space surrounded by gray walls; the one to the left held a two-way mirror. Matt stood in the corner with his arms crossed, still in his running attire, having ditched the water bottle fanny pack.

Ezra Wayman, a young man around his mid-twenties, sat on the far side of the small metal table. He didn't look up as Gio took the chair across from him.

"I'm Agent Crespi, and I'd like to ask you a few questions about your involvement in last night's events and other such things."

Ezra said nothing.

"You've been read your rights, and you understand them, correct?"

Ezra gave the tiniest nod.

"Why don't we start with last night. How did Tim or Trent, however you knew him, talk you into helping hold that family hostage?"

He shrugged one shoulder.

"Come on, man, you need to talk to me. You do know that little girl was my fellow agent's daughter, right? A feisty agent at that. Would you rather I have her come in here and talk to you?"

Ezra finally looked at Gio.

His eyes were the same shade of brown as his brother's. Gio broke eye contact and pulled his pen and notepad out of his pocket. "Ed—I mean, Ezra. Is that your given name?" Heat flashed through him. How could he have almost used his brother's name for this lowlife?

"Doesn't matter."

Gio met his eyes again. Maybe he needed to use a different tactic and treat Ezra like a victim rather than a hardened criminal. "It does. Tell me who you are. You helped us last night by telling us the name of the bar and grill."

"My mom gave me the name, so that must be it." Ezra seemed to relax a touch.

"How do you know Trent?"

"We work together."

"You work at the law firm?"

Ezra's eyes widened.

Gio watched him carefully. "Oh, you mean his other job." A fellow trafficker. His muscles tensed.

Ezra glanced away and shifted in his seat. When he met Gio's gaze again, his expression held a touch of resolution. He leaned forward. "Look, I'd love to tell you all about everything, but that won't save my skin. I tell you what you want to know, I'm a dead man. So I don't really have a choice but to keep my mouth shut." He sat back again.

Gio studied the young man. "I can appreciate that." It had been so hard for his brother to speak up against the people who'd had a vise grip on his life. "But when you let people hold that kind of fear over your life, if they aren't hurting you, they're hurting someone else. You want to live with that?"

"I live my own life."

"Do you? I can't figure it out, Ezra." Gio leaned back. "Are you a trafficker or are you being trafficked?"

"Who says I'm not both?" His words hung with the weight of a thousand boulders.

Bingo. "How many girls do you have? Or do you prefer boys?" Bile rose in his throat at the question.

Ezra sat up straight and glared at Gio. "If I tell you, confess to all my sins, does that mean you lock me up? Out of his reach?"

"Whose reach?" Was Ezra under the grasp of the same man Morgan was?

Ezra shook his head.

"If we take that snake down, he can't strike you."

"Cause sharing a cell with him would protect me. Look, I got brought into the game when I was only a kid. I know how this goes. Those guys never go down for their crimes. Lock me up for mine and live in peace with the fact I can't turn into the same kind of monster he is."

Gio searched his memory. What names had they heard over the last couple of months that could be connected to Ezra? Morgan had mentioned Ezra's name and Trent's. There was another name. Her trafficker. Ronan.

Gio's blood ran hot. "Does the name Ronan mean anything to you?"

A muscle in Ezra's face twitched, but that was it.

Clenching and unclenching his hands, Gio leaned forward. "Who's in charge? Who trafficked you?"

Ezra pressed his lips together as if to keep his face emotionless.

"Come on, Ezra." Gio's blood pounded through his veins like a locomotive through a mountain tunnel. "Tell me. Who is Ronan?"

"I don't know who that is." Ezra's voice cracked.

He knew. Rising slightly from his chair, Gio leaned heavily on the table, close to Ezra's face. "Who do you hand your money to?"

His lips were now clamped shut. He shook his head.

"Give me his name and address, and I'll go take care of him. Once and for all."

The door behind Gio swung open. "Crespi." Warren, their team's agent-in-charge, stepped to the side of the door. "Out."

Gio looked back at Ezra, hoping to see any indication he wanted to tell him the truth.

Unflinching, the man stared back at him.

Gio stalked past Warren and left the interrogation room. Rage boiled beneath the surface. He needed to find out who Ronan was and who had forced Ezra to become what he was now, but Gio couldn't do that from the hallway. He spun toward Warren.

"You're done in there. What's got you so hot about this? We know what he's guilty of. We need to process him and pass it off to the DA."

"There are bigger—"

"And we can catch 'em and fry 'em later. Right now we have to clean up our own house. One of our own was consorting with these scumbags. That entire team needs to be interviewed ..." Warren's sentence continued, but Gio didn't hear it.

What if Ezra was the key to finding Morgan?

"Crespi."

"Sir, at least let me take him back to lock-up."

"No. You just laid out a threat. You aren't going anywhere near anyone who will wind up putting you in jail. Go to your desk and—wait, better yet, convince Harris and Sheppard to go home. She shouldn't be here today."

Warren went into the interrogation room, leaving Gio alone in the hall.

The door both literally and figuratively closed in his face. What was he supposed to do now? Convincing Jacq to leave with no more information was going to be an impossible task.

Jacq picked up a throw pillow off her couch and eased down to the squishy cushions. Ever since Morgan had disappeared this morning, Jacq had been trying to ignore the pain from all her injuries, but five hours was the longest she could possibly ignore them. How was it still Friday morning?

So much and so little had happened. They had no idea where Morgan ran off to. Did she go back to her trafficker, or did she run completely?

"Water or milk?" Gio asked from the kitchen, where he and Dylan poked around trying to find something to eat.

"Water would be marvelous."

Gio filled a glass and handed it to Dylan, who brought it over with a bottle of pills.

"You read my mind." She reached out and took Dylan's offerings.

"You should eat something too."

Gio said, "Pancakes?"

Jacq swallowed two ibuprofen. "My soul would appreciate the carbs. You cooking?"

"Only if you have everything I need."

"The just-add-water protein pancake mix is in the cupboard to the left of the microwave."

"Got it."

Dylan settled on the couch next to Jacq. "Think your hand will be healed enough to sign the papers on the house in a month and a half?"

She studied her right hand, wrapped and splinted from the boxer's fracture she'd gotten by hitting the window of the freezer she'd been locked in. "With Morgan missing, how—"

"Jacq, she's the whole reason you're pursuing the home for freed women."

"I know, but—"

"Nope. None of that." He took her hand and fingered the engagement ring with a princess-cut diamond flanked by two rubies.

"I can't even think about wedding plans right now," she said. "I just want to be married."

"I'm fine with eloping."

She looked away from him and stared at nothing.

"But I'm also fine with waiting. Let's find Morgan and then get married."

"I'm so confused about what I want."

"So not too much has changed since yesterday."

She pulled her hand away and swatted his chest.

He laughed.

It was contagious, so she giggled too, but her rib protested. She moaned. "Bad idea. No laughing."

Dylan slid his arm along the back of the couch. "Take it easy."

"That ranks up there with the stupidest things you've ever said." She shifted closer to him and snuggled against his side.

"We'll find her." The confidence in Dylan's voice soothed her soul, but she didn't feel the same.

"I've been telling myself that for thirteen years."

"Yeah, but you didn't have that guy helping."

Jacq looked over at Gio. The man was a force to be reckoned with. She'd been on the other side of the two-way mirror when he'd interviewed Ezra. The veins in his entire body had seemed to bulge. "Why is he so invested? Because of the dreams? Or is there something else?"

"That's his story to tell."

"So more."

Dylan nodded.

She laid her head on his shoulder and let her mind wander. Because she was confident Harper was safe, well cared for, and would be dropped off in about an hour, the next natural thought was of Morgan. Why had she left? Jacq's entire being hurt with the heartache. They'd had such a wonderful time reconnecting yesterday evening. Had Jacq missed something because of her own excitement? What could possibly have lured Morgan away?

Jacq's phone buzzed with a new text message. She retrieved her phone from the coffee table and opened the messaging app.

Nate Zalman.

Her heart dropped into the basement of the apartment building.

Dylan looked over her shoulder. "Who's that?"

"Morgan's brother."

Gio lifted his head.

Jacq stared at her phone. "I haven't heard from him in years."

Gio asked, "What's the message say?"

She read it aloud. "*I know it's been a long time since we've been in contact, but I wanted to see how you are. This is still Jacq Schumer-Sheppard's phone, right?*"

She dropped the device to her lap. "What do I tell him? 'I saw your long-lost sister, but she ran off again'? I can't tell him that."

Gio gripped the towel in his hands. "I know nothing about this guy, but if you've stayed in contact, it might be worth telling the truth. Is he a believer?"

Jacq nodded.

"Morgan could use all the prayer support she could get." Gio was wringing the towel like it was a chicken's neck.

Dylan said, "That towel's gonna need prayers too."

Gio tossed it at him.

Jacq ignored the guys and picked up her phone. "I was so excited to message Nate and tell him I found her. I didn't do it last night because I didn't think there was a rush, and I didn't know if she'd be ready for them to know, but now ..."

She texted Nate back. *This is still Jacq. I actually have news and was going to text you, but it's not as good news as I'd hoped. Can we talk on the phone sometime soon?*

Now works.

God was going to have to give her the words because she was at a loss, but Nate deserved to be told.

"I'm going to my room to call him. Let me know when the food is ready."

"Guess I shouldn't burn it then." Gio rushed back to the kitchen.

Jacq slowly stood and left the room. She sat on the edge of her bed and prayed for strength before dialing Nate's number.

He answered, and they exchanged "hellos."

"It's been too long," she said.

"I heard about your husband. I'm sorry."

"Has it really been over four years since we talked?" Jacq couldn't believe it. Almost four years since she lost her husband in the apartment fire that almost claimed her life and left her with scars on her back. "I was pregnant when Sean died. I have a daughter."

"Congratulations."

She told him about Dylan and their engagement.

Nate updated her about his wife and kids, then said, "Jacq, you didn't want to talk on the phone just to catch up. What's going on?"

Nate had mostly given up hope of ever finding Morgan alive years ago, so she wasn't sure how he'd take the news. "Morgan's here in Knoxville. At least she was last night."

Nate was quiet for a moment. "Are you sure it was her?"

"One hundred percent." Jacq told him the short version of how Morgan had been helping them, and how she saved Jacq's life.

She went on to tell him how Morgan left that morning.

"You'll find her again." His voice held more confidence than she'd heard from him in thirteen years.

"I hope you're right."

Chapter Three

GIO CAME BACK TO his desk after a briefing Monday afternoon. Sabrina Fritz had been chosen to fill the hole left by Lawrence Levelle. It would be strange not having Sabrina on their team, but she had worked hard for a supervisory position for many years, and Gio had no doubt she would make an excellent special agent-in-charge.

He began sketching on a pad of scratch paper next to the paperwork he was supposed to be working on. Morgan's profile took shape. He'd had another dream last night, and he didn't dare tell Jacq about it. It wasn't good and woke him up and left him unable to go back to sleep at four in the morning.

In the dream, Morgan had been running but not moving. Attacked by drugs and men. Hurting and scared.

It had been brief, but it didn't need to be long to leave him praying down heaven for her.

"You aren't focused." Warren came up behind him.

"No. Sorry, sir."

His boss propped his hip up against Gio's desk and pointed at the sketch.

Gio handed it to him.

"Who is she?"

The team had talked about letting Warren the rest of the way in on the details of their informant. They decided he should know if he asked for more than what their generic reports had given. He'd just asked.

"Our informant."

"I thought y'all never saw her face."

"We did, finally."

Since no one other than their team was in the room, Gio told him how Morgan had been the one to not only give them all the leads that had led to multiple arrests and girls set free, but also the one who saved Jacq from Scar. Gio explained that Morgan had been Jacq's college roommate and was lost to trafficking thirteen years earlier. He left out that he'd been having dreams about her for the last six years.

"But you can't find her now?"

Gio answered, "Jacq, Dylan, and I spent all weekend turning over every cornerstone we could looking for her, but we've come up with zero. We don't know if she ran, went back to her trafficker, or something else."

Warren rapped his knuckles on Gio's desk. "Call the local PD and see if they have any prostitution stings set up, planned, etc. You could at least get her description in their hands. Make sure they know to contact us right away if they find her. But maybe we can join forces."

"I'll do that. I'll talk to TBI as well." The Tennessee Bureau of Investigations often had operations going to fight against human trafficking.

Warren returned to his office, and Gio picked up the phone, invigorated to have on-the-clock permission to move forward with finding Morgan.

Tuesday evening, the door of the upscale hotel room closed, and Morgan strolled to the bed. Duke would be there in about five minutes. She wished she could shake the high before he arrived, but it didn't work that way.

For the last five days, Ronan had given her a daily dose of heroin. He'd waited until late in the afternoon to give her today's dose, and by one o'clock she could feel her body craving the stupid drug. She hated it. No, hated wasn't a strong enough word.

Each time he had strapped the tube around her arm, he whispered how much he loved her and wanted to be sure she'd stay close. She wanted to believe him, but it was difficult when the needle was plunging into her vein.

She slumped to the edge of the bed. *God, it seems like You've listened to me recently. Are you listening now? Can You get me and the other girls out of this life? I had thought Ronan was a rescue, but I was so wrong. Please help me. Or did I turn down Your help when I ran away from Jacqui and her friends? Is it too late for me?*

A soft knock at the door turned her head.

She tossed her purse on the chair in the corner, and despite being sleepy, stood and took her "sexy" stance. "Come in."

The door opened, and Duke smiled at her.

Would Duke do anything for her like he'd alluded to? Or was he as bad as Ronan?

"Hey, beautiful." He shut the door and flipped the bolt locked. "Sorry I couldn't bring you out to the house, but I have a limited amount of time today."

"That's not a problem. What's your pleasure, sir?" She twirled her hair around her finger.

Duke's teeth disappeared as his smile dropped into a scowl. "Are you high?"

She tried to keep a plastered smile. She didn't know how Duke would react to the drugs. "Ronan says it makes me more fun." The lie to cover for Ronan left her nauseated. "Are you ready for some fun?"

He strode across the room and took her chin between his thumb and index finger. Gently, he raised her face until she looked him in the eyes. His other hand lifted her arm. He examined the crook of her elbow. "Heroin." He dropped her arm and met her gaze again.

She nodded.

"Your choice?"

She stared at him. Ronan would kill her if she made Duke mad in anyway, and she didn't know the right answer.

"He forced you?"

She still refused to answer.

He let go of her chin and whipped around and stalked away. "I need to know, Daisy. This could change everything."

Her insides quivered as if she was on speed. "I can't. If he—"

Duke raised his hand and spun back toward her. He considered her for a moment. "Ronan did this to you, didn't he? Don't answer. I must play this right."

He seemed to say that last sentence to himself.

Who was this guy?

He came to her and ran his fingers into her hair. "It'll be fine. I'll fix this, but I need you to trust me."

Warning bells clanged in half of her mind. The other half wondered if he was the answer to her prayer. Could Duke save her? Would he be willing to help the other girls too?

Wearing street clothes with his badge hanging from a ball chain around his neck, Gio crossed his arms and leaned back against the wall of the hotel room that had been set up as the command center of the TBI and KPD's joint task force sting operation. Gio's call to them yesterday had gotten the FBI officially involved too.

Tonight the goal was two-fold, pull girls out and bust men trying to buy sex. Several undercover officers were posing as prostitutes, and the men who offered them money were being arrested. Down another hall women were coming up to meet supposed clients, who were also undercover cops.

Gio, Dylan, and Aliza had come to assist in the arrests. They had asked Aliza to go undercover, but she declined, grateful to be given the choice. She said she would much rather be available to the women being arrested. Their hope was to help them find a way out, not simply throw them into a jail cell.

Aliza leaned up against the wall next to Gio. She elbowed him. "How are you doing?"

He shrugged.

"You seem really focused."

He kept his eyes fixed on the surveillance screen a few feet away. "Yet somehow you're trying to strike up a conversation." He glanced at her.

She covered her mouth with her fingertips.

He finally smiled and let out a deep breath. "I really hope we find her."

"I know. All of us do. But we won't if she left town completely."

"There's that."

"Crespi." A police officer at a computer across the room called to Gio. "A woman with dark hair is walking up the stairs. Fits your description."

Gio pushed off the wall and rushed to the computer. Watching and waiting for the door to open. Who would it reveal? Could it be Morgan?

He gripped the back of the officer's chair so hard Gio's forearms began to ache. And that ache traveled up to his jaw.

Aliza touched his arm. "Relax, or you won't have any teeth left the way you're gritting them."

He forced himself to visibly relax, though every fiber in his body remained coiled.

On the screen the stairwell door opened, and a woman in a tight blue dress entered the hallway. Her straight hair was as dark as Morgan's. Her height and weight seemed about right. But they couldn't see her face.

Look up.

She kept her head down.

"I'm going out there."

Aliza gripped his arm. "If she goes into the sting room, we'll get her."

"And if she doesn't, we've missed her."

"What goes in—"

He wrenched his arm free and dropped his badge inside his t-shirt. Before anyone could stop him, he left.

With fast, determined steps, he strode down the hallway and "accidentally" bumped into the woman. "Oh, I'm so sorry, miss."

She met his gaze. Her blue eyes were sad and scared.

Gio's heart plummeted.

"It was my fault. I am sorry." Her eastern European accent was thick.

"Are you okay, miss?"

She looked away. "I am fine." She headed straight to the designated door for their prostitution sting.

He shoved the door she'd come through open and stormed into the stairwell. If he had to knock on every hotel room door, he would ... until he found Morgan.

Chapter Four

MORGAN ROLLED OVER AND contemplated opening her eyes. Had she really fallen asleep? Where was she? Right. Hotel. Duke.

She bolted upright. Ronan would kill her for sleeping.

"Shh. It's all right." Duke's voice came from behind her.

She turned and found him sitting in a chair in only his boxers, a tiny bottle of liquor from the mini-bar in his hand. She pulled the sheet up around herself. "I'm sorry I fell asleep."

"Heroin can do that. How are you feeling?"

"Fine."

Duke pointed to a large wad of cash on the bedside table. "That should cover everything. Last Thursday too." His eyes narrowed. "Nope, I don't want to know."

"I was supposed to call Ronan when we were done."

"Doesn't look like we're done, does it?"

What did he want now? She faked a smile. "What else would you like?"

He shook his head. "Not like that. If you and I are still in the same room, Ronan can wait."

Her smile became more genuine.

"Daisy, are you ready to leave Ronan?"

Her heart rate skittered around trying to find the right pace. "He wouldn't like that very much."

Duke laughed. "One of these days, you'll realize you could have a better life." He took a swig of clear liquid. "I wanted to tell you I have to leave the country later this week and will be gone for probably about a month. You could come with me."

A knock at the door cut Duke short. His face grew dark. He spoke softer, "Does Ronan know what room you're in?"

She shrugged. She'd been so high when they arrived, she wasn't sure if he'd followed her up or not.

Duke strode to the door and peeked through the hole, then crossed the room and slid into his pants and shirt but didn't button the shirt.

The knocking turned to banging. "Open up."

Ronan.

Morgan moved to put her dress on.

Duke raised his hand, the index finger slightly straighter than the others. "No. Stay."

She froze.

Duke opened the door, and Ronan burst in. Crazy flamed from his eyes.

Morgan tugged the blanket up around herself, willing the bed to swallow her whole.

"What's going on in here?"

Duke straightened his back more, a feat Morgan didn't think possible. "Whatever I want to be going on in here."

"Daisy, get out of that stupid bed and get dressed. You have other clients waiting. Duke here has taken enough time."

"I will take all the time I want." Duke crossed the room, gathered Morgan's clothes, and handed them to her.

What kind of guy paid for sex and then helped the woman with her clothes? She slipped them on beneath the covers and it dawned on her. The kind of guy who didn't want *his* girl to be seen by another man. Maybe Duke wouldn't pimp her out if she left for him?

Ronan fumed. He did not like being talked back to no matter how deep Duke's pockets were.

She slid out of the bed and slipped her shoes on. That's when she noticed Ronan's clothes had a few red stains.

He must have followed her gaze. "A stupid ketchup bottle exploded on me."

She looked away. Why had Ronan answered an unasked question? That alone was suspicious.

"Hurry up!" Ronan was in one of his moods.

How badly Morgan wished she didn't have to leave with him.

Duke took a step closer to Ronan and towered over him. "She can move at whatever pace she needs." Duke pointed a finger right at Ronan's chest. "And if you know what's good for you, you will get her clean and stop dosing her up."

"You don't run this show. Daisy is mine." Ronan grabbed Duke's finger and twisted his arm.

Duke smashed his other hand against Ronan's throat and slammed him into the wall. "Don't touch me." Duke removed his arm and straightened Ronan's shirt. "I am not the kind of man you want to cross. Things will look up for you if you do as I say."

Morgan scooped up the cash and retrieved her purse from the floor, where it had fallen from the chair. Apprehensive to move anywhere near these men, she shuffled to the door.

Duke clutched her arm as she walked past, pulling her to his side. "I will call you when I get back." He let go and looked back at Ronan. "Treat her well, and you'll be rewarded."

Morgan stepped into the hallway. She hated Ronan babysitting her all over again. It had been years since he drove her around as if she couldn't be trusted. Not that he was wrong. She couldn't be.

If she had been certain Ronan didn't have his gun in his pants, she would have risked giving herself to Duke in order to get away from Ronan, but she didn't want any blood on her hands, especially her own. And if she had suggested not going with Ronan, it was fifty-fifty whether he'd shoot her or Duke.

He strode up beside her and gripped her arm, ushering her down the hall faster than her legs could quite manage. "I don't know what that freak thinks he's trying to pull. If—never mind."

She kept her mouth shut and tried to keep up.

Ronan pushed the stairwell door open. A man in a t-shirt and blue jeans was coming down the stairs. Cop. But not just any cop.

Gio. How mad was he that she'd stolen his car? And what was he doing in the hotel?

She stepped back and grabbed Ronan's arm. "Let's take the elevator."

"But—"

"But you want me ready for the next guy. Don't wear my feet out."

"Fine." He put his arm around her waist and led her back to the elevator.

She kept an eye on the little window to the stairwell. Gio walked past. She sighed and leaned into Ronan a little.

As much as she hated Ronan, she hated the idea of being thrown in jail for grand theft auto more.

After a brief walk outside to clear his head, Gio joined the team back in the room, where they continued with the sting. He didn't catch the final totals, but they'd arrested quite a few prostitutes and twice as many johns. It was a very successful sting operation, but they had not found Morgan.

Gio didn't know if they'd ever find her. But he hoped. And he prayed.

Again he pulled to mind the image he'd seen in one of his dreams. Morgan in the future. If that dream was prophetic as Dylan liked to say it was, he would see Morgan again. She would be safe. However, it was nothing but a dream; it definitely wasn't today's reality.

After a debriefing, Gio, along with Dylan and Aliza, left the hotel and went out to Dylan's car. Gio collapsed in the backseat and looked up at the hotel, which stood in the middle of downtown Knoxville.

How many more women and boys were being trafficked through that building here in their city? Stings like the one tonight, while seemingly successful, didn't have much long-term effect on trafficking as a whole.

Half of the women they'd tried to help tonight would end up going right back to their pimps tomorrow, if not sooner. And those johns? It really wasn't much more than a slap on the wrist.

Something more needed to be done.

Aliza turned around in the front seat. "Food?"

Gio half-shrugged. "Not really hungry. I have a feeling she was close, but we missed her."

Dylan turned too. "You have no way of knowing that. I really think she ran. Why would she go back if she's been helping us?"

Aliza shook her head. "I wonder ... the whole reason she started assisting us in the first place was to keep someone from getting caught up in the life. Marrissa. And she wanted to help Natalie. It was all about the other girls."

"Anna too." Dylan's voice was distant, saying his niece's name.

"Exactly." Aliza gripped the seat. "See? Maybe that's in play here. Someone else she feels compelled to save."

"Doesn't she realize we could have helped that someone too?"

Dylan let out a dry chuckle. "That's exactly what Jacq said this morning. Well, not those precise words."

Aliza met Gio's eyes. "We keep praying. But I'm dying to know, why are you taking this so personally? Because she stole your car?"

"I thought you were a better interviewer. Multiple leading questions?"

She narrowed her eyes. "Answer the question, Crespi."

"Might as well fill her in too," Dylan said.

Gio shook his head yet told Aliza all about the dreams he'd had and the pictures he'd sketched. But in telling Aliza, just like when he told Jacq about the dream of the future, he didn't include the detail that it was of Morgan's wedding ... where he was the groom.

"Whoa. That's crazy. I guess you are attached to her in ways very few could understand."

"Especially Morgan. I hope I don't ever weird her out."

Aliza laughed. "I feel I know you decently, but you're still hard to read."

Dylan raised his hand. "When he's *trying* to hide something is the time he's easiest to read."

Gio laughed. "Hence the fear I'll come across as a creep."

Dylan's phone rang. "It's Jacq." He answered and talked to her with joy in his words. After he hung up, he said, "She said she talked to Chloe. We're set to close on the house on June eighteenth. Five and a half weeks. I can't believe this is becoming a reality."

Gio was excited for Jacq and Dylan as they moved forward with marriage and developing a home for rescued women. He hated the idea they would eventually move to that full-time and not be on the team, but he was pumped for them all the same.

A little twang pinged at his heart. He ignored the desire. *God, forgive me for my jealousy. I truly am happy for them.*

Aliza would probably reprimand him if she could hear his thoughts and tell him something about it not being wrong to have your own desires. But he wasn't sure he felt the same at the moment. God had also called him to be an FBI agent, and marriage would be difficult. Of course, he wasn't about to tell that to the happily engaged people.

Gio needed to get out of his head, so he asked, "Anyone set any wedding dates yet?"

Dylan's chuckle hinted at frustration.

Dumb question, Gio.

Aliza bounced in her seat. "We're thinking New Year's Eve." She clapped her hands twice in quick succession.

Gio smiled. "That will be fun. And Dylan, you and Jacq will figure yours out. Of course, that's if you can decide on paint colors. Five weeks might not be long enough for that."

He prayed they'd find Morgan in that time too. If they didn't he wasn't sure if he could recover from the loss.

Chapter Five

Five and a half weeks later

Gio used a flathead screwdriver to pry open the can of light-gray paint. Two days ago, Dylan and Jacq had closed on their home, which sat at the top of a mountain along the edge of the Smoky Mountains. He was glad to spend his Saturday—along with Aliza, Gabe, Matt, and Dylan's brother Chad—helping them fix up the place. And fixing was definitely required.

The house had great bones, and no structural work was needed. But fresh everything would be needed before anyone could move in.

Matt had finished painting the ceiling, so it was Gio's job to edge the kitchen, while Chad rolled the walls.

Gio filled his handheld paint can and climbed the ladder. He needed the distraction. It had been six weeks and one day since Morgan disappeared, and they were no closer to finding her. Multiple sting operations had gone down in Knoxville, but either she was steering clear or had completely left town. He couldn't consider a third possibility.

He tried to push the idea that something worse could have happened to her out of his mind. Jacq was worrying enough for all of them.

Gio dipped the brush into the paint and applied it to the wall with as much precision as his distracted mind would allow. *Heavenly Father, please be with Morgan wherever she is. And help Jacq.*

Gio focused on the task at hand, painting along the sides of all the doorless cabinets and along the ceiling. Chad finished rolling two coats before Gio even completed his first and left the room.

As Gio started back at the beginning to apply the next coat, Gabe came in, face pale.

"What's wrong?"

Gabe gripped the counter-less cabinet frame. "Chloe called."

What about his sister calling brought Gabe to Gio? He was closer friends with Dylan.

"She's out on a SAR call. They stumbled upon a dead body."

Gio's hand began to shake, so he set down the brush and can. "Why call you? Wouldn't the cops on duty respond?"

"They have, but the woman's body ... the description matches Morgan's."

Gio sucked in a sharp breath.

"She called me since she knew I was with you guys today."

"Did you tell Jacq yet?"

"I can't even bring myself to tell Aliza."

Gio moved toward Gabe. But halfway across the kitchen his phone rang. It was Warren.

"Crespi."

"A body was found along the edge of the Pigeon River in the Cherokee National Forest. It appears to be a homicide. The description of the deceased fits your informant, so I've managed to get y'all assigned to the case. I'll send you the coordinates. I want you on scene before they move the body."

"Yes, sir. Everyone is here with me. We're on our way."

He hung up.

Gabe furrowed his brows. "Guess we have to tell them now."

"I'm inclined to not say anything until I see the body. If it's not Morgan, there's no reason to freak Jacq out."

"I can't argue with your logic."

They split up and gathered everyone with a "we have a case," minus any details. They all met outside the front of the house.

Jacq came down the stairs and straight to Gio. "Where we headed?"

"About an hour east. Apparent homicide." He held his breath.

She nodded.

He let his breath out, grateful she didn't ask anything else.

They'd only come up in two vehicles. Dylan gave Chad his keys so he and Gabe could go home after they cleaned up the paint supplies.

The team climbed into Gio's SUV, and, as fast as he could, Gio sped down the mountain.

Matt reached over from the passenger's side and gripped Gio's arm. "Dude, don't take those curves so fast."

Jacq laughed from the backseat. "You shouldn't have eaten so much pizza for lunch."

Dylan said, "Matt just has a weak stomach."

A shuffling sound came from where Aliza sat. "Here." She passed something up to Matt. "Take a couple of these."

"Chewable?"

"The kids call it car medicine. Take two."

For the majority of the trip they rode in silence save the quiet Christian music playing in the background. But Gio's mind was anything but quiet. It screamed at the possibility that the body lying on the shore of the river was Morgan's.

But God, what about that dream of her happy and healthy? Was that the promise of eternity, not here? Is she with you?

Gio had no way of knowing where Morgan stood with the Lord. From what Jacq had said, it sounded like Morgan at least knew about Jesus when they were in college. But was she truly in a relationship with Him, no matter how severed it may be as a result of the life she was forced to live?

As he drove down the two-lane highway, another vehicle pulled out in front of him and did not get up to speed.

Gio smacked the steering wheel. "Come on already." Why did there have to be a double-yellow line?

He drummed on the steering wheel. Finally they reached a passing zone. No one was coming, so Gio gunned it and whipped around the slow vehicle.

"Gio!" Jacq's voice was full of admonishment. "Why are you in such a hurry?"

He ignored her question and didn't slow down, not for another thirty minutes, when they arrived at their destination.

He parked under the interstate overpass and cut the engine. The sound of door handles opening echoed in the SUV. "Wait."

Everyone froze.

"There's something more about this, isn't there, Gio?" Jacq sounded irritated.

He turned in his seat and looked her in the eyes.

She must have read his mind. "No." Her head shook slowly at first, but increased in speed as she repeated the word. "No. There's no way."

"We don't know. We can't until we get over there."

Matt bumped Gio's arm. "Know what?"

With effort Gio broke his gaze from Jacq's and looked at Matt. "The description of the victim matches Morgan."

Jacq practically shoved Dylan out of the car and ran to the water's edge.

Gio met her there and pointed across the relatively wide river, which appeared even more swollen after several days of heavy rains.

A man in a sheriff's office uniform drove a motorized raft across the river toward them. "Nothing to see here, folks. Get back in your car and keep driving."

Gio pulled his badge out of his back pocket and flipped open the leather billfold. "FBI."

"Well, what's one more for a jurisdiction argument." He pulled the boat up to the shore. "Hop in. Nothing has happened yet, as we're still debating about whose case this is."

They climbed in the boat, and Gio said, "If we know the victim, that'll settle it. I promise. But I'd hope we can all just work together."

"I'm in favor of that. Deputy Quinn, by the way."

"Agent Crespi." By the time Gio had introduced the rest of the team, they were on the other side.

They stepped onto the rocky shore. "What can you tell us so far, Deputy?"

"Well, it's not pretty. Although I'd imagine she was at one point. Body is rather decomposed. Exposure. The water. We're guessing she floated down the river."

"Dumped?"

"Doubtful. Lots of dirt, so it looks like she was buried at one point."

A tarp covered the body lying along the shore twenty feet ahead, but the smell was already strong in the air. Every blood vessel in Gio's body constricted. He was glad Jacq was behind him so he couldn't see her face. He needed to stay in work mode and keep his emotions out of this.

Deputy Quinn introduced the sheriff and the park ranger, who stood by the body.

The sheriff said, "I'm fine with handing this case off to y'all, even though it's hard to say where she came from. I'm guessing—now I'm no forensic anthro-whatever—but it's likely she was buried somewhere inland. With all the rain we've had, every nook and cranny became a raging river. Probably uprooted her and sent her flowin' down the mountain, likely in one of the zillion creeks, and into the river."

The park ranger nodded. "She definitely didn't fall into the river on her own."

"What suggested homicide?"

The sheriff answered, "Obviously I'm no ME. but the gunshot wounds to the leg and chest don't suggest anything else."

It was Gio's turn to nod. He couldn't wait any longer. He had to know if it was Morgan.

Kneeling on the rocks beside the body, he braced himself for either recognition or relief. He pulled back the tarp from her face.

He found neither. An unrecognizable face stared back blankly. Her hair was long and dark; however, it was so tangled and matted it was impossible to know if it was naturally straight or curly.

The woman was dressed in a simple, yet filthy t-shirt-style dress. It was torn and tattered, much like her skin.

Someone retched behind him. Gio turned. Matt had moved into the trees and released the pizza to the forest floor.

The regurgitated pizza scent mingled with the dead body, and Gio's pizza moved up his throat. He held his hand over his mouth to restrain himself.

Before turning back to the body, Gio glanced at Jacq, who was glued to Dylan's side. "Can you remember any distinguishing marks?"

Jacq shook her head.

"She didn't have that tattoo in college?"

"What tattoo?"

Gio sighed. "I'm pretty sure I saw a small tattoo on her lower back. She leaned forward to pick something up off the floorboard of the car. I don't know what it was, just that the top was round in shape, maybe a little flowery."

"A tramp stamp?" the park ranger said.

Gio closed his eyes. "Something like that." There was a good chance her tattoo was literally that. A tattoo a pimp had branded her with.

Deputy Quinn snapped on some gloves. "Can I help you look?"

Gio accepted the gloves Quinn offered. Once they were ready, the two men gently rolled over the woman's body. A black tattoo of an elaborate design with what looked like a flower stained her skin.

Gio's hands shook as they lowered the body, returning her to her resting place. He sat back. Was this really Morgan? He couldn't confirm it, but neither could he rule it out.

He thought he'd be sick.

Aliza knelt beside him. "We'll have to wait for the autopsy?"

He couldn't tell if she really meant it as a question.

"Now I wish I had paid more attention to the tattoo."

She slid her hand around his elbow. "But I know you. You looked away like the gentleman you are."

He shrugged and removed the gloves.

A dog barked in the distance. Gio and Aliza looked at one another. Gio glanced downriver where the bark had come from. "Is Chloe still around?"

Quinn asked, "The searcher who found the body?"

Gio and Aliza both nodded.

"Yeah, she's downstream a little."

Aliza pulled on Gio's arm. "Let's talk to her."

They walked around the body, and Aliza released Gio.

As soon as Aliza and Chloe caught sight of one another they embraced. The rest of Chloe's search and rescue team came over, and Gio shook hands with Josh Schneider. He didn't know Josh or Chloe well, but they went to the same church as he did, and he knew they took their roles as searchers seriously.

Chloe released Aliza. "Is it her?"

"We can't tell for sure." Gio's heart felt like a giant rock sitting at the bottom of the river.

Poirot, Chloe's chocolate lab and expert search and rescue K9, nosed Gio's hand.

He petted the dog. "Hey, buddy. Did you find her?"

Chloe answered, "He did. It was as if he was trying to ignore it and continue searching for the missing camper, but he circled back twice."

"That's when I smelled it." Josh rubbed his nose with the back of his hand, then pulled out several folded pieces of paper from his back pocket. "Our written statements."

"Not your first dead body?"

They both shook their heads, and Chloe added, "Lance's statement is in there too. He ran up the hill a few minutes ago."

"Thanks, guys." Aliza took the papers.

"Are we free to go then? They still haven't found the woman we were looking for, so we'd like to rejoin the search."

"Go for it. We'll call you if we have any questions."

They said goodbye, and Gio and Aliza turned back to rejoin their team.

Gio let Aliza walk ahead of him as he hung back. He needed to pray, but he couldn't find the words. Was that Morgan, the woman he was certain would be more to him than an FBI informant in the future? Why would God have given him those dreams and this inexplicable longing for a woman he barely knew just for her to turn up dead, murdered at that? Had he failed? Could he have done something more to save her?

Jesus. That was the only word his mind could put together. The rest of his prayer was only emotion.

Back at the office a few hours later, Gio picked up the pencil from his desk and held the tip against the paper. He doodled. The tattoo he'd seen on the woman's body took shape. It'd be a while before they heard anything from the medical examiner; maybe he could remember the tattoo well enough to aid them in their search for her identity.

"Got 'em." Aliza hung up. She'd been on the phone with the police station trying to get access to all of Gabe's arrest records. He'd arrested Morgan at one time in the past few years, so surely they'd have some records, at least fingerprints.

Gio could kick himself for not dusting his car for her prints. If he had, they'd be able to match them, or better yet not match them, with the body in the morgue. Of course, that was assuming the woman's fingerprints had survived decomposition.

He grabbed his laptop, pushed away from his desk, and rolled his chair across the walkway to Aliza's desk, offering to help comb through the records.

The two of them dove into the search. Twenty minutes later, Gio needed to give his eyes a break and looked up from the screen. Jacq sat with her head on her desk. She'd spent most of the last few hours crying, and while she was so determined to prove the body wasn't Morgan, she was struggling to find that answer. She'd been on the hunt for any bit of DNA Morgan might have left behind when she'd stayed at the Jacobs' farm, but there wasn't anything. Sheets had been washed. The extra toothbrush she'd used had been thrown away.

Aliza elbowed him. "What should we do?"

"Find that arrest record."

She nodded, and they returned their attention to the screens.

Gio clicked on each file and glanced at the pictures, one after another. "How many people has Gabe arrested? Good grief."

Aliza chuckled. "If only we had a narrower timeframe to work with."

"You did ask him, right?"

"Yeah, he doesn't remember arresting her, let alone for what."

"But she clearly remembered him." Gio sighed and leaned back in his chair. "This is going to take forever."

Aliza tapped on his laptop. "Not if you keep working."

He ran his hand through his hair and picked out a paint drip. Had it really been earlier today they'd been putting paint on Jacq's walls?

Jacq's phone rang. She bolted upright and answered.

Gio tried to focus back on the case files in front of him, but he wanted to run over and find out who had called. Maybe the ME had some valuable piece of information.

Jacq said, "Thank you. I appreciate your prayers. I'm a hot mess, so it probably is better if she stays there. I really appreciate it."

Gio clicked open the next report. A woman with a similar look to Morgan came up on the screen. But it wasn't Morgan. This woman had been arrested on a solicitation charge but had been released and the case dismissed.

Jacq finished her phone call and came over to them.

Gio closed the report and opened the next but met Jacq's eyes. "You okay?"

She shrugged. "You?"

"Is it creepy that I'm feeling so messed up about this too? I barely know her."

Jacq planted her hands on the desk and leaned over his laptop. "No. I saw those pictures you sketched. I heard you talk about the dreams. Something about your connection to her is supernatural, not physical. So stop it." Her expression hinted at a smile. "Plus, I like that I'm not the only one so messed up about this."

He distorted his face in an effort to stave off the moisture pooling in his eyes.

"Seeing that woman's body reminded me ... Never mind. Now's not the time."

"Gio?" Jacq pushed his laptop shut.

Aliza spun in her chair.

He looked around. Warren had gone home, and Matt and Dylan were off getting dinner, though they would probably be back any minute. Until then, no one else was in the office.

"Let's just say it wasn't my first body either."

"Who?" Jacq's stance hadn't changed, but her eyes had softened.

"My brother."

"Oh, Gio." Aliza gripped his arm.

Tears flooded Jacq's eyes. He wiped his own away, and both women waited. The office door flew open, and Matt came in talking a mile a minute about the stupid long line at Chick-fil-A that had still moved crazy fast, unlike the traffic on I-40.

Gio had been saved from his vulnerable moment by a chicken sandwich. The Lord's chicken at that.

He opened his computer again and checked the next record. Not Morgan.

Chapter Six

JACQ LEANED HER HEAD back against the headrest in Gio's SUV. Chad had left Dylan's car at their parent's house, which was also where Harper was.

They'd come so far in the last month. Jacq would even say she was close to Dylan's family now. Not something she ever expected to say, and definitely not this soon. There were still moments of awkwardness or frustration, but on the whole, they were all growing closer.

Gio pulled into the long driveway that led to the house where Dylan had grown up and stopped behind Dylan's car.

He reached from the backseat and rested his hand on Gio's shoulder. "You sure you won't come in? My mom probably has some pie or something."

"Nah. I want to go home and sleep. I'll see you guys at church tomorrow."

Jacq wasn't certain she was up to going to church tomorrow. She simply wanted to go back to the office and keep searching for anything that would tell them if that body in the morgue belonged to her friend.

"Fair enough." Dylan patted Gio's shoulder and slid out of the backseat.

Jacq leaned across and gave Gio a hug. "Hang in there."

He let out a dry chuckle. "I'm the one who's supposed to tell *you* that."

"Probably, but it helps me to feel like someone else needs to hear it too."

He gave her a tight squeeze before letting go. "Good night."

Dylan opened her door and held out his hand.

They told Gio good night, and he drove away.

Jacq let go of Dylan's hand and slid her arm around his waist as they strolled to the front door. He didn't say anything, and she was grateful. She needed his strong silence at the moment.

Inside the house, Dylan's mom greeted them both with hugs. "Do either of you need anything?"

"I need to see Harper."

Mrs. Harris said, "She's in Scarlett's old room. You are more than welcome to stay here for the night. The bed in Dylan's old room is made up."

"I'd love to stay. I really don't want to be alone in my apartment, but I'll just slip in bed with Harper."

"I'll stay too." Dylan looked at his mom. "If that's all right, of course."

"Of course. Don't hesitate to let me know if either of you need anything. I'm going to head to bed, but please—"

Jacq gripped her hand. "We will."

She left, and Jacq turned to Dylan. She had no words.

He stroked the hair away from her face. "Go to sleep. I'll be across the hall."

"I love you." She reached up and wrapped her arms around his neck.

He held her tight before easing her back to give her a kiss. "I love you too."

She hated not being able to set a wedding date with this man she loved, but how could she right now? If Morgan really was dead ... She couldn't think about it. Any of it.

Dylan ran outside and grabbed their gym bags from his trunk. At least she had clean clothes.

Once upstairs she tiptoed into the room. She didn't even care about getting ready for bed; she only wanted to see her baby.

A nightlight cast a yellow glow, just enough light for Jacq to see Harper's little foot dangling off the side of the twin bed. Jacq would most likely be kicked from the bed at some point. It was amazing how much space such a little person could take up while sleeping.

Jacq slipped her hands under Harper and slid her closer to the wall. Kicking off her shoes, she lay down next to her daughter. Her shorts weren't exactly clean after working on the house and traipsing around a crime scene, but she had no energy to change into her gym clothes.

She kissed Harper's forehead, and the little girl turned into her and snuggled close. Jacq poked her feet under the sheet, and they came into contact with a stuffed creature. She reached in and pulled it out.

Morgan's bunny.

Jacq rolled onto her back and held the white bunny with purple ribbon around its neck and purple-lined ears up in the dim light.

Her tears were all tapped out. *Please God, don't let that be Morgan we found today. I hate what happened to whoever it is. But I don't think I can handle such a loss. I mean, I know You're always with me, and I can face anything with You. But ... I just can't.*

She hugged the bunny close and fell into a fitful sleep.

Monday morning, Gio and Jacq all but ran down the hallway. The ME had called and said he had results. They'd abandoned the team at the front door of the Knox County Regional Forensic Center and took off for the morgue.

The ME met them in the hall and led them to the room where he'd completed the autopsy. The scent of formaldehyde overwhelmed Gio's nose and burned his nostrils and his eyes.

Before the door behind them closed completely, the ME began talking.

"The DNA is processing, but, as you know, that takes way longer than it does on television. Hopefully we'll have something in a month or two, if we're lucky. Depends on how bad the backlog is. I understand y'all want her identification as quickly as possible, so you'll have to try and pull some fancy FBI strings. But I'm not really sure what y'all want with this Jane Doe."

Jacq opened her mouth, but the ME continued, and his countenance changed.

"In all honesty, this poor woman. She was either a prostitute or in a very abusive relationship. Despite decomposition, there was clear evidence of sexual trauma."

Gio's stomach churned. Jacq wavered, and he caught her by the elbow. She leaned into his hand, so he left it there for support.

The ME continued, "I know, not pleasant. The cause of death was as it seemed—a gunshot wound to the chest. The GSW to the knee probably happened a few minutes prior. She also took quite the beating before she died."

"Do you have a time of death?" That would be key. Maybe this woman had been deceased longer than Morgan had been missing.

"Not more than six weeks. If her body hadn't been washed into the river by the heavy rains, we might have a clearer picture of when she died. We know she was unburied when that second big storm went through, which establishes the timeline. Insect activity matches. And it would have had to be a relatively shallow grave. If it had been less than a foot we'd see evidence of animal activity. On the other hand, she wouldn't have washed out if it had been too deep."

Six weeks. So it could be Morgan.

"Now this tells an interesting story." He grabbed an x-ray and clicked on a lightboard and attached the film.

Gio recognized those bones. He'd broken his ankle in high school. Letting go of Jacq's elbow, he moved closer.

The ME pointed at the image of the bone. "There is some significant perimortem damage to the ankle here, as if she'd been chained. The other ankle"—he clipped up another x-ray—"shows similar damage, but there is remodeling. So she was probably chained by one ankle, and when that one broke, she would most likely have walked with a significant limp while it was healing."

"How long before death?"

"Based on the amount of remodeling I'd guess the break occurred around April, making time of death early to mid-May. There's at least a month's worth of remodeling. Of course, I have to factor in the malnutrition."

Jacq stepped closer. "Malnourished? How bad?"

"Pretty bad. I'd say it'd been at least three months since this woman ate enough to sustain her."

Gio's mind sorted through the information. There was no way Morgan would have been walking in those high heels if she'd had a broken ankle, even a partially healed one. A tiny bit of hope flickered inside him. Morgan did not have a broken ankle. But malnourished? He spoke his thoughts. "She was thin, but—"

"Not that thin," Jacq said.

"Not your lady then?" the ME asked.

Gio felt an odd combination of relief and continued worry. "I don't think so, but whoever she is, we'll figure it out and bring her killer to justice."

The ME looked puzzled. "Even if she's just some hooker who—"

Jacq put her finger in the ME's face. "Especially. She's not just some hooker. She's someone's daughter, sister, friend. No one deserves to live like that or to die like that, except maybe the man who did all this to her."

The ME's shoulders drooped. "Of course."

Gio wanted to smile at Jacq's fire, but the question still remained: where was Morgan? Was she all right?

Chapter Seven

MORGAN SANK ONTO THE hotel-room bed. She couldn't believe how relieved she felt to spend the evening with Duke. Maybe it was because Ronan hadn't had her working so hard in the last twenty-four hours.

As soon as he heard Duke was back in town and wanted to see "Daisy," Ronan had let her take it easy and ensured she'd pampered her body to be ready for Duke. Mani, pedi, wax. The whole nine yards. But it made her feel as cheap as she was. It didn't negate the revolving door of men he'd had her "treat" over the last six weeks.

She was tired, sore, and ready to give up. The heroin was starting to cause sores on her skin, so no amount of "pampering" would make her feel a man like Duke, let alone anyone better, would want her.

Standing, she walked to the window and looked out while she waited for Duke to arrive.

For a Monday evening, downtown Knoxville was bustling. From the third-story window, she watched people stroll down the sidewalk, going about their normal lives. Why couldn't she have had a normal life? Why in all the times she'd been passed from pimp to pimp had she not been able to escape? Now with Ronan's drug-hold over her, it would probably never happen.

A black Dodge Charger parallel parked down the street from the hotel. Two men with dark hair stepped out. Gio. Dylan.

Without thinking she banged on the window. "Look up."

She was too far away.

But what if they did see her? What could they do for her? Nothing.

She raised her fist to bang again anyway, but a gentle knock sounded on the door behind her. Then it opened.

Gio and Dylan were walking toward a restaurant, and Morgan glanced over her shoulder.

"Hey, you." Duke's voice was smooth. The door clicked behind him.

She looked back at the street. The guys disappeared into the building.

Swallowing, she faced a very tan Duke. "Hi."

"I missed you."

She tried to smile, but she couldn't find the fake grin she normally pulled out.

Duke closed the space between them and stroked the side of her face. "Are you feeling well?"

No one ever actually cared how she felt. She half-shrugged.

He took her arm and inspected the crook of her elbow. "No needle marks."

She used the other shoulder this time for her half-shrug.

"But he's still dosing you, isn't he?"

She looked at the floor.

He ushered her to the bed and made her sit down. Kneeling in front of her, he ran his hands down her leg and slipped off her pump. As he inspected between her toes, a shadow crossed over his face.

Why did it make Duke so angry that Ronan was giving her heroin? What did he care?

"I'll deal with him later." He eased her foot down and stood. He unbuttoned his shirt and ripped it off, tossing it to the chair with too much force. He kicked his shoes across the room. Each one slammed into the wall.

What should she do? If she tried to run away from him, would he just grab her and be even rougher than it appeared he was going to be? And where would she go? To Dylan and Gio? Maybe.

If only they had seen her. Would they have run up here to rescue her? Maybe they did see her and would bust through the door at any minute.

Who was she kidding? They didn't care what was happening to her. Why would they?

Gio sat at the table across from Dylan, who had insisted they go out for a bite to eat after work. No doubt Dylan would try to get him to talk about and process the reality that the woman in the morgue was not Morgan. But what good would that do?

"So why'd you look over your shoulder when we walked in?" Dylan asked.

"What are you talking about?"

"We've been friends too long for that." Dylan's attempt at sounding stern was comical.

Gio laughed. "It was worth a shot." Why did his friend always have to observe his behaviors?

"Did you really expect it to work?"

"Do you really expect me to talk about everything that goes through my mind?"

It was Dylan's turn to laugh.

Gio gave up on the idea of keeping his thoughts from his best friend. "I got one of those feelings that Morgan was close by."

"Are you getting those regularly?"

"Eh. Not necessarily, but that one was strong. If it doesn't help save her, though, what's the point?" Some days he wished God would take this supposed gift away.

"Does she even want to be saved?"

Gio leaned on the table. "You interacted with her prior to identifying who she was. Now tell me, did that woman who wanted desperately to save others from the life really want to stay in it herself? Was that the impression she gave you?"

One side of Dylan's mouth turned up. "I phrased it wrong. She probably wants out, but she doesn't think she ever can."

"True. I wish I knew how to convince her she can be free. There is always hope."

"That's because you have Christ," Dylan said.

"We have to share Him with her."

"That's the whole heart of the home Jacq and I are going to start. There is hope in Jesus, even in the most hopeless situations."

The waitress dropped off water glasses and took their drink order. When she left, Gio removed the straw wrapper and stuck the straw in his glass. "When do you think you'll have the home up and running?"

"Are you trying to ask when Jacq and I are leaving the FBI?"

Gio tilted his head.

"I probably *won't* leave. I don't mind a commute. It's just under an hour, and my mom has convinced me I can always stay at the house overnight if we're on a big case or have to work late."

"Your mom has come a long way in a short time."

"Don't I know it. But about the home. We've got a ways to go. Jacq's drafting up a business plan, and then we'll look for donors and ministry partners."

"You can count on my financial support."

"We appreciate that. Sure you don't want to be more involved?"

Gio's insides prickled. What more could he do? Being an FBI agent was important to getting these women out of the game. "We'll see."

The waitress came back and took their order. They moved on to other topics, but a nagging feeling weighed down Gio's heart. When his food arrived, he could barely eat. That woman in the morgue might not be Morgan, but she was out there somewhere. If she was still alive, he doubted she was safe. The money she'd taken from his wallet wouldn't last her long if she did run, and if she hadn't run ...

He took another reluctant bite. The hairs on the back of his neck stood on end, and he looked toward the door. A muscular man with black hair and tanned skin ambled into the restaurant and went to the bar only about ten feet from where Gio and Dylan sat. Nothing in particular gave Gio reason to feel suspicious, but nonetheless ...

He searched his memory. Did he have a run-in with this guy? Or was it something else?

Morgan strolled out of the hotel and onto the sidewalk. Duke had only wanted an hour tonight, but he promised he'd be in touch very soon. He hadn't been as rough as she was afraid he would be. Duke was nothing like Ronan. He'd paid her enough for two hours. Even though he'd already left, she would take her time before she called the escort service, looking for work.

Maybe a little stroll would be good?

She walked without really thinking about where she was going. She spotted Dylan's car. The guys were still in the restaurant. She aimed in that direction.

But why was she going toward them? What was she going to say? Maybe Gio was still mad about the car and money. Dylan probably hated her for upsetting Jacqui. Morgan was sure Jacqui did not take her running-off well.

It made no sense to look to those guys for help. They were men after all. And didn't men only want one thing? But were these two different? They had seemed to be.

With their guns, maybe they could protect her from Ronan. She snorted a laugh. No one could protect her from Ronan. Probably not even God Himself. Because didn't Ronan think he was god anyway?

But still, she walked. Right toward the restaurant.

What would she say to them? Maybe she could sit with them and explain why she'd left. They could tell Jacqui she was fine and Jacqui didn't need to worry.

Of course that would be a lie. She was anything but fine.

Nevertheless, Morgan reached for the handle on the large glass door that led to the restaurant. Her hand gripped it. She could see the side of Gio's head.

An older couple pushed the door from the other side, blocking her way. She stepped aside to let them pass, then glanced through the door.

At the bar, only twenty feet away, stood Ronan.

Her heart thundered.

She spun and plastered herself to the side of the building. No!

What was he doing here? Why? There really wasn't any hope of escaping him. She had to get away from here before he saw her. He might question what she was doing wandering around instead of working. And what if he recognized Dylan and Gio as feds? Even if he didn't realize she knew them, he'd be mad she'd been so close to them.

It wouldn't matter. He'd been so uptight about cops lately. He didn't use to care, but since Ezra had gone and gotten arrested, Ronan had been paranoid.

She turned the corner and breathed a little easier and laughed at herself. Who was she kidding? Ronan was paranoid because of what she'd done. This was all her fault.

Ronan being so rough with Iris that she couldn't work for two days, all the drugs, the constant hovering over all of them and taking their cars away—it was all her fault.

If she'd stayed in pocket, no one would have gotten hurt. Except those girls she'd helped save. Marrissa. Anna. Even Natalie was out now. That was all her fault too.

Wasn't that worth it? They were free because of her.

But not "Daisy." She'd never be out. This was her life.

Chapter Eight

GIO DUMPED HIS SUPPLIES out on his desk the next morning. Sketch pad, tracing paper, pencils, sharpener, eraser. Next, he grabbed a lightbox, the photograph from the coroner, and his FBI Facial Identification book. He pulled out his chair and sat.

He'd figure out who this Jane Doe was. Her family deserved to know she was gone. How long had they been looking for her, hoping she was okay?

They needed to know she was not suffering.

Anymore.

At the thought of all this poor woman had endured, his stomach churned. He didn't know this woman's story, but it wasn't pretty. She needed someone to tell it and bring her murderer to justice. He would do everything he could to make that happen. And first up, he had to discover what her face really looked like.

He switched the lightbox on and laid the photograph and a piece of tracing paper on top. After clipping them in place, he sharpened his pencil and stared at the photograph.

Thankfully, her lower mandible had remained with the body. Having the whole jaw would make this an easier job.

He began tracing.

The door opened behind him, but when he looked, no one was there, so he got back to work.

Ten minutes later, a cup of coffee appeared on his desk.

Jacq stood beside him. How hadn't he heard her come in?

"Figured you could use one of these. What time did you get here this morning?"

"Thanks." Gio looked at his watch. It wasn't even eight yet. "Less than an hour ago."

"How can I help?"

"Start narrowing the search parameters for the missing person. Let's find her."

She nodded and went to her desk.

As Gio worked on the sketch, flipping through the Facial Identification book and making educated guesses as far as soft tissue, the rest of their team members trickled into the office.

Warren was last. He set his hand on Gio's shoulder before he went to his office. "That's looking good. What's this?" He tapped on a sketch Gio had laid to the side.

"Jane Doe's tattoo. Matt was going to run it through prison records and see if there are any hits."

"Perfect." Warren turned and went to his office.

"Aliza?" Gio called across the aisle.

"Yep?" She looked up from her laptop.

"Will you look at this? Do you think I'm on the right track?"

Aliza also had training as a forensic artist. She came over to his desk and examined the sketch.

Gio waited.

She unclipped the sketch and the photograph and held them next to one another. "It's pretty close, but based on the ME's report, you may want to give her a little less flesh in the cheeks."

"But if her malnourishment had only been toward the end, she may have not been quite so thin."

"True. Run it as-is then."

"Okay." He made a few more tweaks and called it good.

Jacq took the sketch and scanned it. "All right, here goes nothing."

After hours of waiting for facial recognition to match it with a missing person, that's exactly what they had: nothing. He rubbed his aching forehead; his frustration increased the pain. Had he failed to sketch her well or was she a ghost?

Wednesday evening around eight, Morgan stepped out of the room and walked down the open-air stairs of the cheap motel. Ronan had dropped her off about a half hour ago, yet she'd already seen one trick. Time to find another.

She wandered around the front of the building, one always ready for the picking. Guys would drive into the parking lot and catch a girl's eye, and then it was working time.

This was the worst way to do the job. Even working a party was better than this. At least at those parties there was a better chance of the guys having showered. She wanted a shower after that last guy.

A shudder worked its way through her body.

A man with a runner's build and only a few inches taller than her turned the corner. She sized him up. Clean cut. No wrinkles in his t-shirt or jeans. Ball cap covering surfer-blond hair.

She shot him a smile. "Are you looking for a little fun around here?"

He kept his eyes on the ground. A nervous fellow. The ones who were unexperienced at picking up a hooker were always entertaining. She strutted closer to him.

"I like having fun."

"What kind of *fun* are you offering?"

"Depends on how much money you have."

He looked up and met her eyes. His sky-blues grew wide, and he drew his lips in tight.

She forced her chin down and shot him a suggestive gaze.

He swallowed and lifted his hand. A room key dangled between his fingers. "I already have a room."

"Perfect." She slid her arm around his elbow and snatched the room key. "Let's go."

They strolled to the room, and she unlocked the door. He hung behind her. She pushed the door open.

She was not met with a dark room.

Faces appeared.

"On the ground. Hands behind your back."

Before she could react, she was pushed to the ground and patted down.

One of the officers said, "Do you have any weapons or anything sharp we should know about?"

She lifted her face from the cheap, stinky carpet. "No."

Why was this happening? Ronan would kill her. He always hated it when his girls got arrested. But he, and all her guys before him, had drilled it into her well: Say nothing. Only cooperate enough to keep yourself alive.

Someone gave a spiel about her being arrested for prostitution and solicitation. Once they'd cuffed her, they gently lifted her off the floor.

Her eyes met familiar ones. Officer Gabe Jacobs.

His smile was a touch too big considering she was being arrested. "Olsen, call Gio."

Gio and not Jacqui?

Morgan turned to see the man who had lured her into the trap. He nodded at Gabe. Then he met her eyes. "Sorry, Morgan." He turned and left the room, closing the door behind him.

"My name is Daisy. Daisy Smith." Her voice shook from the lie. But she couldn't be arrested as Morgan. No, she was Daisy right now.

"Morg—Daisy." Gabe touched her arm. "Come sit down."

She moved to the chair Gabe indicated and sat.

Another officer picked up her purse from the floor. "Anything we should know about?"

She shook her head.

Her insides burned as they went through her belongings.

"Are you using?"

She didn't answer. She didn't feel high right this minute.

"No crack cocaine?"

"Nope." That one she'd answer.

Gabe sat on the edge of the bed near her. "You know everyone has been really worried about you."

Her gaze locked with his. "I don't know why."

"People care about you."

She snorted. "That's laughable. Just take me to lockup. I know this routine so don't try and pull anything emotional with me. Don't get me killed."

Chapter Nine

Gio walked into his kitchen. The guys from church, including Dylan, were over for Bible study. They'd wrapped up their discussion and were ready for snack time.

Whenever they met, they rotated who was in charge of snacks, and one guy's wife had made them some killer dip to enjoy tonight.

Gio pulled the dip out of the oven, where it had been warming. He had hoped tonight's Bible study would bring more peace to his soul, but Hosea didn't exactly help. Instead, it stirred up frustration in his heart. What was God calling him to do? Love a woman who didn't want to be loved or at least didn't think she should be loved?

He set the dish on top of the stove.

"Ah, man," Dylan said. "I was supposed to bring cups and plates tonight. I totally forgot."

Gio shrugged. "Whatever. You'll just have to stay and help do dishes."

Dylan laughed and went to the cabinet where Gio kept his plates. Gio went to grab the glasses. One at a time he removed the glasses from the cupboard and set them next to the two-liter root beer the snack guy had brought. But there were only three. Not the seven he needed.

Dylan came up beside him. "Where are the rest of your cups?"

"Umm ..." Gio looked around the kitchen. Dish drainer was empty. The dishwasher was empty. He didn't have any more. "I have mugs."

He opened a different cabinet and pulled out four mugs.

Keeping his voice soft, Dylan said, "Where'd all your glasses go? You used to have a full set of eight."

"Let's not talk about that."

"And now you don't have a choice but to talk about it after *that* statement."

Gio's phone rang. Relief washed over him. He did not want to talk about the glasses. He pulled his phone from his pocket. "It's Matt."

Dylan's brow furrowed. "He was working the sting tonight."

Gio's heart leaped. Slipping into the living room away from the other guys, he answered the call. "Crespi. What's up Olsen?"

"We found her."

His lungs stopped working. He gripped one of the kitchen chairs they had moved into the living room. "Seriously?" Not that he thought his friend and fellow agent would joke about something like this. "Where is she?"

"I'm sorry, man. I wouldn't have arrested her, but she solicited me before I recognized her."

"Who's she with now?" He couldn't ask fast enough.

"Gabe Jacobs."

"Are they taking her downtown?"

"That's the plan. Really, I'm sorry, I hope it doesn't make things more complicated. I can't even think about calling Sheppard."

"Don't worry about her. Dylan's here. He'll go get Jacq." Gio forced himself to take a deeper breath.

"I have to get back to work. The sting is going well, and I'm the undercover."

"Well, bringing them in beats the alternative. Maybe more of these girls are being trafficked and not hooking on their own. Do what you can to get them out."

They hung up, and Gio turned to Dylan, who had followed him into the living room. Gio didn't have to say anything. The smile on Dylan's face told him he'd followed Gio and Matt's conversation.

Dylan said, "I've got to call Jacq."

"Just drive over there. I'll get everyone out of here and then go downtown." After so many weeks of not knowing where Morgan was, he couldn't wait to see her. But what if she wasn't receptive to him?

"What are we going to do? Bail her out?"

Gio shook his head. "Depends on how she's acting." *Lord, give us wisdom.* "If she's resistant to being pulled out, it would probably be better if she's still technically in custody. She's our witness. I think we have grounds to take her into protective custody."

"So take her to the field office?"

The office would feel so cold and uninviting. "Perhaps we can secure a safe house. Maybe a more neutral home-like situation would be best anyway."

"Perfect." Dylan grabbed his Bible and rushed straight out the door.

Gio chuckled. He went back to the kitchen where the rest of the guys were and loosely explained the situation. They gobbled down what was on their plates and made a quick exit. Within twenty minutes of receiving the call from Matt, Gio, anxiety building, was in his car and driving toward the downtown police station.

How would she react to seeing him? To his taking her into custody? It could go terribly wrong, but he hoped for the opposite. And what had she endured the last six weeks? What if—he cut himself off. *Lord, I'm casting all my anxiety on You.*

In the interrogation room, Morgan, with back straight, sat across from a police officer who identified himself as Detective Buckley. The interaction between this clean-cut Black man and Gabe made her wonder how far back their friendship went. Gabe probably trusted "Buck," as he'd called him, with his life, but Morgan didn't.

"Daisy, we want to cut you a deal; talk to us about your pimp."

She stared at the wall.

"What's his name?"

"Who said I have a pimp?"

"Then tell me your husband's name."

She tried not to laugh. "Husband" was exactly what Ronan called himself. But she still held high esteem for the actual institution of marriage. As much as she could, she refused to actually call Ronan her husband. He didn't deserve that title. Not that she was sure anyone would. Wasn't Christ supposed to be the husband of the church? Isn't that what she was taught in Sunday school? He was probably the only one worthy of that title. How could any man on earth be decent enough to love her the way a man was supposed to love a woman?

"Daisy?"

She looked at Detective Buckley.

"You didn't hear anything I said, did you?"

She blinked but made no other indication of anything.

"Please talk to me." His voice was kind and not sickening in his plea. But she had nothing to say. She cared more about living to see the next day than she did about giving up Ronan. They could arrest him, but he'd still find a way to control her or even kill her. That's just how he rolled.

The detective finally surrendered to her stonewalling and indicated to the officer to take her.

Morgan allowed the officer to lead her back to the group holding cell where all the girls they had caught were being held. She went inside when told and slid her hands through the opening for her cuffs to be removed.

Another working girl Morgan had seen around a few times came up to her. "Did you tell them anything? What did you say?"

"I kept my mouth shut. And you should too." Morgan turned away from her and took a spot on the bench that ran the length of the cell, as far from the other girls as she could get. She'd been arrested enough times over the years to know she should keep quiet and keep her distance. That last one was more of a personal choice.

She crossed her arms and closed her eyes. A couple more of the girls were taken out and no doubt questioned to give up their pimps. Hopefully, if any of them spoke out against their guys they wouldn't get too hurt.

Someone banged on the bars. "Daisy Smith."

She opened her eyes. "I'm not going to say anything, so unless you're letting me go ..." She looked at the officer.

Gio stood behind him.

She sucked in a rapid breath. Why did he have to see her here? Her cheeks, no, her whole body warmed. She tugged on her skirt to try and make it longer and stood.

"Hands out."

She kept her focus on Gio but refused to look him in the eye. What a horrible person he must think she was. He probably hated her for stealing that money and his car.

The officer cuffed her and opened the cell. She stepped out and waited for more instructions.

"This way." Gio's voice was soft but held so much strength.

She followed him with the officer right behind her.

Maybe she could pretend she really thought that agent, whatever his name was, was her boyfriend—no, Gio was too smart to believe that. What else could she say so maybe he wouldn't think as poorly of her as he must?

They exited the cellblock.

Who was she kidding? He knew exactly what she was. Why should she try to play some game for him?

He led her to a window, where he signed some papers and took a large Ziploc bag that held her purse. "Thank you, officers."

They brushed off his gratitude and went back to their work.

What was going on? Why were the officers leaving her with Gio? And why did he have her stuff?

"Come with me." He turned and trekked toward the outside door.

She didn't move. "Where are you taking me?"

"Federal custody."

"Did I commit a federal crime?"

He looked up and down the hall. "Just come with me. I'll explain."

She pursed her lips but stepped forward.

He took her elbow and led her outside to his SUV. He opened the passenger door.

"Not the back?"

He shook his head. "Climb in, and I'll remove the cuffs."

She slid in but settled her cuffed wrists on her lap.

"Don't you want me to take those off?"

"I'll probably run if you do."

He leaned his forearm against the upper frame of the vehicle. "Now why would you do that? You haven't even heard what's going on."

Why did his hovering presence unnerve her so much? "Then tell me."

"Before I came in to get you, I got off the phone with Jacq. She and Dylan are at a safe house waiting for us."

"A safe house?"

"You're our witness. Was it true you knew Ezra and Connor were both involved in kidnapping Harper?"

She picked at her fingernail polish. "Why would that matter? You caught them in the act, didn't you?"

"That's not the point."

She turned and poked her finger into Gio's chest. His strong, tight chest. "The point is, you don't need me, so why on earth would you take me into federal custody? Are you trying to get me killed? Because that'll be what happens when Ro—what Ezra's boss will do if I rat on him. Unless of course he's done with Ezra, then Ezra can count his days."

"Ro ... who?"

"That's all I'm good for, finding the big bad guy?"

"Is Ezra's boss the big bad guy? And no, that's not all you're good for. We care about you."

She snorted. Nobody cared about her, only what she could do for them.

Chapter Ten

Gio couldn't believe he'd been stupid enough to ask about the big boss first instead of acknowledging she was who they really cared about. *Lord, give me wisdom and patience.*

He lowered his arm from the car's frame. "Are you sure you don't want me to remove the cuffs?"

She turned straight ahead and stared.

Apparently, that was a no. "Well, let's go. Dylan and Jacq are waiting for us." He closed the car door and went around to the driver's side.

When he opened his door, she wiped a tear from her face. He was certain he wasn't supposed to see that.

The radio turned on with the car, and he lowered the volume, but not before noticing the song playing. A song that reminded him the battle wasn't his and he needed to fight with prayer and praise. The battle belonged to God.

Heavenly Father, soften Morgan's heart before we get to the safe house. Give me the right words to switch her out of the defensive mood she's in. I don't know how to help her. Show me. How do I show her Your love?

Not knowing what the right thing to say was, he said nothing. So he drove.

Until his stomach growled. It had been a few hours since he'd eaten a tiny smidge of chips and dip. Maybe Morgan was hungry too.

"Would you like something to eat? Jacq was going to grab food for breakfast tomorrow, but I'm hungry now."

"I'm fine." She kept her gaze trained out the window. Until a grumble louder than his own sounded from her stomach. "Fine. I'm a little hungry."

That was something. "Not too many places are open. McDonald's? Taco Bell? Your choice."

"Doesn't matter what I want. You pick."

The shoulder where they drove was wide, so he pulled over and put the car in park. He turned toward her and waited patiently for her to look at him.

Silence lingered.

"Morgan?"

She finally relented and met his eyes with a huff.

"What you want matters. *You* matter."

She blinked. Her mouth opened but shut. It happened again.

He tried to keep from smiling.

"Taco Bell." Her voice was soft. She looked away. "Chicken quesadilla with black beans and a side of sour cream."

"You got it." He righted himself and rejoined traffic. "Anything to drink?"

"Dr. Pepper, if they have it."

He drove to the nearest Taco Bell and pulled up behind a car in the drive-thru.

"Morgan, it's going to be hard to eat with those cuffs on."

"Whatever." She fidgeted with how her arm lay around the seatbelt, which couldn't be worn properly because of the handcuffs.

"You know, Jacq's going to yell at me if we show up at the safe house and you're wearing cuffs. You want to explain it to her?"

"What do I care if she yells at you?" She gazed out the side window.

He narrowed his eyes and glared at her. A smile toyed with her lips, but disappeared when she realized he was looking at her. He pulled the cuff keys off his keychain and faced her.

"Fine." She lifted her hands toward him.

He removed the cuffs and hooked them back on his belt.

Morgan rubbed her wrists but stayed quiet.

The car in front of them pulled ahead, so he inched up to the speaker and placed their order, including two orders of cinnamon twists. He didn't know if she'd want them, but maybe she would.

Once they had their orders, he pulled into a parking spot. "The safe house is another fifteen minutes away. Mind if we eat first?"

"In your car?"

He shrugged. "We weren't going in when you had the cuffs on, so this was my plan."

Her defenses let down a little further, and she released a snorty chuckle. "Not afraid I'm going to make a mess?"

"Not as much now that your hands are free."

Her lips parted with a smile. "Thank you for this." She lifted the quesadilla he'd handed her.

"These are for you too, if you'd like them." He offered the cinnamon twists.

"Really?" Her eyes brightened.

"Of course."

"Thank you." She took them and popped one in her mouth.

His heart decided it was time to perform some elite acrobatics. He wished he knew what to talk about. He was comfortable with silence, but he didn't want her to feel awkward. What could he say to help befriend her a bit? Everything he could think of was stupid or would sound like an interrogation, so he kept his mouth full of food.

After a few bites, she took a sip of Dr. Pepper, then asked, "If you could have any food on earth what would you choose?"

"Mmm. Good question. I tend to be a steak and potatoes kind of guy, but I could really go for my mom's homemade mostaccioli right now. It's been too long."

"Your mom's Italian?"

"Actually, no. But my dad is third-generation. It's my dad's grandmother's recipe, but Mom worked really hard to figure out how to make it just like GG did."

"That's neat. She sounds like a wonderful woman."

"My mom? She is. Speaking of which." He picked up his phone and set a reminder. "I need to remember to call her tomorrow."

"You have to put it on your calendar?"

"It's how I do things. We normally talk about once a week, but last week ended up busy, so I want to make sure we connect."

Morgan popped the last bite of quesadilla in her mouth and balled up the wrapper.

Gio really wanted to ask about her mom, but he was afraid if it wasn't a good thing or she missed her too much the question would send Morgan to a dark place. He wanted to keep the focus off her personally, but he wasn't one to talk about himself or the weather, so he had no idea what else to say.

"This really hit the spot, but I think my dream meal would be pad Thai. I've tried to make it before, but it's never as good as from a real Thai restaurant. There was one down the street from Jacqui's and my dorm. Ah, it was so good."

He tried to squelch the delight that filled him as to not make it awkward, but he was thrilled to hear her open up to him. "I've only eaten Thai a few times, but I think that's what I ordered. Whatever I had, it was good." She smiled at him, ate her final cinnamon twist, and licked her fingers.

"Ready to go see Jacq?" He put the SUV in reverse.

Her smile faded. "Does she hate me?"

"No. She's been really worried about you." A car drove past, so he waited.

"Don't you hate me? I did steal your car and money."

He put the car back in park and sucked in a quick breath. "Not at all. I got my car back. Was I happy to be out of that money I'd been slowly collecting every time I got groceries? No. But hate you? Absolutely not."

She stared at him.

"But I have to say I don't understand. Why did you go back? We thought maybe you ran off completely."

She looked at her feet and shrugged. "I told Jacqui I can't be saved. Y'all need to put your effort into people who can be."

He reached over and touched her forearm with the tips of his fingers. "That's not true."

She shifted her arm away. "We should go."

With an anchor on his heart, he backed out of the parking spot and drove to the safe house. But oh, how he wished she'd talk, give him a chance to understand. Then again, maybe she couldn't explain it. It's difficult to articulate what you don't comprehend.

Morgan glanced at the clock as Gio turned down another street. Almost one in the morning. She wasn't making the money she should be, but she also wasn't in prison. If Ronan found out she'd been arrested, but not that she'd been taken by the feds, she had up to twenty-four hours before he freaked. Unless someone got wind she'd been moved. He'd flip if he knew she was with the FBI, and that was if he didn't know *anything* more. If he knew the full extent of her trespasses ... she shuddered.

They entered a familiar neighborhood, one directly behind where she lived with Ronan. Gio pulled into a driveway in front of a modest ranch home in the middle-class neighborhood. The houses weren't showy, but there was a decent amount of space between each one. Tall trees surrounded the property, giving it plenty of privacy. Once in the driveway, he entered the garage. He got out and came around the car before she could even reach for the door handle.

This man confused her completely. He seemed so genuine, but could he really care like he claimed? Was he lying about not hating her? Hoping to pull her in so she'd spill the beans about all her associates?

He opened the door and offered her a hand out. He grabbed a bag out of the back hatch and nodded for her to go with him into the house. Once he clicked the button to close the garage, he opened the door, and she followed him inside.

Jacqui appeared around a corner and bombarded her, wrapping her arms around Morgan in a fierce bear hug. "I'm so glad you're okay."

"I won't be if you suffocate me."

Jacqui released her but stayed close. "I missed you."

"Me too." She really had. Why had she run back to Ronan? At the moment, that seemed totally stupid, even if it hadn't when she made the decision.

"I have comfy clothes if you'd like to change."

Morgan smiled at her friend. "I'm fine." She pinched her dress and pulled it away from her body. "This one is really stretchy and super cozy." She pulled it down a little so it wasn't as short. She remembered how modest Jacqui had always dressed, skirts to her knees.

"Are you hungry?" Jacqui dragged her to the kitchen. "We brought over some food."

"Gio fed me."

"Then water, hot chocolate?"

"Tea?"

"Herbal or—"

Morgan tugged Jacqui to a stop. "Just show me."

Jacqui brewed hot chamomile tea for all four of them. They all went to settle on the pair of couches in the undecorated living room. Gio settled on one end of a couch, and Morgan took the other half of it, while Dylan and Jacqui sat close on the other sofa.

Morgan let the three of them chat while she blew on her tea, waiting for it to be a sippable temperature.

Jacqui, cupping her mug in her hands, asked, "Why did you go back?"

Morgan darted her gaze to her tea. She shrugged.

Turning toward her, Gio put his arm across the back of the couch. "We aren't going to judge you. We're curious and want to understand."

"I'm not sure I understand. I know I had a particular reason, but I honestly can't remember." The heroin had scrambled her brain too much, but she didn't want to say that.

Goosebumps covered her arms. She tried to rub them away.

Gio jumped up and disappeared briefly. When he came back, he offered her a pullover sweatshirt.

"Thank you."

While he held her mug, she slipped on the softest sweatshirt she'd ever felt. It smelled like him. Fresh and clean, slightly masculine without being overbearing. She never wanted to take it off.

Dylan squeezed Jacqui's shoulder but met Morgan's eyes. "You're safe now. You can be free of that life."

She shifted on the couch. Everything was catching up to her, and she was exhausted. "I don't know what to say. I want to believe it, but I don't know what life would ..." She picked at the hem of her dress. "Sorry, what was I saying?"

Gio touched her shoulder. "Are you all right?"

"Getting tired, I guess." She rubbed her forehead. Her brain felt mushy. She ran a checklist in her mind. Chills, restlessness, brain fog. Shoot. These were withdrawal symptoms.

"I talked to Nate," Jacqui said.

Her brother's name grabbed her attention.

Jacqui bit her lip.

"Really? How is he?"

Jacqui told her about her brother, his wife, and their children. Morgan had missed so much, but Nate would never want to see her.

She shifted again and rubbed her face.

Gio leaned closer. "You could probably use a little sleep. Why don't we call it a night?"

She nodded. Her hand shook as she lifted the mug to Gio's waiting hand.

The withdrawals were starting early. It would be a rough night. Could she handle it? Sure, why not? She'd done it before. Of course, she remembered very little of the last time she'd gotten clean. Hopefully, she could sleep through the worst of it. It was wishful thinking, but she really didn't want Jacqui and the guys to know.

Still, she honestly had no idea how she was going to make it through. If only Ronan hadn't taken to shooting her up in the middle of the night too.

Gio started from sleep at Jacq's nudging. Must be five o'clock.

"Your watch, sleepyhead."

He swung his feet down from the couch. "All's quiet?"

"Seems to be."

They'd taken a fairly lax approach to guarding the safe house since there wasn't anyone actually after Morgan at the moment, at least as far as they knew. Still, one of them was staying awake throughout the night.

Jacq said, "I don't understand why you didn't just sleep in the bedroom."

"This way the sheets are still fresh for you. And I can sleep anywhere."

"Apparently. I'll be awake for at least another ten minutes if you want to do a perimeter check."

"I will. Thanks."

They exchanged goodnights, and Gio slipped his shoes on, checked his weapon, and went out the back door. Once he'd completed his walk around the perimeter, he let Jacq know all was clear.

He went to the bathroom. When he came out he put his ear near Morgan's door, which was propped open. Morgan and Jacq had fought briefly about leaving the door open and had compromised with leaving it cracked.

From the other side, Morgan sounded miserable. He could hear her thrashing in the bed, moaning in pain.

He didn't know what to do. Was she having a bad dream or was she in withdrawal? They had hoped she was clean, but it hadn't been clear if she was or not.

The door opened and Morgan flew past him and into the bathroom. She barely got the door shut before the toilet seat banged against the back of the commode and the sound of her retching met his ears.

His heart crumbled for her.

Not knowing what to do, he stood there like a fool, waiting.

The toilet flushed, the water ran for a long time, and she finally emerged.

"What do you want?" She swiped at the sweaty hair plastered against her head.

"Nothing. Is there anything I can do to help you? Can I get you anything?"

Her eyes narrowed. "Unless you can get me some heroin, I don't think so. I'll be fine."

She pushed past him and went back into the room.

When she started to shut the door, he shoved his foot in the way. "Leave it open so I can hear if you call for help." She grunted and crawled back into bed.

He paced up and down the hallway, praying and debating about what he should do. He did a little research on his phone regarding heroin withdrawals. Goosebumps, trouble concentrating, restlessness, agitation—all symptoms he'd seen in her. Vomiting, diarrhea, rapid heartbeat, muscle spasms. The more severe symptoms were appearing. Potentially fatal seizures could be next. She required medical attention.

Morgan darted into the bathroom again.

He needed to tell Jacq.

Across the hall, he knocked on Jacq's door. A massive groan resounded from the other side, but a moment later, Jacq appeared. "What's wrong?"

"She's not clean. Heroin. Her withdrawals are in the severe range."

"Are you saying we need to take her to the ER?"

"That's exactly what I'm saying."

"She's not going to like that."

"I think she's past the point of being allowed to have an opinion about it."

Jacq pointed to the bathroom with a question in her eyes.

He nodded.

She knocked. "Hey, Morgan. Let's talk."

Silence.

Jacq knocked again.

There was no sound. No water, no retching. No answer.

Something was off. He knocked and called out, "Morgan, are you all right in there?"

He stepped aside and let Jacq try the door handle. It opened.

The bathroom was empty, the window open. His sweatshirt lay across the windowsill.

"Get Dylan." Gio ran to the back door and flew outside.

"Morgan," he called, but there was no reply.

He pulled his flashlight out of his pocket. First, he ran to the bathroom window.

He found impressions in the dirt from where her bare feet had hit the ground, yet there were no more footprints. The ground was soft, but not that soft.

Where would she go? And why?

He swept around the house. Would she try and steal his car again?

"Morgan?" He didn't want to call out too loudly and bring unwanted attention from the neighborhood.

The garage door was closed.

He checked his pocket. He still had his keys. And Dylan's car was still in the driveway too.

He darted toward the street and checked the sidewalk. Empty. A vise gripped his chest, squeezing hope from his heart.

Where did she go?

Chapter Eleven

Morgan slid between the trees along the back of the property. She heard Gio call her name, and it killed her. But this withdrawal was going to kill her first.

She stepped on a pokey branch. "Ouch."

Why hadn't she figured out a way to find her shoes?

She wasn't thinking straight, but she was trying. She'd go back to the house. Maybe Ronan would be busy, and he wouldn't see her. She could dose, just a little bit, and then go back to Jacqui and Gio.

Yeah, that's what she was doing. She'd be back. And just a little dose; wouldn't that help ease her off better anyway? She found a wooden fence enclosing the yard behind the trees. Skirting around the side of the fence, she kept her body close to it as she slipped up the side through another yard.

A few large trees worked as cover. The sky was shedding its blackness for a shade of dark blue. It was way too early for her to be home, but if she was lucky, Ronan wouldn't even be there.

Once she was on the sidewalk, she plodded along normally, but checked over her shoulder with every sound. Her stomach wanted to retch again, but it was completely empty. She fought off heaving until she couldn't any longer. Thankfully, a bush along the property lines hid the remnants.

Only one more block.

It must have been the longest block known to man. Her feet hurt, which probably meant they were in bad shape. All she really felt was the need for more heroin. It drove her forward like a vulture to a dead body.

One step then another. The house came into view, despite the towering pines that tried to hide the front of it. Even if she could see the garage, the door would hide whether Ronan's Escalade was there or not.

She wouldn't know until she was inside. What she did know was exactly where the security cameras were and how to avoid them.

Morgan snuck around the outside of the house and squeezed through the tightly planted evergreens to get to the back patio. Ronan kept a spare key there for the girls, should they end up losing theirs.

But if Ronan did catch her, she'd need a really good reason for not having any of her things. The shoes would be the trickiest one to explain.

She retrieved the key, unlocked the door, and replaced it before slipping inside.

The drugs were in Ronan's bedroom. If he was sleeping, she might have to do one more job before escaping again. Maybe she could—

She couldn't focus enough to come up with a plan. Hopefully, her quick wits would help her on the spot, because they didn't want her to plan right now.

She just needed a fix, and she'd be fine.

As she tiptoed through the house, it seemed like no one was there. It was dark and quiet.

Putting her ear to Ronan's door, she listened for any sound.

A hand snaked around her neck and shoved her against the wall. The deep voice connected to the hand swore at her. "What are you doing here?"

"Ronan." She could barely whisper his name. "I just ..." She couldn't breathe.

He loosened his grip and glared at her, waiting for an answer.

"I got arrested, and they let me go." The muscles in her arms spasmed.

"I guess that explains why you came back here instead of getting to work. Apparently you like your night-time dose."

"Ronan, please."

He released her throat but gripped her upper arm instead. "Where's your purse?"

"With the cops."

"Those losers didn't give you back your shoes either?"

"Umm, I used those to pay for a cab. They didn't even let me make a call." Where had those words come from? Whatever, at least he seemed to buy them.

"Come on, let's get you hooked up so you can get back out and work. A whole night wasted. You're going to have to make up for this."

A shiver shook her entire body, and it wasn't because of a withdrawal. No, she'd had to "make up" for a "wasted" night before. It was never good. The exact opposite, in fact. He'd put her in a room and line up the guys for her outside the door.

Once she got her hit, she had to get back to Jacqui. She couldn't stay here.

Tears ran down Morgan's cheeks as she woke up in Ronan's bed. Why had she come back? How stupid could she be? The bright red digits on his clock read eleven o'clock. She hadn't had near enough sleep, but at least she felt somewhat human again after the euphoric feeling of the heroin dissipated.

The doorbell rang.

What on earth? No one came to the door in their neighborhood.

She rolled out of bed. Not seeing her dress, she found one of Ronan's t-shirts on the floor and pulled it on.

She couldn't distinguish Ronan's words, but he sounded surprised and a little put out, though not angry.

She eased the door open and walked into the foyer.

Duke stood by the door talking to Ronan and smiled when he spotted her.

But Ronan turned and glared at her, then returned his attention to Duke. "She can't. Her diddly-squat night last night—"

"She'll make it up. With me. I'll pay you well." Duke pulled out a wad of cash. "But she'll be clean when she comes back, and if you force that poison into her body"—Duke stepped closer, emphasizing the height difference—"you will pay."

"Are you threatening me?" Ronan puffed up his chest.

Duke stepped to the side. "Let's go, Daisy."

"I need to change."

"You don't. I'll get you whatever you need."

She still felt frozen in place. What was happening? Her groggy mind couldn't quite handle it. Part of her wanted to run to Duke. Was he really promising to get her clean? But if she went with him, would she be able to escape and get back to Jacqui and Gio?

Gio. What was it about that man that had her wanting to run from this life? The realization of the truth made her heart ache. He felt so much safer than either of these two loose cannons.

But she knew Ronan. And she knew how to deal with him. What if Gio was just as volatile?

And Duke? Too many unknowns, and as gorgeous as he was, he scared the crap out of her.

"Daisy." His voice was serious.

She met Ronan's angry eyes. He thumbed through the stack of cash Duke had given him. "There'll be more?" Ronan asked.

Duke nodded. "That much for each day it takes her to get clean."

Ronan jerked his head toward Duke. "Go with him."

She shuffled across the foyer.

When she passed by, Ronan gripped her elbow and hissed in her ear, "You will come back. If you don't, each one of these girls will make up for your getting arrested last night. Understand?"

Her stomach churned violently. She nodded. He knew exactly how to ensure her return. Lily. Iris. Violet. Even Celeste.

Morgan's nature had always been to care for others. That was why she'd come back in the first place. And it would keep her coming back.

Gio chucked his pack onto the floor at the foot of his desk. Dylan and Jacq had finally made him give up searching and go to the office. The rest of the team looked at him but said nothing.

Jacq slapped his arm. "Chill out. I'm just as upset, and you don't see me throwing things."

"Yet you hit me." He rubbed his stinging arm. She was right. After searching for an hour, Jacq had broken down and sobbed. They'd failed to help Morgan.

Again.

They had a case to work, though, and couldn't spend all day looking for someone who had run away from them.

Gio sorted through the piles of paperwork on his desk until he found his doodle of Jane Doe's tattoo. He stared at the pathetic excuse for a sketch before putting it down and logging into his laptop. He pulled up the photograph of the tattoo and redrew it with more accuracy.

What little he remembered of Morgan's tattoo didn't seem quite the same, but there was definitely a similar design. He wished he knew what was different, but he simply hadn't seen enough of it. Best he could guess was that it was the same artist.

He turned the sketchbook around toward the team and tapped it on his desk. "Anyone seen a tattoo similar to this before?"

Matt's eyes narrowed, then he stood and wandered over. "I did last night."

"Arrest her?"

"Nope. She apparently was quick to feel my cop vibe, either that or the guy with her did. I'm guessing it was her pimp with the way he pulled her away. But she was wearing a tube top and low-rise skirt. The tat was in the same location as Jane Doe's."

"Exactly the same?"

"Nope. Same swirly shape, but different flower. What are those?"

Aliza came over. "Roses."

Gio asked Matt, "What flower did you see last night?"

"I have no idea. I didn't even know that was a rose," Matt said.

Dylan came up behind Matt. "Guess we don't have to wonder why your ex left you."

Matt rolled his eyes.

Gio pointed the eraser end of his pencil at Matt. "Can you sketch it?"

Matt laughed. "Drawing is even less of an option. I'll go see if I can find it." He spun around and went to his desk.

While he waited, Gio sketched a few different flowers. A tulip, his mother's favorite. An iris. A pansy. Another one he didn't know the name of. A daisy.

His pencil stopped when the daisy was only half done.

Daisy. Daisy Smith. Morgan.

He changed the flower in the tattoo to a daisy. That was Morgan's tattoo, he was sure of it. "Jacq?"

As soon as she looked over, he held up his sketchbook and tapped on the tattoo.

Her eyes widened, and she nodded. "I bet that's it."

"Found it." Matt turned his screen.

"A lily?" Aliza asked.

"If that's what you call it. That's the flower I saw in her tattoo."

Gio turned the page and sketched the shape with a lily. When he was done, he rotated the book again. "This?"

"More or less."

Gio sat back and flipped between the two pages. "Do you think it's some sort of branding?"

Aliza came up beside him. "Sure seems like it."

Dylan asked, "Matt, any chance you heard the guy call her Lily?"

Matt shrugged.

Aliza ran her finger along one of the sketches. "Do you think this part is a letter?"

"I've thought that. But which? Maybe a K or a B?" He wiggled the pencil back and forth in his hand.

"Not a B. K is possible, but look at how this comes back at the top. An R perhaps?"

"That's it!" Gio smacked the pencil down. "We heard an R name at one point in all of these cases, didn't we?"

"Ro was the guy at the club," Dylan said.

Jacq held up her index finger. "Ronan."

Gio nodded. "That name means something."

But what? He searched his memory. Ezra. "That's the name that made Ezra flinch." But who was he? Wait, Morgan had slipped and said "Ro" the other night. Gio dug further into his memory from months ago. Wasn't Ronan the name of Morgan's pimp? Was he also Jane Doe's? If only Gio could ask Morgan.

But he'd have to find her first.

Chapter Twelve

MORGAN ROLLED OVER IN a plush bed. Where was she? What time was it? With a little struggle she opened her eyes and looked around. An ornate bedroom. To her right, a giant set of windows revealed a view of the mountains upon which the setting sun cast a pink-and-orange hue. It must be pushing late into the evening. Was she at Duke's house?

She tried to get her mind to play back the rest of the day, but all she could hear was Gio calling her name in the dark.

Come on, Morgan, remember.

Then it came back to her. Ronan. Duke. Leaving with Duke. He'd given her a bag of clothes from the backseat of his car. A stupid-expensive car. The man was outrageously loaded. She'd pulled on a pair of leggings, but she still wore Ronan's shirt.

It made her want to puke.

Her mouth tasted like she'd done plenty of that. She wiped her forehead. Sweat.

She was in withdrawals. Ronan had given her an even larger dose than normal this morning. Not the small dose she'd been hoping for to get the edge off.

Sorrow deeper than she'd ever felt overwhelmed her. Why had she run? Maybe Jacqui and Gio could have actually gotten her help like they'd been talking about in the hallway last night. What was Duke going to do to her?

How was she ever going to give him enough to make up for the cost of caring for her through this, let alone all that cash he'd given to Ronan this morning. Was he going to want something so weird even she wasn't comfortable with it? She'd played along with fantasies before, but she'd hated it. Her whole body shook. What was she to do?

The door opened, and Duke walked in holding a tray. "You're awake. How are you feeling?"

"Awful."

He nodded. "That's to be expected. It's been what, about twelve hours since your last dose now?"

"I have no idea."

He set down the tray, which was filled with an assortment of breads and fruits, along with a huge water bottle and a cup full of pills. "All of this is essential to get you feeling like yourself again."

"What are those?" She pointed at the pills.

"A few supplements and medications that will ease the withdrawal symptoms and help you detox from the heroin, which I legitimately procured, if you're concerned."

"Illegal activity is my job. You think I care?"

He chuckled. "I kept the food light because you're probably not up to eating much, but you need to eat something."

"Food sounds disgusting."

"Everything you could need is in the bathroom." He pointed to a door against the same wall as the bed. "Including a toothbrush."

Brushing her teeth would be liberating. "May I?"

"Of course." He gestured toward the bathroom with a sweeping motion of his arm.

She disappeared, and after using the restroom and cleaning her mouth, she came back out.

Duke was laying out a pair of leggings, a long t-shirt, and undergarments. "Clean clothes. After you eat and take your meds, you can shower if you'd like."

"Then what?"

"You should probably try to go back to sleep. Getting clean is going to be rough. And sleep may become difficult. There's plenty around to occupy you when the insomnia kicks in." He pulled open a drawer in the nightstand. Puzzle books, a deck of cards, and a TV remote.

She looked around. There wasn't a TV to be seen.

He chuckled and strolled to the wall across from the bed. He took hold of a giant-framed painting of a lighthouse and slid it along the wall, revealing a television.

She had never been in such a place. This guy really had it all. He sat on the end of the bed and motioned for her to join him. She obeyed. "Eat up and take your meds," he said.

Fear crept in. What was in this? Was he going to poison her? Was he some mad scientist who wanted to experiment on her? "You've never told me what you do for a living."

He smiled with a slight chuckle. "You can trust me."

She picked up a piece of bread and nibbled on it. It was delicious. She inhaled the rest of the piece. Then ate the apple slices. She was hungrier than she'd expected. Eventually, she took the pills. Even if he was a psychopath, it couldn't be worse than dosing heroin and dealing with Ronan.

"Good job, Angel."

Her heart stopped. Why did he call her that? She hated that name. Now she was scared to look at him. Would he have a sinister glint in his eye?

Despite her fear she met his gaze. His eyes were tender and caring, but that almost made him look more psychotic. But what if he actually just cared about her? Like legitimately.

He stood and kissed her forehead. "Keep eating and drink plenty of water. I'll be back to check on you soon. I love you."

Did he really? How was she supposed to know if someone actually loved her and didn't want to abuse her?

He walked out the door, leaving her to ponder love and abuse in her mentally and emotionally weak state. She didn't even know what love was. Never had really. Something about the way Gio bought those cinnamon twists for her last night seemed more genuine than anything Duke was doing for her.

And Ronan. He was all talk. He'd showered her with praises and supposed love, but it was nothing more than lip service. He wanted something from her and sold her to get it.

But Duke. Why was he taking care of her like this? What did he want from her? There was always a catch. Ronan had taught her that, and Vincent before him, all the way back to her college boyfriend. No one ever wanted to love you just for who you were. Not Morgan anyway.

Morgan.

A voice seemed to whisper in her heart.

She didn't remember schizophrenia being a symptom of withdrawal. But maybe it was. It's not like she remembered the last time she got clean. Or did she?

She searched her memory. Something seemed familiar, but she wasn't sure what.

She shook it free from her mind and finished another slice of bread. The carbs soothed her aching stomach. With another gulp of water, she got up to shower like Duke had encouraged her to do.

The warm water running down her weary body felt amazing. Like maybe it would wash away the past. She slathered soap all over her skin, but no matter how hard she scrubbed the past wouldn't leave. She sank to the floor of the stone-tile shower.

"I want a guy like Gio to love me, not Duke. But that's not possible, I know. God? Am I so far gone that You can't love me?"

Why did it feel so fruitless to pray? Didn't she used to believe God heard anyone's cries? Hadn't He heard hers when she was a little girl and needed saving from her stepdad?

Tears and sweat mingled with the rushing water of the shower, but she didn't feel any cleaner. She felt dirty down to her very soul.

Gio sipped his coffee and stared at the sketch of Jane Doe Thursday morning. Surely someone somewhere was missing this girl. Didn't her parents want to know what happened to her? A sister? A friend? Didn't someone report her missing?

"What's going through your mind, Gio?" Jacq's voice projected across the bullpen without shouting.

"I can't believe no one reported Jane Doe as missing."

"And you're one hundred percent on the sketch?"

"Yes. I know it's accurate."

"Could her features have changed with age? Think about your sketches of Morgan versus her missing-person photo versus the woman we know today. Could that change your sketch? Maybe she's been missing longer than we thought."

Gio sat up straight and, after setting his coffee down, grabbed his pencil. "Good point. Let me try a few things."

Jacq smiled. The first one he'd seen grace her lips in more than twenty-four hours.

Everyone went quietly about their business while Gio got to work. He made various versions of the girl, keeping all of the features congruent with the skull and postmortem photograph. In one, he simply made her younger. In another he added about twenty pounds.

In less than an hour, he held up the sketchbook, open to the younger version of Jane Doe. Jacq jumped up and crossed the room.

"This is good." She scanned the image into the computer, then stared at the screen as the program ran the new sketch against missing-person photographs.

The software flipped through thousands of photographs. Despite how fast it was sorting, it felt like an eternity.

"While that's searching ..."

Gio wanted to tell Matt to shut it and wait. But he kept his thoughts to himself.

Matt continued, "I've been combing through the prison database looking for other similar tattoos. I found one."

Gio went over to Matt's desk with everyone else.

The tattoo was no doubt exactly the same as Jane Doe's but with a large multi-petaled flower. Though similar to a daisy, this one had thinner petals.

Matt looked at Aliza, who stood behind him. "What flower is that?"

"I think it's an aster. What's the owner's information?"

"Amber Erickson. Also known as Aster. Served one year for assaulting an officer when picked up for prostitution."

Gio said, "Sounds like there's a connection. Any chance we have a current address on her?"

"Let me look. Go back to staring at your missing-person search." Matt shooed them all away.

They turned back to the screen flashing through missing-person photographs.

A match popped up.

Gio took a step closer and studied the picture. She was so young, even younger than Gio had sketched her. No wonder she hadn't shown up with his earlier sketch.

A runaway who went missing fifteen years ago from Des Moines, Iowa.

Jamie DeRozan.

She'd only been fourteen when she left home.

Gio's heart broke. So young. When had she ended up in a trafficking relationship? That early, or had it been a few years before she fell victim to this despicable game? Half her life hadn't been spent with the family who loved her. Maybe her family situation hadn't been great and perhaps she'd made bad choices, but she hadn't deserved to have her life end so violently.

Father, please be with this family when we have to deliver the news that this daughter—who I'm sure they hoped was still alive—and had been until recently—was now gone. I can't imagine. Comfort them.

Jacq gripped his elbow.

He squeezed her hand. "Let's find the bad word who did this to her."

"Please."

Jacq let go of his arm.

Aliza said, "I found her mother's address. Looks like she still lives in Des Moines. I'll focus on notification, and you guys find out who she knew here in town."

Gio turned to Matt. "Anything more on Amber Erickson or Aster?"

"Nothing. She never showed up to meetings with her parole officer after she was released. It's like she disappeared completely."

Gio asked, "Is there an active warrant for her arrest then?"

"Looks like it, but it's older."

"How old?" Gio rubbed his chin.

Matt said, "Three years."

"So when she left prison, she dropped off the face of the planet?"

Matt shook his head. "I can't find any record of her after that, but I'll keep looking. Though if she went right back to the streets, there's a good chance she wouldn't come up."

Gio couldn't help but consider the other possibility; perhaps she'd met the same fate as Jamie DeRozan. "We should search unsolved homicides, especially out in the area where Jamie was found."

Jacq said, "If she was buried too, she may have never been washed out."

"We should still look."

Jacq nodded. "I'll take care of that." But she didn't move.

"Jacq?" He stepped closer to her.

She shook her head. Apparently she didn't want to share her thoughts. But she didn't have to. "Afraid this could be Morgan's fate?"

"Yeah." She met his eyes.

With his head, he motioned for her to follow him to his desk. He pulled out a different sketchbook and flipped to the drawing of Morgan from six months ago, before he even knew who she was. "Remember what I told you when I sketched this one?"

"You thought it was an image of the future."

"Exactly. If this is her future, that"—he pointed to the photo of Jamie's corpse—"is not her fate. Cling to that."

Jacq took the sketchbook in her hands. "But if this is her future-future—as in heaven?"

"I don't think so."

"I don't understand your optimism."

"Me neither. I'm reminding myself as much as I'm telling you."

Jacq chuckled and handed back his sketchbook. "Fair enough. If we keep reminding each other of that, maybe one of us will actually believe it."

Gio squeezed her shoulder. "Exactly."

Chapter Thirteen

MORGAN RUBBED HER EYES and tried to figure out when it was. She had no idea. Everything had been a blur of working through withdrawals. She was so tired but couldn't seem to sleep.

"You awake?"

She rolled over in the bed and found Duke sitting in a chair by the window. It was dark outside. How long had she been in bed? She remembered a bit of sunlight at some point since she'd arrived. Had it been a full two days? "What day is it?"

"Friday, well, it's almost Saturday."

Had he been sitting there watching her? She was fully clothed, so unless she didn't remember getting dressed, nothing had happened. Right?

"You're handling the withdrawals well, Another twelve hours, maybe, and you'll be feeling completely normal for the most part."

"Then what?" She wasn't sure she wanted to know the answer. Was he going to ship her back to Ronan? Lock her inside this room and tell Ronan he's out a girl? Neither of those possibilities appealed to her.

Duke stood and crossed to the bed. He sat next to her, leaned over, and stroked the side of her face. "You're going to feel amazing when you're clean."

Her stomach twisted. It wasn't from his touch or from the continued withdrawals.

Another feeling had appeared. This exact moment felt familiar. It was the strongest déjà vu she'd ever experienced. The situation, the feeling in her gut, the drugs washing from her system, Duke's face and words all felt the same, but something was different. The location. His name. It wasn't a memory from yesterday. Why did this feel so familiar?

Duke's voice stole her away from the feeling. "What do you think about staying here instead of going back to Ronan?"

"To what end?"

Duke's eyebrows rose. "To be with me, of course. Do you really want to go back to that rotten man who sells you to anyone who will give him a buck?"

Her chest tightened. She absolutely did *not* want to go back to Ronan, but the idea of being a prisoner in this room, no matter how amazing the view, horrified her.

"I don't know," she finally said. It probably didn't make any sense to him, but it didn't make sense to her either. He was offering her a way to get away from Ronan. Wasn't that what she needed more than anything?

No, she needed freedom. How often had she looked for a way out of the game? Every time she'd gone to a new pimp, whether by choice or force, she'd hoped the guy was different. Duke wouldn't be any different, would he?

He leaned down and kissed her cheek. "Think about it. I told Ronan you'd be home tomorrow, but say the word, and you can stay with me."

"What about your wife?"

He closed his eyes, his face emotionless, and shook his head. "Don't concern yourself with anything like that."

She didn't understand, but her heart sped up. Something was off. She just didn't know what. "I want to go back to Ronan when I'm strong enough." The words tasted like acid, but at least in Knoxville she stood a chance at getting away. Up here in the mountains, she'd be at Duke's mercy, and she wasn't sure that was somewhere she'd want to be.

The next day, Morgan really did feel amazing. Whatever drugs Duke gave her made a huge difference. And as he'd said, he came in to take her back to Ronan.

She had nothing to pack. She didn't even have her purse, but Duke had said she could wear some of the clothes he'd bought her instead of Ronan's dirty t-shirt.

"I'm ready."

"Say the word, Angel, and you don't have to leave."

There was that name again. She hated it. If only she could remember why. "If you want me to stay so bad, why are you taking me back to Ronan?" She swallowed, hoping she wouldn't regret her boldness.

"You're right, I want you to stay more than anything. But I want you to desire the life I can give you."

"May I ask another question?"

"I'm not Ronan. I won't hit you because you have a brain."

"Why do you call me 'Angel' sometimes?"

He tilted his head and raised a single eyebrow. "You don't know?"

She opened her mouth to respond but closed it. What did he know that she didn't? "Never mind." This was getting too weird.

She walked toward the door.

Duke gripped her arm, not letting her pass. "I have one request before you leave."

Her heart sank. He'd paid for her for more than three days. She was a fool to think she wouldn't have to give him a good time too. Didn't she need to "thank him" for getting her clean?

She let him lead her to the bed, but dread gripped her throat with a death squeeze. Why did men always only want her body? Couldn't she just leave? Wasn't it bad enough she would be forced to go out on the streets and work again tonight? As she lay down on the bed, she could no longer hold back the tears.

Morgan helped Lily clear the table after dinner Saturday evening. Ronan had announced he'd take them all to work in one hour and then disappeared to another part of the house. The other girls left too, leaving Lily and Morgan to clean up. At least Ronan hadn't made Morgan prepare dinner after she got back.

Duke hadn't pleaded with her anymore to leave Ronan and stay with him, other than a simple "call me if you need me."

A glass clattered on the counter. Morgan turned and caught it before it rolled to the tile floor.

Lily's eyes were bloodshot.

"What's wrong?"

The girl shook her head.

Morgan closed the space between them and gripped Lily's arm. "Talk to me."

"I'm late. Ronan hasn't figure it out yet, but I really think I'm—"

Morgan put her finger to Lily's lips. "Shh." She glanced around to make sure no one was around. "Are you sure?"

"I haven't bought a test, but you know how some people say you just know?"

Morgan nodded. She pulled Lily into her arms. This was the worst best news ever. Ronan never let his girls be pregnant. Babies were not allowed. One of Ronan's old girls had actually hit a police officer in hopes of getting arrested so she wouldn't have to have an abortion. She'd ended up having the baby in prison. Ronan said he sold her off when she got out because he wasn't going to put up with that kind of playing out of pocket.

"What do I do? I don't want another abortion." Lily's voice cracked.

"I don't know. But keep quiet about it for now. And hopefully Ronan lost count of your days. If he asks, say you think the drugs messed up your cycle. Whatever you do, don't take a test yet. If you don't know the answer, you don't have to lie if you are."

She hugged Lily tight for another moment, then let go. "Hang in there. But let's finish cleaning up."

Lily nodded.

They did the dishes, and Morgan racked her mind about what to do. Could she get Lily out somehow without Ronan knowing? But how? He didn't let her use her car anymore. Maybe Jacqui could help? But how was she going to get ahold of her?

All day Saturday, Gio helped Dylan and Jacq at the mountain house. Some very generous people donated furniture to the ministry, including a couch, a kitchen table with chairs, and several beds, even though the ministry hadn't officially started yet. But God was working already, and the house was nearly livable.

They went back to Dylan's apartment for dinner. After eating, Gio set the stack of plates in Dylan's sink. "Thanks for having me over."

Dylan slapped his shoulder. "Uh duh. I'm glad you came."

Jacq's three-year-old daughter ran into the kitchen. "Uncwa Gio come." She grabbed his hand and tugged him toward the living room.

"What is it, Harper?"

"Come looky." She pulled him to a pile of Jenga blocks she'd dumped on the floor. "Build with me."

He sat on the floor and, with Harper's professional assistance, built the biggest castle they could with the fifty-four rectangular blocks.

Playing with Harper was one of his favorite things to do. He hoped he'd have a family one day, but until then, he'd adopt all of his friends' kids as nieces and nephews. His heart hurt for his mom. She longed for grandbabies, not that she ever said much to Gio about it. She never wanted to push him. But with his brother gone, he was the only chance of that ever happening for her.

"Five more minutes, Harper. You too, Gio." Jacq's eyes sparkled as she suppressed a giggle.

He shook his head. "You don't really expect to tell me to go to bed?"

Her face turned serious. "Have you slept at all this week?"

"Who needs sleep?" He turned to Harper. "Let's clean up these blocks."

They picked up the blocks and slid them, plastic guide and all, back into the box.

He stood and plopped down on the couch beside Jacq. "Have you slept much this week?"

She snorted. "Not hardly. Though I was so tired last night I fell asleep at like eight, but it was broken, and I was up multiple times."

He nodded. "Same boat."

"Dylan's been great, though."

"Good. You tell me if he's ever not, and I'll kick his butt for you."

"What would I do without a friend like you?"

"I don't know, but I will always have your six."

She put her head on his shoulder. "Do you think we'll find her?"

"I do. I have to."

Harper ran over and jumped on his lap.

Jacq sat up. "Time to go home, kiddo."

Harper threw her arms around Gio's neck. "Night." She bounded off and launched herself into Dylan's arms.

He said to Gio, "I'm gonna walk them out. Don't go anywhere. I'll be back in a minute."

"Take your time."

Gio leaned his head back on the couch and prayed while he waited for Dylan to return. Once Dylan came back into the apartment, he grabbed a pair of PlayStation controllers and tossed one to Gio.

"Talk to me."

"There's nothing to talk about."

All through the next hour of mindless gaming, Dylan pressed Gio to talk. Instead of answering, Gio focused on mercilessly defeating him.

After an hour, Dylan yawned.

Gio beat Dylan in one final game, then handed the controller to his friend. "I'm out. You need to go to bed." He stood.

"So much for getting you to talk about the black dog hanging out on your shoulder."

"It's not that bad, is it?"

"I guess not. Others might not notice, but as your best friend ..." Dylan held out his hands as if to state the obvious.

"I'll see you at church in the morning."

They said goodbye, and Gio left.

But Gio couldn't bring himself to go home, so he drove aimlessly around Knoxville. He headed downtown and through the sketchier areas, being sure to drive past corners where prostitutes liked to hang out.

Part of him was tempted to show Morgan's sketch around and ask if girls had seen her, but then he risked getting her in trouble with her pimp. Of course that was assuming she wasn't already in trouble from being with them the other day. Hopefully, being arrested was enough to keep him from beating her.

It was foolish to look for her here. She was a high-end girl, one who worked swanky hotels and rich parties. But something drew him to the area tonight, and he wasn't sure if it was the Holy Spirit or his stupid, messy heart of flesh.

Turning down another road, he saw about five girls hanging close to a corner. Their body language screamed "working girls." He slowed the car. One woman caught his eye. Her perfectly straight, long, dark-brown hair flowed over her shoulder. She looked in his direction. Morgan!

Chapter Fourteen

Morgan's feet and legs ached. Duke had sent meds with her, and they helped, but the lingering withdrawal symptoms would last a while. And it didn't help that Ronan had put her on a corner tonight. She couldn't believe it. But he was mad she'd been with Duke for so long, and probably even angrier that she was clean. He'd control her in any way he could.

She'd already been picked up twice, and they were sleezy lowlifes who only wanted ten minutes each. She could be working a party or calling the escort service to meet up with higher-paying tricks. But Ronan wanted her to remember her place, so here she was.

"Daisy, here comes another. Nice clean car. I want this one," Kim said.

Morgan looked at the SUV driving slowly toward them. Gio.

Her heart spazzed like a junkie on speed. She grabbed Kim's arm. "No. He's mine." Her spasming heart skipped. If only she could actually have Gio.

Kim wrenched her arm free. "I don't think so, girl. You always get the good ones."

She had no idea how good this one was. So good none of these girls was going to get him.

But what was he doing out here? Looking for her? Was he going to arrest her? Better that than going back to Ronan. Even if he arrested her, Gio felt safe. Unlike Ronan or Duke.

Morgan shoved Kim aside and strode to Gio's car as it came to a stop.

The passenger window rolled down. *Gio.* He genuinely looked happy to see her. What on earth?

"Here to arrest me again?"

"Again? I never arrested you."

She raised her eyebrows. "Um, just the other day?"

"I took you into *protective* custody. I got you out of jail. I think that's the opposite of arresting." His smile didn't fade. "Come with me."

She deflated. "I can't."

"Is that really true?"

"Yes. I've been off the job too long this week, and I have to ... work."

"Please come with me."

"Are you really trying to pick up a pro?"

"You know, I could arrest you."

"Maybe you should."

He tilted his head, then moved it side to side as if to shake loose a thought. "Can you look at something quick?"

She glanced around. Another girl got picked up, but at least Ronan wasn't nearby. "Quick."

He reached into his backseat and produced a sketchbook. "Have you ever seen this woman?" He turned it around so she could see a pencil sketch.

Her fumbling heart skidded to a stop. "Rose." The name barely escaped her lips.

"So you have?"

Morgan glanced over her shoulder, then grabbed the door handle and yanked it open. She jumped inside.

Gio's eyes were wide.

She found the button to raise the window. "Let's go." She put on her seatbelt and stared at the sketch as they drove away. It was almost perfect. "Why do you have a sketch of her? And why are you asking about her? What happened?"

He turned down another road before answering. "We found her body a week ago."

Morgan's stomach found her mouth. "Rose is dead?" She wished she was more shocked.

"Who is she, Morgan?"

Her real name. Why did it sound so good coming from Gio? "She was supposed to have a house of her own and be working her own schedule. At least that's what he said. I can't say I'm surprised it was a lie." She looked at Gio. "She used to live with me. Wife-in-law is the lingo."

"I wondered. Who is *he*?"

"Ronan."

"Your pimp?"

She nodded. For whatever reason she couldn't lie to the man sitting next to her. "Why did you think I knew her?"

"Her tattoo. I saw a bit of yours once and thought it looked similar." He pulled up to a stop sign at an empty intersection.

She scooted forward in the seat and turned slightly. Her skirt and shirt didn't quite meet tonight, but she pulled the waist of her skirt down a touch to show Gio.

"A daisy."

"Yep. That's me. Daisy."

"Did Ronan have a girl named Aster?"

"How'd you know that? She was in jail when Ronan brought me in. When she got out, he sold her to the highest bidder, supposedly."

"Supposedly?"

"If he killed Rose, there's a good chance he killed Aster too."

"I didn't say she was murdered."

"But she was, wasn't she? Did he beat her to death?"

"No. Gunshot."

"His second favorite weapon."

He drove again. "I'm worried about you, Morgan."

"Seems reasonable. If he knew what I've done ..."

Gio reached across and took her hand in his. "Exactly. If he's the one who killed Rose, as you call her—"

"What's her real name? He won't let us say them to one another."

"Jamie DeRozan." With a gentle squeeze, he released her hand.

"Jamie." She let the name linger in the air as she remembered the hardened but kind woman. How had she wronged Ronan? How far out of pocket had she gone?

Gio let the silence linger as he merged onto I-40. She didn't know where he was taking her, but she didn't care.

She couldn't breathe. "Gio, I'm scared."

Gio's heart shattered for the woman sitting in the car next to him. "Let us—Jacq, Dylan, our team—protect you."

She nodded.

"Do you have a cellphone?"

"Yeah, why?"

"Does Ronan track you with it?"

She drew her lip between her teeth. "Yep."

Gio opened his hand.

She dug a small smartphone out of her purse and gave it to him.

He debated what to do with it. If he turned it off, it would stop the tracking, but then Ronan would know something was up immediately.

Gio turned off at the next exit and drove back toward where they'd been.

"What are you doing?" The caution in her voice confused him. Was she afraid to ask the question?

"Don't hesitate to ask me questions. I sometimes forget to tell people what I'm thinking."

She chuckled. "You seriously don't care if I ask questions?"

"Why would I?"

"Where I'm from, questions result in a blow to the head, if you aren't careful."

He pushed the brake down too hard at a stop sign. "That's awful."

She shrugged. "It's just the way it is. Unfortunately, I've never learned my lesson."

"I'm sorry. We're going to ditch your phone, but in the area where he thinks you should be."

"Smart. I like it."

"Every once in a while I come up with a good idea."

"Then what?"

"I don't know yet. But I'll call Jacq."

Morgan smiled, making his heart take wing.

He drove slower as they approached the area where she'd been.

"There." She pointed under an overpass. A dirty man with scraggly hair pushed a shopping cart.

Perfect. He opened his phone and searched for the closest fast-food place. They swung through McDonald's and bought a cheeseburger combo. Then went back to where they'd seen the man.

Gio said to Morgan, "Stay in the car."

She nodded. He hopped out and, meal in hand, went to the man. "Sir, I'd like to give this to you."

The man's eyes lit up. He stretched out his gnarled hands and took the bag.

Gio continued, "The food is totally yours, but I have a request."

"Sure, sonny. Though I don't know what I could do for you in your fancy car."

"Would you carry this phone around for the rest of the night and then sell it at the pawn shop down the street tomorrow as soon as they open? Whatever money they give you is yours."

"Really?"

"Absolutely. Just don't wait too long in the morning."

"Thanks!"

Gio jumped back in the car and drove off. "Thanks for not stealing my car again."

Morgan laughed.

Gio was pretty sure her laughter was the most beautiful sound he'd ever heard.

"You know, Morgan, you look like you feel a lot better than the last time I saw you."

"I'm clean."

"How's that possible? It's only been three days."

"Almost four. But it's the weirdest thing. I have a regular trick who has this thing against heroin, so he made Ronan let me get clean. It's so weird, but I'm glad. I hate drugs."

"But three days?"

"The last three days have *not* been pleasant."

"I'd imagine not. You sure you're all right? We can go to the hospital."

"I really am fine." Rose's sketch caught her eye again. "Just scared. He will find me."

"I'll protect you."

"I don't get you, Gio."

"Eh, me neither." He winked at her. It was hard to tell in the faint glow of the streetlights, but it appeared as if she blushed.

He drove on in silence, but really wasn't sure where to go. No one wanted a call at almost midnight to ask about a house guest. They'd burned the bridge to get a safe house. *Got a place for us to go, God?*

Your place. The idea did not come from his own mind, of that Gio was certain.

Seriously? You know how that would look.

He could imagine God furrowing His eyebrows at Gio and almost laughed out loud. Since when did God care about the opinion of man?

Morgan shifted in her seat. Gio had grown quiet and the slight smile on his lips seemed to reveal he was amused at the conversation going on in his head. He was forgetting to share his thoughts again.

"Where are we headed?"

"My apartment. Hope that's all right."

She fiddled with the seatbelt. His home? Was he really the same as Duke? And what was with that last part? Did he really care what she thought?

"I'll of course call someone else to come over and be there too. Probably Dylan. And Jacq too. She'll have my head if I don't. But Harper is probably asleep."

"Wait, why call someone?"

"It wouldn't exactly be proper for me to have a woman in my house in the middle of the night."

She pressed her lips together to keep herself from bursting out laughing. Once she composed herself, she said, "Really? That's a first for me."

"I'd imagine, but I guess I'm ruled by a different playbook."

"Apparently." She relaxed back into her seat. Maybe he really wasn't *anything* like Duke.

He swiped in the code to his phone and, with the speakerphone on, called Dylan, who said he'd meet them at Gio's place. Then he dialed Jacqui's number.

With a groggy voice she answered with, "I told you to get some sleep."

"But then I wouldn't have been driving around Knoxville and run into a certain friend of ours."

"Wait, what?" Jacqui sounded awake now.

"Morgan is sitting in my car with me. We're headed back to my apartment. Dylan's meeting us, but I knew better than to not tell you."

"I'm coming over too."

"Isn't Harper asleep?"

"Yes, but she'll keep sleeping even if I move her."

"If you insist. You know I'm not going to tell you no."

"Mwahaha. I've got you right where I want you."

"You need sleep, Jacq."

"See you guys shortly."

After Gio hung up, Morgan laughed. "You two aren't just colleagues then, huh?"

"Jacq's the closest thing I've got to a sister. Doesn't hurt that Dylan is my closest friend."

"Have they set a date?"

Gio took a deep breath and glanced at her for as long as he could before he had to look back at the road. "She refuses to as long as your safety is uncertain."

"Oh." Morgan shrank in the seat a little, and the conversation lulled.

Eventually, she spoke again. "Gio, I'm really sorry I keep running off. The last time I was planning on coming back. I needed a hit, but Ronan ..." She looked out the side window of the car.

Gio's hand gripped her arm, but he quickly removed it. "We could have helped you."

"I know. It was stupid."

"We all do stupid things. You aren't alone in that."

She couldn't trap the tiny giggle that escaped. "Like you've ever."

"I ain't perfect. Sinner, like everyone else."

"Some of us more than others."

"Quantity is irrelevant. One sin was enough to send Jesus to the cross. Sorry, not trying to get preachy."

"You're one of those kind of people, aren't you? Just comes out because it's who you are?"

"Exactly."

"I remember Jacqui being like that. Is she still?"

"Absolutely." Gio pulled into an apartment complex not too far from Jacqui's and Dylan's homes.

"Do all FBI agents live in apartments?"

He looked at her sideways.

She gave him her cheesiest smile.

He parked, and, like last time, was at her door before she could even reach for the handle.

She handed him his sketchbook, and he scooped up the bag from his backseat.

They trekked up the open stairwell to his second-floor apartment. After inserting the key, he looked at her before turning it. "I wasn't expecting company, so, well, I make no promises. I left in a hurry to help Jacq and Dylan at the mountain house this morning."

She squeezed his arm. "I'm sure I've seen worse."

Once inside, he switched on the light. "Welcome to my humble abode."

A strange feeling washed over Morgan. She couldn't identify it. The living room and dining room, which flanked the sides of the door, were a touch messy—the living room with chord charts scattered near an acoustic guitar and the dining room table with a few books and dishes—but mostly the place was warm and inviting. Nothing stood out as to why it was that way, but immediately she felt herself relax. This really was a safe space.

"Thank you, Gio." The words almost caught in her throat.

Why did she have such a strong urge to walk into this man's arms? She literally never felt that way about anyone. She only ever walked *to* Ronan because she wanted something or wanted to avoid his wrath. With Duke she was playing a game. But with Gio … she couldn't explain it.

He motioned for her to follow him, and he gave her a tour. Past the dining room was a galley-style kitchen, where he said she was welcome to whatever she could find there. They strolled down the center of the apartment. Past the living room and across from the kitchen was a bedroom she could sleep in.

Then a bathroom on the same side as the kitchen, and his bedroom and bath were at the end. He shrugged. "It's not much, but it's home."

"I don't suppose you have anything I could wear?" She hated the outfit Ronan had made her put on tonight. The skirt was impossible to sit in.

He went into his room and pulled open a drawer. "I don't really have anything. A t-shirt?" He held one up and opened another drawer. "Gym shorts?" He dug a little deeper.

She crossed to him and took the t-shirt. It was super-soft cotton with an outline of mountains.

"Ah, these. They don't actually fit anymore. Will still probably fall off of you. I can call Jacq."

"This is fine." Her hand brushed Gio's as she took the shorts. His touch made her skin tingle.

She laid her hand on his chest for a moment before catching herself and pulling away. "These are great. Thanks."

As fast as she could without running, she turned and bolted to the bathroom. What was it about Gio?

Chapter Fifteen

GIO STOOD IN HIS room reeling from Morgan's hand on his chest. Oh, how he'd longed to pull her into his arms. Maybe he just needed to take a cold shower. Good thing the others were coming over.

A knock sounded on the door.

He went and opened it, revealing Jacq and Dylan, who was carrying a sleeping Harper.

Jacq held up a sleeping bag. "Which corner should I put her in?"

"Morgan can have the guest room, so why don't you and Harper take my bed. I promise I changed the sheets yesterday. Dylan and I can crash out here."

Dylan and Jacq disappeared down the hall. Gio forced himself to sit on the far end of the couch against the wall, opposite of the guest room.

God, what are we doing here? Show me the next step in all this. Help her feel like a guest and not a prisoner. Will that help her stay and not run off again?

He stretched his arm across the back of the couch.

Morgan came around the corner, his baggy clothes hanging off her thin body. She was even more attractive now that she looked relaxed.

"They're a little big." She bit her lip.

"You look comfortable though."

"I am. Thank you." She came and sat next to him. Not at the other end of the couch, but actually next to him.

He squeezed her shoulder briefly as he moved his arm to his side.

She took a breath, and her body language changed. "Is there anything I can do to thank you?"

Her words seemed to hold a different meaning than what she said. What was she asking? "Morgan, you're a guest in my home. Let this be your retreat. There's no need for you to thank me at all."

She tilted her head, then pointed to his lap. "Not even a little—"

"Definitely not."

He turned to face her, but words escaped him. How would he tell someone who's spent over a decade doing sexual favors for men in exchange for money and such that he'd never abuse her like that?

He resisted the urge to reach out and touch her. "What I have done is because you are a woman worthy of respect, honor, and a safe place. You deserve it all, at no cost, and I will accept nothing in return for it."

Tears brimmed in her eyes.

He wanted to embrace her but didn't. He needed her to know he was different than all the other men in her life.

She sunk deeper into the couch and wrapped her hands around his arm. She melted into him.

He laid his head on top of hers.

But Dylan and Jacq's voices pulled their attention. Morgan stood and hugged Jacq. The women held each other for a long time before finally joining Gio on the couch again. Dylan took the armchair.

Jacq asked Morgan, "How are you doing?"

Morgan told them about how the trick took her to the mountains and got her clean.

Jacq said, "No matter how weird he is, I'm glad he helped."

"I'll be glad if I don't have to see him ever again."

"No doubt." Jacq then pressed for more. "How are you really doing? You're out, for real. You don't have to go back."

"I know. I don't want to, really. But it's what I've known, so you kind of reach a point of acceptance, I guess, where you just survive day to day. Although sometimes I do wonder if it'd be easier not to live."

A brick slammed into Gio's heart.

"A few times I hoped Ronan had filled the syringe a little too much. Then maybe it could all be over, and I'd be done."

Gio's hand started to quiver. It broke his heart to hear her talk like this. He knew too well how hopeless trafficking leaves its victims.

Morgan grasped his hand. "Are you okay?"

He squeezed her hand then slipped his away and leaned his elbows on his knees. "I pray you don't ever feel like that again. There is hope."

"I want there to be. But what good am I now? No one wants a washed-up hooker. I'm not going to be able to find a job. I can't ever get married and have a family."

His heart felt as though it was being crushed. How could he help her see there was hope in Jesus? *Please show her Your hope and love, Lord.* "You can have those things."

Tears forced their way out of Jacq's eyes.

Morgan's voice was tight. "You can't know that."

"I have a pretty good gut feeling that you will. Don't let despair take root; it leads people to do ..." His voice trailed off. He couldn't finish the thought. He couldn't let the despair root in his heart too. But he didn't dare let anyone in this room see the place he went when he fought the grief and hopelessness that threatened his heart. Focusing that energy in the opposite direction always led somewhere equally ugly. Images of what he wanted to do to the traffickers filled his mind.

Morgan gripped his forearm.

Gio opened his eyes and realized his fists were clenched, every vein in his arms visible.

He met her eyes. Fear flickered there.

Releasing a shaky breath, he forced himself to relax his hands. "Sorry."

"Where'd you go?"

"A dark place." Gio looked to Dylan, who gave him a little nod. "I don't know."

Dylan said, "Just tell them. Jacq's been wanting to know, and the hope you found is what Morgan needs to hear."

How did he talk about the very reason he was an FBI agent? The reason he had such a heart for trafficking victims. The reason a thirst for vengeance swelled up within him so often. "My brother." His throat closed.

"What was his name?" Morgan asked.

"Eddie. Great kid, but he was taken advantage of." Gio turned on the couch toward Morgan and Jacq, who had both pulled their legs up.

But Gio couldn't seem to go on.

Jacq prodded this time. "What happened to Eddie, Gio?"

"He was trafficked by his friend's parents for a few years. People he was supposed to be able to trust. And it was hard to spot. He went about his normal life. My parents and I thought he was in a bad phase with his attitude and whatnot, but I was taking a psychology class in college when I realized something more had to be going on. I confronted him, and he broke down and told me everything. I went to a police detective in our church, and we were able to get him out. The man who had raped and sold my brother was finally behind bars. But just like where you are right now, that was the beginning of the journey."

Gio looked at the women. Jacq's hand covered the bottom portion of her face. Morgan's lips were tucked into her mouth. Had she heard similar stories before?

Morgan asked, "Eddie didn't find the hope you have, did he?"

Gio shook his head. "I tried to share with him, and he went for counseling, but I don't know. He let the despair overwhelm him." Gio didn't want to speak the next part. He'd only told a few people in his life, including Dylan. "That's why I challenge you, Morgan, to not dwell on the awful. There is hope in Jesus."

"It's so hard to walk with Jesus when I haven't been allowed a Bible or to go to church, but I want that. He's the only thing that's kept me alive so far. Did Eddie take his life?"

How was Morgan so perceptive? "Yeah, he overdosed on prescription drugs. I found him, but it was too late."

"Gio." Jacq's voice barely made it across the couch.

Morgan threw her arms around him and held him tight. He embraced her. "I'm so sorry, Gio. You don't have to explain anything else."

"But God's sustained me through it all. And He can do the same for you."

Morgan loosened her grip but didn't remove the arm across his back. "What was that verse? Hope and a future or something?" She turned slightly to Jacq. "You had it in our dorm room."

He knew the one. "'For I know the plans I have for you,' declares the Lord, 'plans to prosper you and not to harm you, plans to give you a hope and a future.'"

Jacq added, "Jeremiah 29:11 but verse thirteen is my favorite. 'You will search for Me and find Me, when you seek Me with all your heart.'"

Morgan's hand slid from his back as she sank into the couch. "I want to learn to seek Him again."

"You will. And we're here to help." Gio hoped she'd really let them.

Jacq said, "All you have to do is call out to Him."

"Like Bilbo in *The Hobbit*, running after Gandalf and the dwarves, yelling, 'Wait, wait.'" Morgan snickered.

Gio laughed. "Yes, but you don't have to chase God like Bilbo chased Gandalf. He's right there waiting for you."

She released a contented sigh and became quiet.

The conversation turned less serious as everyone grew tired. Eventually, Gio pulled out the air mattress for Dylan and made sure everyone had what they needed for the night.

Jacq had said goodnight to Dylan and disappeared into Gio's room. Gio made a final trip to the bathroom, but when he came out, Morgan stood in the hallway.

"Everything all right?"

"I'm still struggling with insomnia from the withdrawals. And I'm a little afraid of lying in there unable to sleep. All the thoughts about what Ronan ..."

"I have some melatonin."

"Would you stay with me?"

"I can't. It wouldn't be appropriate."

She tilted her head to the side. "I don't think I've ever had a guy not want to be with me."

"It's not like that." Quite the opposite really.

"You sure?"

He stepped closer. "You are very desirable. And not just your body. You've got a great sense of humor and an infectious laugh. You're kind and—"

She put a finger on his lips.

He took her hand and moved it away from his face. "Are you testing me?"

One shoulder came up to her ear, and she smiled.

"Melatonin?"

"Sure."

He got the sleep aid for her, and she went to bed without any more words.

Once in the living room, he collapsed on the couch.

"She's really taken with you." Dylan's voice surprised him.

"I thought you were already asleep."

"Kind of thinking one of us should stay awake. No matter how much she likes you, she's still a flight risk."

Gio stood. "True. I'll stay awake for a while if you'll go to sleep now."

Dylan said goodnight, and Gio went to the dining room and picked up his Bible from the table. He flipped it open. It fell to where his brother's suicide note was tucked inside. He unfolded it and read it for the thousandth time.

Hey Gio,

I'm sorry, bro. I can't do it anymore. I've tried. I really have. I don't know who I am anymore. I don't even know if I'm gay or straight. I don't know anymore. I don't want to be that *son. I can't bear to disappoint Mom and Dad. They'll be better off without me. Take care of Mom.*

I want to be whole again, but I can't be. That was taken from me. Too many times.

Thanks for being the brother I could always count on even when I didn't know it. Thanks for getting me out. I wish I could have lived up to your rescue.

I love you.

Goodbye. Maybe I'll see you in heaven, if God hasn't forgotten me. I hope He still accepts my prayer from when I was a kid. Bye.

Eddie

He'd bought into so many lies from the devil.

For the next hour, Gio tried to focus the grief into prayer instead of rage against the men who had taken advantage of his brother and forced him to do unspeakable things to the point of robbing Eddie of his life.

Gio prayed for Morgan and for himself, that he would have the ability to show her God's love and not the flawed version the world toted around. But did he even know what love was? He opened to First Corinthians chapter thirteen. "Love is patient" caught his eye.

I think I can do that, but only with Your help.

Morgan wandered out to Gio's living room Sunday morning. It had taken forever, but she'd finally slept. Before sleep came, her mind tossed around so many things. What if Ronan found her? Had he really murdered Rose? Why was she so drawn to Gio? All questions but no answers. She eventually drifted into a thankfully dreamless sleep, that only sort of left her feeling rested.

The television was running a countdown and playing what sounded like a worship song.

"Morning." Gio came out of the kitchen beside her with a cup of coffee in his hands. "We thought virtual church might be a better option this morning."

"Good morning." She pointed at his mug. "Got any more of that?"

"Absolutely." He nodded toward the kitchen. He set his mug on the counter and retrieved one for her. "Did you sleep all right?" He poured the black liquid into the mug.

"Well enough. You?"

"Same. Would you like any breakfast? I don't have much, but I could whip something up." He opened the fridge. "I have eggs or yogurt. I might have stuff for pancakes if you want to get fancy."

"Yogurt would be good."

He gave her two flavor choices, and she picked the strawberry.

After he offered ingredients to doctor her coffee, she made it a little sweet and creamy, and they went to the living room.

Harper and Dylan played on the floor, and Jacqui sat in the armchair.

Harper jumped up. “Pretty lady!” She wrapped her arms around Morgan’s legs.

“Hey, there. How are you, little friend?”

“Uncwa Gio got me a new coloring book.” She picked up the Peter Rabbit book, sending crayons flying across the carpet.

“Very nice.”

The music from the TV changed. “Ooh, singing time.” The three-year-old’s energy was delightful.

Morgan took a seat on the couch, where she’d sat the night before, with Gio by her side. She only knew the one hymn they sang, but it had been so long she barely remembered the words.

Gio knew them all, though, and sang with an amazing, deep voice, full of passion and conviction.

Once the singing was over, a couple came up on the stage and talked about things happening in the church. “Today,” the woman said, “is pro-life Sunday.”

Morgan’s heart panged as guilt washed over her. Only once had she been forced to endure an abortion, but she hated thinking about it. She hated abortion. She hated the loss of life, but what choice had she had? Her pimp at the time gave her none. Have the “simple procedure” or she’d be living on the street.

Gio lightly touched her arm, concern in his eyes.

She tried to smile at him, and it was just the distraction from her own mind she needed. She tuned back in. The woman was still speaking.

“I had an abortion when I was twenty-two. I thought I’d feel so relieved by the fact I wouldn’t have to face my family, who I was sure would turn me away. It was exactly the opposite. The guilt was immense. I still wrestle with the regret, but I have found freedom and healing in Jesus. Forgiveness is available to all who cry out to Him.”

God, can You really forgive me for everything I’ve done?

The man spoke next. “Do you know someone who is experiencing an unexpected or unwanted pregnancy? What can you do to encourage them and help them as they face the challenges of this life change?"

He continued, but Morgan couldn't focus anymore. Lily. She would be in so much trouble once Ronan figured out she was probably pregnant.

More dread filled her stomach. What would he do to her since Morgan had disappeared? All of the girls? What should she do?

She tried to listen to the sermon, but her brain rattled with the idea that she somehow needed to get Lily out at the very least. Every time she refocused on the sermon, Lily's face danced in her mind. So she started to formulate a plan.

Ronan would be sleeping now, probably until around three. That was his norm anyway, especially lately as he was keeping such a tight rein on all the girls. They would also be asleep. If she could slip in and wake Lily, they could simply walk out and come back here.

Her last sneaking attempt had failed, but that was probably because she'd been jonesing. It wasn't her first attempt around Ronan, just the only time she'd ever been caught. She set her mind to it. But the biggest question was how to duck out of here?

Her opportunity came after lunch. Harper begged all through the meal to go to the playground. So Dylan and Gio offered to take her to the park.

Morgan said, "We can clean up."

Jacqui took everyone's plates. "Yay, girl time."

Morgan screamed silently behind her smile. She hated that she was planning to slip out, but she had to. Lily needed her.

The guys left with Harper, and Morgan and Jacqui put away the sandwich fixings.

Morgan forced a yawn. "Oof. I guess I'm still tired. My days and nights are so confused."

"I can only imagine. Go take a nap. Maybe I'll hop in the shower while you sleep, and when you get up, we can chat."

"I'd like that." It wasn't a lie. She would much rather sit and talk with Jacqui than sneak past Ronan.

A few minutes later, Morgan went into the guest room but didn't shut the door completely. She lay down and listened. The apartment was quiet. She wasn't really tired so closing her eyes wasn't a risk.

She sensed Jacqui peeking into the room, then heard a door shut at the back of the apartment. Slipping off the bed, she tiptoed to the hallway.

The shower kicked on.

It was now or never.

She glanced down at her bare feet. That wouldn't work, and her heels wouldn't work either. Glancing into Gio's room, she spotted Jacqui's tennis shoes. They'd worn the same size in college, it must be time to share shoes again. She slipped them on. *Sorry, Jacqui. I'll be back.*

Quickly and quietly she moved through the apartment. She reached for the door. How was she going to get anywhere? Steal Gio's car again? No, surely Gio and Dylan would spot her, and she didn't have time to explain. She glanced around.

Gio's phone was plugged in on the kitchen counter. Perfect. At least she could use the map app to find her way. Maybe she could call an Uber. She had enough cash in her purse. She grabbed Gio's phone, slipped out the front door, and padded down the stairs opposite the playground.

Chapter Sixteen

JACQ SQUIRTED SHAMPOO INTO her hand, then heard what sounded like a door. Did one of the guys come back? She thought she had spotted Gio's phone on the counter.

She lathered her hair, but something nagged her. Maybe she should hop out and check on Morgan.

She rinsed the shampoo, and the feeling didn't let up, so she climbed out and wrapped a towel around herself.

Cautiously, in case it was Gio, she wandered out into the hallway. She didn't want to yell and wake up Morgan. She made it to the dining room and didn't see anyone. Gio's phone wasn't on the counter. He must have slipped in and out quickly.

Back to the shower. As she padded down the hallway, she peeked in on Morgan.

The bed was empty.

She spun. The bathroom was empty.

"Morgan?"

Silence.

"Morgan?"

No! Jacq ran back to the bathroom and threw her clothes on her damp body. Found her phone and called Dylan while she searched for her shoes.

"She's gone. Please tell me she came out to join you guys."

"Morgan? No. What happened?"

"She laid down, so I jumped in the shower. How could I be so stupid? Where are my shoes?"

"We'll look for her out here."

Dylan hung up.

Jacq's shoes had vanished. "Forget it." She ran out the door barefoot and considered the stair options. She chose the ones that led away from the playground and parking lot. She yelled when she reached the bottom. "Morgan!"

But her friend was nowhere to be seen.

Jacq ran out across the grass toward the street that was parallel to the building. Nothing. No trace of where she could have gone. No cars pulling away. No flashes of brown hair. She'd disappeared. Again.

Morgan eased the back door closed behind her. She'd paid the Uber driver after she had him drop her at the end of the block, then snuck around to the backyard like she had before. So far all seemed quiet. Getting to Lily probably wouldn't be the hard part; getting out with her would be. She took the back staircase by the kitchen.

At the top she waited, listened. Still quiet. Everyone must be sleeping, but it was pushing two o'clock. Before entering the house, she had double checked that Gio's phone was on silent. If only she could put her own breathing on silent.

The phone was in the pocket of the gym shorts. She was nervous about having it there because if she did run into Ronan ... but maybe she could dial 911 quickly.

Who was she kidding?

God, help me. Direct my steps. And more than anything, help me get Lily out of here.

She crossed the hall to the room Lily and Celeste shared. She eased the door open. Celeste was asleep, but Lily wasn't there.

Hopefully, she wasn't downstairs with Ronan.

Maybe she'd gone into Morgan's room. Even when she was home, Lily often crashed with her to get away from Celeste.

Morgan tiptoed down the hallway and turned the handle as slowly as she could.

Lily!

She shut the door with as much care as she had opened it, then ran to the bed. The phone banged against her leg, so she reached in and grabbed it. She sat on the edge of the bed and shook Lily. "Lily, get up. Quick."

Her heart thundered in her chest.

"Daisy, let me sleep."

"No, you have to get up right now."

Lily rolled over and opened her eyes. "What is going on? Where have you been?"

"Shh. I'm going to get you out of here. I know some people we can trust, and they can help us—keep us safe from—"

The door crashed against the wall. *No!*

Using her body to block his view, she slid the phone between the mattress and box springs, then turned toward Ronan.

A string of expletives flew from his mouth. "Where have you been?" He grabbed her arm and yanked her to her feet. "What in tarnation are you wearing?"

She swallowed but refused to say anything.

His other hand gripped her throat.

She couldn't breathe.

"You weren't where you were supposed to be this morning." He let go of her throat and jerked her purse up and open. "Where's the money you were supposed to be making all night long?" He dumped the contents of her purse all over the floor.

At least she hadn't put Gio's phone in there.

He slapped her face. "Speak."

Her head snapped to the side and the skin stung. But she remained silent. What was she supposed to say? She needed to get out of here. With Lily.

"Do you really think that because some rich guy insists on getting you clean that you are better than the other girls? That you can just waltz around and do whatever you want? That's not how things work here. You do as I say, or you face the consequences. And you will face the consequences."

He grabbed both of her arms and threw her against the wall.

Her shoulder hit, leaving an indent in the drywall. "Lily, run."

"Don't move, Lily." Ronan drew his gun from the back of his pants and pointed it at Lily.

A vise tightened around Morgan's lungs. "No!"

"Is she why you came back? Should I kill her? Would that teach you a lesson?"

"No, don't. Leave her alone."

"Fine." He redirected the gun at her, his finger dangerously close to the trigger. "Lily, go to your room and don't come out until I say to. Obey, or Daisy dies."

"Yes, Ronan." Lily's voice shook, and she darted out of the room.

Ronan stalked toward Morgan until the barrel of the gun was in her face. "Daisy, you will learn to behave. No more coddling you and treating you like a princess. No, I'm going to treat you like the whore you are."

Everything in Morgan screamed to fight back, but he'd shoot her, just like he did Rose. And if she was dead, she couldn't help Lily.

Ronan pressed the cold metal of the barrel against Morgan's temple. "I can't shoot you with this or with heroin, otherwise Duke's pockets would find another coffer to fill. But there are other ways to keep you under control. Start by taking these stupid clothes off, immediately."

She pulled Gio's shirt and shorts off, dropping them to the ground. For the first time, in she didn't know how long, she wanted to cover her body, but she couldn't.

"Good." With his free hand, Ronan gripped her arm again, fingers digging in between muscle and bone. He hauled her across the room and shoved her into the hallway.

She stumbled but managed to keep her feet beneath her. If only she could get to Gio's phone and call in the cavalry. But she couldn't. At least with Ronan's attention on her, he wouldn't bother with Lily. Lily and her baby were all that mattered.

Ronan pushed her forward again. "Downstairs."

She walked, but apparently not fast enough.

"Would you move, you little—"

She blocked the slurs he hurled at her.

"I said move."

The barrel of the gun pressed into her back along with his other hand. He shoved her.

She reached for the handrail to try and catch herself, but that only wrenched her arm worse as she fell. *God, help.*

Her side collided with the carpeted stairs. She skidded down a couple, burning her exposed skin, before she tumbled, feet over head. Her hip hit the tile at the bottom. Pain radiated through her whole body. She took a quick assessment. Nothing felt broken. Bruised, but not broken. Even so, she couldn't move, couldn't get up. Not before Ronan made it down the stairs.

Why did I think I could do this on my own? Give me endurance, God.

Heart racing and body throbbing, Morgan tried to push herself off the floor, but Ronan kicked her shoulder to the ground. "Get up."

"I could if—" She shut her mouth.

"That's right, think twice before you say anything." He grabbed her hair. "Now get up."

Her legs screamed as she put her weight on them.

Ronan dragged her toward his room.

What was he going to do to her? It would be hours before he put her up in a motel room, which was bound to happen. Maybe they could get out once Ronan had his way with her. Take off running. Maybe.

She just had to make it through whatever Ronan would do. She needed to not provoke him to something worse. This would be bad enough. She tried to shut her brain off from the fear that wanted to consume her. *Block it out. Don't think about it.*

Once in his room, he whipped her to the ground. She skidded on his oriental rug, and her cheekbone slammed into the bed frame.

She touched her cheek. No blood. But her knees were raw and a bit bloody.

Ronan locked his gun, and her only chance of getting away, in the safe beside his bed and turned back toward her. He removed his belt. "Somehow along the way you forgot the rules to this game, and now you need a reminder. One, I'm in charge. You are nothing. Worth nothing more than what a man will pay to spend an hour with your sorry carcass. You are trash to be swept up and thrown away when *I'm* done with you."

Gio's words from last night echoed. "A woman worthy of respect, honor, and a safe place." Whose words were true? Because they couldn't both be.

She closed her eyes and endured all Ronan threw at her verbally and physically. Maybe this was penance for all the horrible things she'd done over the years. She may be damaged goods, but if she could figure out a way to get Lily out, she could do something right. She had to save Lily and the baby, no matter the cost.

Gio ran down the road, but Morgan was gone. This was fruitless. They'd been searching for an hour. He stopped at the corner and wiped the sweat from his forehead. Early afternoon in late June was not an appropriate time for running.

But where was Morgan?

He checked his pocket. Where was his phone? Must have left it on the charger.

Dylan's car pulled up, window down. "Want a ride?"

Without words, Gio got in the passenger's side. "Where's Jacq?"

"She jumped in her car with Harper as soon as you took off. She couldn't run around barefoot. I just got off the phone with her. She's dropping Harper off at my mom's."

They went back to Gio's apartment and looked around for any clues about Morgan. About five minutes into searching, Jacq arrived.

How had Morgan slipped away again? And why? She really acted like she was going to stay. Was that a show? He went into the guest room. Her skirt and shirt from yesterday were still draped across the dresser. He ran his finger along the crop top.

What if Ronan had found her? What if he'd gotten his filthy hands on her and hurt her? What if he was selling her off again? If Gio could get his hands on Ronan, he'd wish he'd been born a eunuch.

The shirt crumpled in his grasp. He pressed his hand back out against the dresser, flattening the shirt.

"Gio?" Dylan's voice made him turn. "Anything in here?"

Gio shook his head. "She left her clothes, but her purse is gone."

"Why would she leave her clothes?"

"Guess she thought it was easier to get away in what she was already wearing."

"Did you find your phone?"

"I forgot to look. I think I left it on the charger, but who knows?" He strode past Dylan and toward the kitchen.

The phone was not on the charger where he could have sworn he'd left it. "Where'd I leave it this time?"

He pulled his Bible off the shelf and checked inside. A few times he'd left it in his Bible. Not there.

"I'll call it," Jacq said.

"It's on silent."

Jacq dialed anyway.

He glanced at his watch. The call didn't register. Weird. Where'd he put the stupid phone? Why'd he have to lose it again? He stalked to the couch and flung the cushions off. Surely it had fallen in. What-if questions bombarded his mind and rattled him more.

Jacq sank into the armchair. "What if Ronan ..."

Dread filled Gio's entire being. "He'll get what he deserves."

"I'm with you." Jacq's voice was tight. "If he hurts her, trust me. You won't be the only one going for him."

Dylan said, "But maybe she didn't go back to him."

Abandoning his search of the couch, Gio met Dylan's eyes. "Where else do you really think she went? I really thought ..."

"We all did."

With overly forceful movement, Gio shoved the cushions back on the couch. Controlling his anger was increasingly difficult. Gio wanted to kick or throw something. And where was his blasted phone?

Chapter Seventeen

Naked, battered, and bruised, Morgan fell to the floor in her room, catching herself with her arms. Ronan towered over her. "Go to bed. You need to be well-rested for tonight."

Tonight. Never had a word held such dread. The way he spit it out made it clear what his intention was. As much money made as possible, filing men through a room as fast as possible.

He slammed the door shut and locked it from the outside with the bolt he rarely used.

She collapsed the rest of the way to the floor, unable to cry. Her emotions were shut off as much as she could manage. She couldn't let herself feel anything right now, otherwise she'd ... she wasn't sure what, but it wouldn't be good.

Because the floor bit at her rug burns, she pushed herself up. Logic told her the bed would feel better. *Get up.* Her knees hurt too much to crawl, so with effort she got on her feet.

Gio's shirt on the floor caught her eye. She waddled over to it and scooped it up. Holding it close to her body, she went to the bed and collapsed onto the soft mattress. She held it out and read the print for the first time. Beneath an outline of a mountain range were the words, "Faith can move mountains," and the reference Matthew 17:20.

God, will You listen to me, even after that? I hope so. Because I've got a huge mountain that needs moving. Please move it. Rescue us. Please.

Emotions she thought were shut off welled up. She wanted out of this. She didn't want to be here. Why hadn't she thought of a better way to get Lily? *I need help.* She hugged the shirt to her chest and rolled to her side.

Gio's phone! How had she forgotten? But what could they do? Just calling and saying she was in trouble wouldn't be enough for a warrant or whatever they might need. Would it?

Still, maybe she should at least apologize.

She reached around the side of the mattress and felt for the phone. Where'd it go? Ronan had been with her the whole time. He wouldn't have found it.

Did someone else come in here?

She moved her hand down farther. It bumped into something.

Relief.

Gio's lock screen was a Bible verse. Of course it was.

When you pass through the waters, I will be with you; and through the rivers, they shall not overwhelm you; when you walk through fire you shall not be burned, and the flame shall not consume you. Isaiah 43:2

Why would Gio have a verse like that? What fire would he experience?

His brother. That memory had to be rough to walk through.

She swiped open the phone using the pattern she'd seen Gio use last night. She couldn't risk calling Jacqui and being heard, but she could text her.

She opened the text app and typed a few words. Then she deleted them. She didn't know what to say. What could she tell them? Ronan threw her down the stairs and raped her? They didn't need to know that. They needed to know she was alive and would contact them when there was an opportunity. When that would be she had no idea.

So what do I say?

The bolt on the door slid open.

Morgan rolled to her side and stuffed the phone back under the mattress. She yanked the sheet up, covering herself and Gio's t-shirt.

The door opened.

Ronan came in and threw his phone on the bed. "Duke wants to talk to you. Tell him you can't see him until tomorrow. I'll be back in two minutes to get my phone. No funny business. I'll know if you call anyone other than Duke." He pulled his gun out of his pants. "One for Lily and one for you if you do."

Once Ronan left, relocking the door behind him, Morgan grabbed the phone and called Duke.

He answered immediately. "Hello."

"Hey, it's Daisy."

"Good. Can I see you tomorrow?"

She would be so sore by then. She was already sore; a whole night like she was about to experience would do her in. "Late tomorrow?"

"Sure, I suppose I can wait a little later than I was thinking. But I actually have a better idea."

"What's that?"

"You leave Ronan and come be with me."

"You know Ronan will kill you for talking like this, right?"

"Not if I kill him first."

"You'd do that?"

"I'd do anything for you."

A shudder worked its way down her spine. "Anything?"

"That's what I said."

"Would you take Lily too?"

"We can talk tomorrow. I'll see you at our regular place. Ten p.m." The phone clicked.

Talk about it? He hadn't actually answered the question.

Freedom in any form wouldn't come tomorrow.

But at least she could count on an evening with Duke instead of another night of a revolving door. Maybe she could convince Duke to keep her until morning. But if he wouldn't take Lily too, she wouldn't leave with him.

She set the phone at the end of the bed and lay down as she waited for Ronan to come back.

The wait was short.

"So when does deep-pockets want you?" He picked up his phone.

She told him.

"Lucky you, just one night like tonight. Unless he only wants an hour, then ..." He laughed as he walked out the door.

Once the bolt was locked, she retrieved Gio's phone.

Gio collapsed on the couch. Beyond frustrated. Not being able to find Morgan *and* his phone was driving him nuts. He rested his head on the back of the couch.

Jacq's phone dinged with a text message. "Well, that explains why you can't find your phone. You just texted me."

He bolted upright. "What? Morgan? What's it say?"

"Chill, opening it now."

Gio watched her intently. Her face dropped, and she put her hand over her mouth.

"Jacq?"

Dylan came back into the room. "What's going on?"

They both ignored his question.

"Read it, Jacq."

Her eyes brimmed with tears, and she shook her head. She handed him her phone.

This is Morgan. I'm so sorry. I wasn't going to leave, really. Wanted to get someone. Was going to come right back. But he caught me. It's bad. He locked me in, so I can't get out at all now, and he'll lock me in a hotel room tonight. Pray for me. Tell Gio I'm sorry, again. I'll be in contact, at some point. Have to hide the phone pretty well, and I'll turn it off to save the battery.

Gio stood and raised the hand holding Jacq's phone, but Dylan snatched it away before he could do something stupid.

"Anyone going to tell me?" Dylan asked.

Gio let Dylan have the phone and moved toward the kitchen. Each thudded step reverberated with the force of Gio's fury.

The images of what Morgan's pimp might have done to her when he caught her flooded his mind, fueling his anger into rage. With a shaky hand, Gio pulled one of his last three glasses out of the dishwasher and filled it with water. He chugged it.

Gio raised his arm, glass in hand, ready to send it flying. But Jacq's voice from the other room halted his movements. The muscles in his arm trembled. If he could get his hands on Ronan, he'd—

Gio slammed the glass down on the stone counter. The glass shattered in his hand, but he couldn't stop clenching his fist.

"Gio, are you—" Jacq rounded the corner. "Oh my. Gio!" She gripped his arm. "Let go of it. Oh my word. Dylan!"

Gio felt frozen.

"Come on, Gio. Relax your hand." She massaged his arm.

He finally released the cup and shards fell to the counter, though not all of them. Blood dripped among the pieces of glass.

Still he felt no pain. It should hurt, but he was too angry to feel anything.

Jacq grabbed some paper towels and cradled his hand with them.

Dylan came up to his other side. "Hey." Dylan put his hand heavily on Gio's shoulder. "Chill. You need to relax."

Jacq pulled on his arm. "Come sit."

He obeyed and sat at the dining room table.

"First aid kit?" Dylan asked.

Somehow he managed to get an answer out. "My bathroom."

Jacq made Gio lay his hand on the table while she examined it. "You may need to go to urgent care for this."

"I'm fine."

"Don't argue with me. You could have cut a tendon or something."

"Fine. Then call Josh Schneider. He owes me one anyway."

"I don't have his phone number."

"Chloe will have it."

"Don't go anywhere." Jacq turned. "Dylan, where's my phone?"

"Coffee table."

Gio laid his head down on his other arm. All he could think about was Morgan. If Ronan touched her, she was probably hurting more than he was right now.

His insides quivered, but he tried to pray. *Protect Morgan. Show me what we can do.*

Ten minutes later Josh Schneider, a family doctor, arrived. About six months ago, Josh's car battery had died on the coldest day of the year after a church event. Josh had insisted on owing Gio for helping. And today it was time to collect.

"Thanks for saving me from trying to explain this to some random urgent care doc."

Josh took in the chair next to Gio. "No problem. I won't ask too many questions. But what happened?"

"Lost my cool with a glass."

Dylan sat opposite of Josh. "And now he's down to just two glasses. What happened to the other ones, Gio?"

"What happened to not too many questions?"

"Josh said that, not me." Dylan gave him a best-start-explaining look.

Gio shook his head at his best friend and turned his attention to Josh. "How bad is it, doc?"

"Doesn't look too bad, but I won't know really until the glass is out."

Josh set to work and had Jacq assist him with flushing out the wound at the base of Gio's thumb.

Dylan was unrelenting. "What happened to the other glasses, Gio?"

He winced at the pain. "Seriously? What do you think happened?"

"Do you normally throw them rather than smashing them against the counter?"

"Do guitar strings snap if you strum them too hard?"

"Only if they're wound too tight."

Gio gave him a well-there-you-have-it look.

Josh poked Gio's thumb. "All the nerves and such seem unscathed. A little surgical glue and bandaging and you'll be fine, but no more fights with drinking glasses."

"If you insist."

Josh laughed and wrapped his hand. "Random question: do you have room in your Bible study for another guy?"

Gio said, "Sure, we're studying the minor prophets. Currently, we're in Hosea." The word pricked at Gio's heart. Hosea.

"Great. I'll get the details later. If you develop any fever, oozing, or red streaking, call your doctor." Josh finished up the bandage and left.

Once he was gone, Gio sank back into the chair. "Hosea. Why do I get the feeling I know exactly how Hosea must have felt? It's not like she's my wife, but good grief."

Jacq and Dylan sat at the table with him. Jacq said, "Because she keeps going back, just like Gomar did. Just like we all do."

Gio snorted a rueful laugh. "Don't we though?"

"What if"—Dylan rubbed his chin—"we played this like Hosea?"

Jacq looked as confused as Gio felt.

Dylan's eyes were intensely focused on Gio. "What did Hosea do in chapter four?"

"He went and bought Gomar back."

"Exactly. If that's what it takes, maybe that's what we need to do."

"How? This pimp isn't going to sell one of his girls to a bunch of feds."

"No, but maybe we buy the right to see her. Pose as a john. We're a phone call away, and we get her out of there."

Jacq raised her index finger. "One problem. How do we find her?"

"Surely we have enough connections."

Jacq said, "We can ask Natalie, Sydney, and Lexi."

"We can always talk to Ezra again too."

Gio tilted his head. "Can we?"

"Last I heard he was still sitting in lock-up since no one paid his bail."

"And there's always Bobbi." Jacq shivered.

Gio nodded. "I think we have enough sources that perhaps we can get a lead on where he'll have her. Might be able to call escort services and see if they can connect us with Daisy."

"Connect *you* with Daisy." Jacq's eyes were intense.

Could Gio really pull off going into a hotel to supposedly meet a prostitute?

As if reading his mind, Jacq grabbed his uninjured hand. "You can do it. And we'll be right around the corner."

"Wondering if I should leave my gun behind."

"Probably your badge but not your gun." Dylan raised his eyebrows.

"Indeed."

God, help.

Gio was back at the office, sitting at the conference room table, laptop at hand around nine that night when Dylan dropped a bag of food on the table beside him. Next to the bag he set down a wad of cash.

"That's what I could get. Now eat."

"I'm not hungry." Gio pushed the bag away. But the movement let loose the scent of fried rice. His stomach growled.

"You were saying?"

Gio tapped the money. "Hopefully, we won't need this."

"Would you eat? Warren says we're a go."

Jacq came into the room. "I've got ears." She dropped an earpiece on the table for him. "But, of course, I won't be offended if you turn it off at some point."

"What's that supposed to mean?" It came out more defensive than he had intended.

"Talking. Duh. What did you think I meant? I know you better than that."

Gio shook his head and pulled the food back to him. Everything was in place, but they were still trying to narrow down where Morgan would be tonight. By the time they had been able to track Gio's phone it had already been turned off, and while they had the general vicinity of where she had been when she sent the text, they didn't know the precise address.

Since getting his hand bandaged, they'd also gotten him another cellphone, talked to the girls they'd helped save back in April, talked to Bobbi and Ezra, and called a few escort services looking for "Daisy."

They had a good idea of possible locations, but not the exact one.

"I could go back to the corner where I found her yesterday and ask if the girls there know where she is tonight."

Dylan shook his head. "They'll sniff you out as a cop and keep their mouths shut."

"But somehow I'm supposed to convince the pimp at the door I'm a legit john?"

Jacq said, "You'll be fine. Just remember: Morgan."

Dylan raised his index finger. "You didn't see this guy trying to get into the club we busted a couple of months ago. He almost didn't get admitted."

Gio laughed. "I didn't know Morgan then."

Dylan slapped him on the shoulder. "I take it all back. You got this."

While Gio ate, he continued his search of the dark web, and Dylan made a few more calls.

Morgan's picture came up on the screen. There! With a mouthful of fried rice, Gio said, "Found her!"

He clicked on it. It was a web ad for "Daisy" at a discounted rate, tonight only.

With difficulty, he swallowed his food. But it threatened to come up again. He grabbed his water and took a swig.

"Do you need to call?" Dylan asked.

"Nope, address given. Just show up." Gio stood. "Let's go."

"We need to hurry; she started already."

Fifteen minutes later, Gio ambled around the backside of a sketchy motel, one of the very motels Ezra had told them was a regular location for Ronan to set up business. Dylan and Jacq dropped Gio off around the block so they wouldn't be seen together. He then spotted Dylan's car coming into the parking lot of the adjacent restaurant.

Gio adjusted his baseball cap and wished he wasn't wearing a polo shirt over a t-shirt, but the goal was to sneak Morgan out and the shirt and hat would hide her at least a little.

A few doors down, a huge man sat in a lawn chair straight out of the eighties. The ad said "talk to Scissors."

"You Scissors?" *This is for Morgan. This is for Morgan.*

"Probably."

"I'd like to see Daisy."

Dylan's voice resounded over the comms. "This time you need to act nervous."

Gio checked over his shoulder and scanned the area.

"You got money? It's pay upfront."

"Yeah, how long does this give me?" Gio pulled out cash from his pocket.

The guy laughed. "Barely ten minutes."

Gio doubled it. "So twenty."

"Yep. The last guy just left, so she's all yours. I'll knock on the door when your time's up. You'll have one minute to put your pants on. Then I open the door. Capiche?"

Gio nodded. He wiped his stupid sweaty palms on his jeans.

He followed Scissors down a few more doors. Interesting. He wasn't stationed right outside. "You sit over there when she's here?"

"I don't need to listen to your pleasure, man." Scissors inserted the key and turned it. Then he pushed the door open. "Clock starts now. Have fun."

Gio stepped inside and let the door close.

Perched on the edge of the bed, sheet over her lap, with her back toward him, was Morgan.

"What's your pleasure?" She pulled her hair over her shoulder, revealing her back. Giant purple bruises spotted with raw red patches appeared.

He couldn't talk, couldn't think, couldn't breathe.

Chapter Eighteen

Less than five minutes since the last trick left, yet another guy entered Morgan's room. She hurt from head to toe, but especially in the middle. If she wasn't careful, she'd throw up from the pain.

Why wasn't this guy responding?

She threw her hair back over her shoulder and turned to the man. Might as well entice him to get it done.

Gio!

She froze. Why was he here? Was he not the guy she believed he was? "I thought you were different." The words came out with more bite than she meant.

His cheeks burned bright red, a shade she didn't know a man's face could achieve. She pulled the sheet up over her chest.

He stepped farther into the room. "I'm here to rescue you."

Rescue? He'd come to save her, to get her out of here? "A little short for a storm trooper, aren't you?" A giggle worked its way out from deep in her soul.

He came closer. "I've been accused of many things in my life, but being short has never been one of them."

Another giggle came out. She yanked the sheet from its hospital corners, wrapped it around her backside, and stood. Her body screamed. She stumbled a little.

Gio darted to her. "Are you all right?"

She shook her head. "But I will be. I'm so sorry I left."

"I know. We got your text. What happened?" His hand hovered near her elbow, but he didn't touch her.

"Ronan. He caught me sneaking into the house." She turned slightly and, while holding the sheet to her chest with one hand, used the other to reveal the wounds on her side. "I don't think anything is broken, but this is what happens when you fall down the stairs naked."

"Oh, Morgan." His hand moved closer. "May I? I'd like to be sure nothing is broken."

She nodded. Did he really ask permission to touch her?

His hand was warm and gentle. "Your ribs don't feel broken. Although we probably should get x-rays to be sure."

"How exactly is that going to happen in here?"

"We leave. I give Dylan the signal, he and Jacq cause a diversion, and we sneak out. Where are your clothes?"

"Ronan took them so I wouldn't leave."

"That complicates things."

"Gio." She reached out to him but stopped shy of touching his chest. "I'm not leaving. I can't. The whole reason I went back was for Lily, and I don't know where Ronan has her. If I run, he'll kill her."

"Then we find her first. Did he have the same set up for her tonight?"

"I don't know. But it's likely. Punishing her also punishes me."

He looked over her head. "Did you guys catch that? Yeah, find a girl named Lily. I think that may be the girl Matt saw. So get him searching for her. Thanks, guys."

Gio met her eyes again.

She stepped closer to him and ran her fingers along his chest. "Thank you. Please let me give you a little something."

"No, Morgan."

She toyed with the buttons on his polo. "But it's the only thing I know how to do."

"That's not true. You know how to make me laugh."

"And blush."

"I bet you make lots of men blush."

"Nah. Most of them barely look at me. But you, you looked at *me.*"

His hand hovered close to her face. "May I?"

"Are you asking to touch me?"

"Yes, you deserve to be honored and respected."

Her lip quivered, and she bit it, nodding.

He brushed the hair away from her face and traced her chin. "I'm sorry he hurt you. How's your cheek?"

"It's fine." She reached down and unbuckled his belt.

"Whoa." He jumped back.

"Gio, if he's going to believe something happened, you probably should look a little disheveled." She pulled the belt.

"Good thing my gun holster isn't dependent completely on my belt."

She stepped toward him. "You don't want to give into temptation?"

"Not until I'm married, and you aren't my wife—" He barely finished the word "wife" before snapping his mouth shut.

"You cut yourself off. What else were you going to say? Yet?"

The bright red color returned to his face.

"Why on earth would a guy like you ever marry a girl like me?"

"Why not? If God can love any of us, can't I? You deserve to feel loved and cherished as much as the next person. You aren't less because of what other people have made you do."

"I want to believe you."

"I hope you will one day."

He tossed his hat on the foot of the bed and pulled off his polo shirt.

Her pulse increased. Had he changed his mind?

"Here." He handed her the shirt. "So you don't have to struggle to hold the sheet so much."

"I could just let it drop."

"You are trouble. Don't think for a second my refusal is anything akin to a lack of desire."

She waggled her eyebrows. "So you *are* actually a man?"

"You have no idea."

A knock sounded on the door.

"How long did you pay for?"

"Twenty minutes. I thought that'd be long enough to convince you to leave."

"I don't want you to go." She gripped his arm.

"I'm not going anywhere."

He kicked off his shoes, untucked his t-shirt, and covered his gun. The door opened. Morgan dropped Gio's shirt to the floor.

Gio stepped to the doorway and put himself halfway outside but kept a foot inside.

Morgan moved closer to hear.

Gio spoke. "Look, man, this wasn't enough. I want longer. I can pay."

"Boss wants to keep 'em moving through here tonight. Your time's up. More guys'll be coming."

"What's your cut?"

"Enough."

Cash rustled. "Well, based on the rate you said earlier, which was twice what was advertised, this should pay for the whole night, plus some."

"You're nuts, man. Boss said—"

"Boss wants money, so do you. When he asks, tell him whatever number you want about how many guys came through. You've got the money. Isn't that what really matters?"

"True."

"This way, you can take it easy. Win-win."

"Fair enough. Nothing funny, though. I'm still sitting out here."

"No problem. You leave us alone; we'll leave you alone."

Gio came back in, closed the door, and let out a whoosh of air.

"How much did you pay to spend the night with me?"

"Doesn't matter. Now you don't have to worry about having sex with anyone tonight."

The irony was not lost on her. She was about to spend the night with the one man who wouldn't have sex with her, even though he was the one man she would like to have sex with.

Gio took a seat at the little table by the window in the motel room. Morgan still stood by the door where she'd taken her stance while he talked to the guy outside, the sheet barely wrapping her slender, battered body. He wished he could fix everything for her. *Heal her body, Lord. Only you can fix this.*

She moved toward the bed and picked up his shirt, then slipped into it. It was huge on her, hanging past her bottom. She looked adorable, but without the sheet around her waist, he could see the bruises on every side of her legs.

With pained movements, she sat on the end of the bed.

"I feel like a broken record asking if you're all right."

Her smile electrocuted him.

"I really will be fine." Her smile faded. "I've been through worse."

He clenched his fist, but the cuts stung with the movement. He winced.

"What happened to you?" She motioned for him to show her.

He scooted his chair closer and offered her his hand. "The glass didn't like being slammed on the counter. But I was so angry that Ronan hurt you."

"This is because of me?"

"No, because of Ronan and his ..."

The anger welled up again.

Morgan stroked his hand. "Do you get angry much?" Fear darted through her eyes.

Was he really any different than Ronan? "More than I should. I take it to God, but occasionally I lose it before I make it to the foot of the cross. The glasses in my kitchen typically pay the price."

"What makes you lose it?"

"Most of the time it connects to someone hurting another person or a case gone south. A triple homicide made me punch a hole in a wall. A mom and her two kids—sorry, you don't need to hear that."

She traced the veins in his arm. "Have you ever hurt someone when you got angry?"

Her touch was driving him crazy, but he didn't want her to let go. "Maybe my brother when we were kids."

She chuckled. "That doesn't count." Her hand stopped and cradled his. "My poor brother was my human punching bag when we were little. Guess I've never really known what to do with my anger either."

Silence fell between them. He couldn't believe how easy it was for her to draw him out. He barely talked to Dylan about these things.

As much as he wanted to sit here silently with her, he needed to ask a few questions too. "Would you tell me more about Ronan? Things that would help us catch him?"

Her neck moved with a hard swallow. "I'm scared."

"I know. But if we play this right, we can get him out of the way and that would be the best way to keep you, Lily, and any other girls safe."

She nodded. Letting go of his hand, she shifted back on the bed and pulled the sheet over her lap. She grimaced and held her side.

"You need medical attention."

"I'm just sore."

"Oh, wait." He pulled out his wallet and found the little package of pills he kept there. "I get headaches regularly enough that I always have some Advil. Here." He stood, unwrapped a clear plastic cup, and filled it with water from the sink at the back of the room.

"Aren't you supposed to eat with these?"

"It helps." He walked back toward her.

"I haven't eaten since lunch."

The Chinese he'd had sat uneasy in his stomach. "I wish I could get you some food."

"Oh, I'll be fine." She reached for the tiny plastic cup, popped the pills, and finished off the water.

He took the cup, set it on the table, and settled back in the chair.

Morgan fiddled with the sheet. "I'm not sure what to tell you about Ronan. I honestly don't know if that's his real name, but it's the only one I've ever heard. I've never actually seen his driver's license."

"Any last name?"

She shook her head.

"That's all right." He asked for their address, and Dylan acknowledged over the earpiece that he wrote it down.

"Tell me about what he looks like." He raised his index finger. "Actually, hold on a second." He searched the drawers and found a notepad and pencil. It wasn't his normal drawing tools but would get the job done. He returned to his seat.

"He's about five-ten-ish. Caucasian but fairly dark—dark hair, dark eyes, tan. Spends a lot of time in the gym."

"How old is he?"

"I'm not real sure. He's never said, but based on how long he's been at this, I'd guess he's around forty."

He pulled out his phone.

"New phone?" There was a bounce in her voice.

"Yeah, some lady stole my other one." He winked at her.

She bit her lip.

He brought up a composite website, not quite as thorough as his FBI book. "Can you look through these images and tell me which one is closest to Ronan's eyes?"

They went through all the features and turned out a decent replica of Ronan. "Not my best since my hand hurts, but how is it?"

"That's him."

Perfect. Now Gio knew exactly who he wanted to hang upside-down and use as a punching bag.

"Thank you, Morgan. This will go a long way in being able to identify him. Now we need a plan." He folded the sketch and tucked it into his wallet.

Morgan was quiet. "Gio?"

"Yeah?" He met her eyes. She looked tired. "I'm sorry. Too much?"

"No. I appreciate what you're trying to do. But I have a question for you." Trepidation filled her voice.

"Anything." He set the pencil and pad on the table and turned more fully toward her.

"Will you hold me?" The vulnerability in her words and expression pulled on his heart.

"Of course." He stood.

When he reached for her, she grasped his hands and pulled herself to her feet.

He drew her against his chest. She fit perfectly.

But he could tell she was weak. They couldn't stand here the whole time. It was only eleven o'clock and going to be a long night. They might as well get comfortable.

He stepped out of the embrace. "Give me a second." Grabbing the extra pillows from the shelf by the bathroom, he tossed them at the head of the bed. He sat against the headboard and got comfortable with the pillows propping him up. When he motioned for her to come, she crawled across the bed and tucked herself under his left arm. As she hugged his waist, she laid her head on his chest.

With firm, steady hands, he wrapped his arms around her and held her close. He could stay like this forever.

Morgan listened to Gio's heartbeat. Thump. Thump. Thump. It helped calm her weary soul. She traced the word "Smoky" on his Smoky Mountain National Park t-shirt. His heart rate increased. She flattened her hand and stopped. She didn't want to tease him; well, maybe a little. But his convictions were strong.

"Talk to me, Gio."

"That's like asking a monkey to go swimming. I'm not much of a talker. Although, you've gotten more out of me in the last hour than I normally say in a day."

She snickered.

"How 'bout I read something?"

"I'd love for you to read to me."

"Is there a Gideon's Bible in the drawer? If not, I can read from my phone, but there's something about a physical book."

She turned over and pulled the drawer open. "Yep."

His hand never left her back. The way he touched her was so different than any other man. His hand felt supportive, not obsessive.

She turned back and handed him the hardback Bible. She winced a little as she settled back against Gio.

"Is this position comfortable?"

She burst out laughing.

"What?" The naivety in his voice made it even funnier.

She pushed herself off him and met his eyes. "You don't even know what you said." She cupped the side of his face with her hand. "I like you, Gio."

"What did I say?"

She shook her head. "This *position* is fine." She intensified her touch on his face. "Thank you for tonight."

"I'm going to put Ronan behind bars, so you can have as many nights like this as you want."

She nudged his head down and kissed his forehead. Then settled against him again. Was she crazy? Or was she really falling for this man?

How many men had she fallen in love with? How many men had she thought were different from the last? But Gio really was different. Every other guy in her entire life with the exception of her brother would have had sex with her by this point.

Gio flipped through the pages of the Bible, then stopped. "Oh."

"What?" She lifted her head.

His cheeks were bright once again.

She snickered. "You realized the *other* way what you said could be taken?"

He nodded. "I ... I—"

She put her finger on his lips. "Don't even try." She couldn't contain the chuckle that erupted.

He leaned his head back and laughed too. After a moment, she settled back against him, and he found a page in the Bible.

Strong and steady, Gio read from the Psalms.

"Praise the Lord, O my soul ..."

The inflection in his voice drew her into the words. She glanced at the page. Psalm 103. A Psalm of David.

"... Who forgives all your sins, and heals all your diseases, who redeems your life from the pit ..."

She wanted to believe the words for herself. But could these words written so long ago by King David really be for her too?

"The Lord is compassionate and gracious, slow to anger, abounding in love ..."

Love. What was that, really?

"... He does not treat us as our sins deserve or repay us according to our iniquities. For as high as the heavens are above the earth, so great is His love for those who fear him; as far as the east is from the west, so far has He removed our transgressions from us ..."

Morgan buried her head a little deeper against Gio's chest. *God, I want that. Can you really forgive me? Love me like that?*

More than any other moment in her life, Morgan wanted to escape the life she'd been trapped in for so many years. She wanted to steep herself in Scripture. To talk to God every day.

By the time she realized Gio was no longer reading but praying for her, his shirt was damp from her tears.

He prayed *for her*. That God would heal her injuries and her heart. That God would help them capture Ronan. That God would protect Morgan and Lily and the other girls.

Gio brushed her hair away from her face and let his hand rest on her head. Then he kissed her hair.

"In the name of Jesus, I pray these things for my dear friend Morgan. Amen."

Dear friend. She squeezed him tighter.

As he pulled his hand away from her head, the bandage on his hand stuck to her hair.

They both chuckled, releasing a bit of the emotional weight that had rested on them.

Gio said, "You can go to sleep. I'll be right here."

"I think maybe I could." She closed her eyes.

Gio started to sing softly.

Morgan drifted off.

Something woke her. They'd slid down farther on the bed to the point where she couldn't say they were sitting anymore. Gio's arms tightened around her.

Banging at the door registered. Someone was trying to come in.

Chapter Nineteen

MORGAN SAT UP. WHO on earth was banging on the door?

"I want a turn. Get out of there!" a gruff voice called from the other side of the door.

Gio removed his arm from around her and stood. "I'll get rid of him."

She grasped Gio's arm. "Take your pants off or he's going to think—"

"I am not taking my pants off. I'll act like I'm pulling them on."

She jumped up on the bed, a motion her body was not happy with, and reached over Gio's shoulders to grab his shirt. "No shirt then."

"Fine." He allowed her to yank it off.

She dropped onto the bed, and he opened the door.

Gio put his hand on the hilt of his gun still tucked in his waistband. "Get lost. She's with me."

Those words tickled her heart. *With me.* Something about the way Gio said it gave a sense of protection versus the possession everyone else who said it had meant.

"It's not fair, man. I wanna see Daisy."

Morgan sank a little deeper into the pillows and pulled the sheet up to her chin, grateful she couldn't see who it was. She didn't recognize the voice.

"You can't, so get lost."

The man tried to push past Gio.

Not wanting to arouse more questions, she pulled Gio's shirt off and pulled the sheet back up.

"Daisy, remember me? Don't you wanna see me again?"

A chubby face appeared, despite Gio's effort to push him back. Morgan didn't recognize him at all.

She waved to him and plastered on her fake smile. "Tomorrow, sweetheart, I'm all booked up tonight."

Gio called for Scissors.

The burly man appeared, and Gio and Scissors were finally able to get the fat man out of the doorway.

Chubby shoved the guys off. "Fine, but I *will* see you later, Daisy. You won't get away with refusing to see me."

Scissors pushed the man. "Get outta here." He turned back to Gio. "I'm sorry about that, man. He's so fat, he just got past me."

"Make sure it doesn't happen again." Gio closed the door and leaned back against it. "Glad that's all that was. Jacq, Dylan, what on earth? A little warning would have been nice."

She wanted to laugh, but she was still overcome by the fear that Ronan had been at the door. In some ways she wished it had been, then maybe Gio could have arrested him or pulled his gun. Although Ronan would have his gun, and she did *not* want Gio to get shot.

Instead of grabbing the polo, she snatched Gio's t-shirt and slid it on.

He came back toward the bed. "Apparently, Jacq and Dylan muted themselves, and that's why—" He narrowed his eyes.

"This one's more comfortable."

"Yes, it is."

He reached for the polo, but she pulled it away. He dove for it, coming close to her.

"Come on, Morgan."

She giggled. Placing a hand on his chest she shoved him but didn't pull away. He was built like he spent time in the gym, but not obsessively like Ronan.

His face flushed and eyes widened.

She let her hand slide down to his abs. The movement revealed a small tattoo on Gio's chest she hadn't spotted a moment ago. "That's unexpected." She touched a tattoo barely the size of half of her index finger. It was a semicolon, but the dot was actually letters. "EC."

He sat beside her. "Eddie Crespi."

"Your brother."

He nodded.

"A semicolon stands for solidarity regarding suicide and depression, right?"

"Addiction and mental illness too. I have it to remember Eddie, but also to remind myself to pause and look to God when life feels too heavy."

"I want my tattoo removed if possible."

"And you can, or we can design something to cover it. Maybe to represent the change God is working in your life."

"We?"

"I'm handy with a pencil." He took her hand off his chest and cradled it. "But I need to put my shirt on." He raised his eyebrows.

She handed him the polo. "If you must."

"I see the way you're looking at me."

She shrugged and lay down on the bed, patting the pillow behind where Gio sat.

After turning off the light next to the bed, he lay down beside her, and nudged a strand of hair away from her face. "Go back to sleep."

Under Gio's watchful care, she let herself sleep again. But this time her dreams were fitful, confusing, and downright scary.

She woke with a start from a dream. She'd been running for her life, and her heart pounded as if she had actually been running. Gio still slept soundly beside her. She lifted his arm, which lay limp between them, and slid beneath it, rolling until her back was against Gio.

He tightened his arm around her. "Are you all right?"

"Just a bad dream."

"I've got you."

She closed her eyes. *God? Is this what Your love feels like? Strong and protective? Thank You for sending Gio to protect me tonight. That really was You, wasn't it?*

Gio started singing again. "What a fellowship, what a joy divine, leaning on the everlasting arms; what a blessedness, what a peace is mine, leaning on the everlasting arms. Leaning, leaning, safe and secure from all alarms; leaning, leaning, leaning on the everlasting arms."

She fell asleep.

"Morgan." Gio squeezed her hand, which had at some point slipped into his. "It's morning."

"I was afraid you'd say that. I don't want this to end. I don't want to go back."

"You don't have to."

She rolled onto her back to see his face. "If I disappear, the first thing he'll do is shoot Lily." She shook her head. "It's not worth that. Her life is worth more than my freedom."

She tried to read the expression in Gio's eyes.

"What are you thinking?" she asked.

He took a deep breath. "You are so brave. While it frustrates me, and I want to argue with you, I love that you put her safety above your own. The life you have could easily have hardened you not to care about anyone but yourself, yet you haven't let it."

"But I go back with the hope that you can, with God's help, save us all."

"Hope keeps us both going."

"Why are you so good to me? I don't deserve it."

"None of us deserve much other than eternal condemnation. But you, and me too, were created in the image of God. Sorry, I'm preaching again."

She put her hand on his cheek. "Don't stop."

"You were made in the image of God. Anyone bearing that image deserves honor, respect, and love. I hope I can show you how much God loves you."

She soaked in his words. She wanted it so bad. God's love, Gio's love. Real love.

Gio's expression shifted, and he closed his eyes briefly. He must have heard something in his earpiece.

"Scissors is coming."

She nodded. An intense urge to kiss Gio overcame her, but she resisted and stood instead.

Gio threw his legs over his side of the bed and sat with his back to Morgan, putting on his shoes.

A knock sounded on the door. "Time's up. Boss is coming to get you, Daisy."

Gio said, "Be out in a moment."

Morgan slipped off his t-shirt, wrapped the sheet around herself, and tossed the shirt at his head.

"Hey!" He turned and smiled at her. But the smile held sorrow. She felt it too.

She strode around the bed and threw herself against his chest.

He held her tight. "I will come as soon as I can get a warrant. Be careful. And text me if you need us sooner. I will come on my own if I have to. Jacq too."

She nodded.

Another knock. "Open or I will. You need to get lost, lover-boy."

She picked up his ballcap, popped it on his head, and walked him to the door.

He opened it but turned back to her and cupped her face with his hand. He leaned close, kissed her cheek, and whispered. "I *will* rescue you."

He left her reeling. It was so hard to stay strong and let him walk away, but she had to. For Lily.

Gio forced himself to take one step forward, then another. But he'd left his heart with Morgan. He wondered if he'd die by the time he got to the end of the motel. It was the hardest thing in his life to not look back, to not turn around and whisk her out of the hellhole she was headed back into.

"You guys keeping eyes on her and Scissors?"

"We are." Jacq's voice was heavy with sorrow too. "Matt's waiting for you around the corner."

"Keep an eye out for Ronan. Scissors said the boss was coming to get her."

"We've got it, Gio."

He turned the corner.

A Cadillac SUV drove into the parking lot.

Gio lowered his hat over his eyes. "I think that's him pulling in now."

Matt's car sat on the other side of the building.

Once the SUV was around the corner, Gio jogged over and jumped in. "Hurry. Ronan's over there."

"Good morning to you too." Matt drove out of the parking spot. "You know, not all of us got to sleep with a beautiful woman in our arms, or, for that matter, sleep at all."

"Still, this is the guy we're looking for. We need eyes."

Jacq's voice came into his ear. "We've got eyes on him. And Dylan's taking pictures."

In less than a minute, Matt parked next to Dylan's Charger. Matt pointed at the guy talking to Scissors. "Does he match your sketch?"

Gio retrieved the sketch from his wallet. "I'd say so."

"Wow. That's impressive, considering your hand."

"What didn't they tell you?" Had they told Matt about his faux pas too?

Matt snickered but stopped short. "Your guy doesn't look so happy."

"Oh, man, I hope Scissors didn't tell him about me at all."

"They're shaking hands."

Scissors and Ronan seemed to part amicably, and Gio let a tight breath loose. Gio snapped a few pictures with his cellphone. Ronan went inside, a small bag in hand.

Matt grabbed his laptop from the backseat and typed for a moment. "There. It *is* the same SUV we searched for before, the one Morgan aka 'Daisy Smith' left Walmart in that one day."

"I figured." Gio didn't move his eyes from the door, waiting to see Morgan.

About five minutes later, she followed Ronan out. Her hand was touching her red cheek.

Flames sparked to life in Gio's gut. "Remind me why we can't run over there and take him down?"

"Warrant," Dylan said.

"Lily." Jacq's voice held the same agony he felt. "We have to get Lily too."

Matt pointed at his screen. "I searched all night but didn't find her until an hour ago. By then it was too late. When I got there, she was already gone."

Matt's words punched Gio in the gut. They'd been so close.

Ronan drove away with Morgan.

Matt asked, "Do we tail him?"

Gio shook his head. "No, we know where they live. Let's get the warrant in order as fast as possible."

Chapter Twenty

Back at the field office, the team met up with Aliza and Warren and debriefed the night, minus Gio's increasing connection to Morgan and, thankfully, minus his faux paus.

While Matt owned finding Ronan's legal identity, Jacq and Aliza worked on the warrant, and Gio and Dylan set to making a plan of attack.

They looked up the address Morgan had given them.

Gio shook his head. "No wonder she snuck away from the safe house; it's only a few blocks from there."

"That house is huge." Dylan pulled the inactive listing up on a home sales website. "There aren't a ton of pictures, but it helps give a little feel of the layout."

"Perfect." Gio glanced at Dylan's screen. Those were the rooms Morgan called home right now. It was a strange sensation. He could *never* provide her that kind of house, but he could give her a home of warmth and love. One where she wouldn't be starved or abused.

"Gio." Dylan rested his arm on his back. "We'll get her out. We can probably pull all of this together in a few hours and have her out of there by dinner."

He hoped that would be soon enough. "I should never have let her go back."

"Put your foot down, so she can think you're exactly like all the rest of the men in her life?"

"No."

"I know you don't want it like that. You are showing her respect by doing this the right way. We'll get all the girls, not just Morgan and Lily."

"And take Ronan down in the process."

"Exactly. Without anyone getting hurt."

Gio felt like he was going to burst out of his skin. They needed to move faster. A deep sense of urgency and dread filled his gut. What if they didn't get there soon enough?

From across the bullpen, Matt said, "This guy's a ghost. I can't find anything about him. Not even a fake driver's license. No facial matches. No one named Ronan that looks like him even remotely. I'll keep looking, but I'm not too hopeful."

Gio's agitation grew. It shouldn't matter too much once they had him, since they had pictures and eyewitness statements, but hopefully, they'd be able to get a warrant without his given name. They should at the very least have one to search the premises as long as they found a decent judge to sign. Being the middle of the day should give them an advantage on which judge Jacq and Aliza could get.

God, help this all come together soon.

Morgan rolled over in bed. In the last two hours, she had slept on and off, but she wasn't really tired after sleeping part of the night, plus the pain was back. The ibuprofen Gio had given her last night had really helped. Ronan had let her take a shower before he locked her back in her room.

She hugged Gio's t-shirt. The waiting was torturous. And she was hungry. She got up, went to the door, and knocked. "Ronan? May I come out and get some food? Ronan?"

She waited a few minutes and then called out again.

Footsteps. Someone was coming. She stepped back. The bolt was removed, and the door opened. Ronan appeared; he was on the phone.

He covered the mic of the phone with his hand. "Hungry?"

She nodded.

"Fine." He pointed down the stairs with his head, then grabbed her jaw. "But behave, or you'll pay."

Again, she nodded. She walked ahead of him down the back staircase where he'd indicated.

He spoke to the person on the other end of the phone. "Yes, I understand. Well, I can call you when Daisy has an opening. Hold on a moment."

Ronan grasped her elbow. "What time are you starting with Duke tonight?"

"Ten."

Ronan let go and she continued down the stairs.

"How's nine o'clock?" Ronan paused. "Yes, I'll give you an extra fifteen minutes since you've had to wait." Ronan hung up and stuffed his phone in his pocket.

She went to the refrigerator and grabbed a yogurt. When she reached for the drawer that held the spoons, Ronan stepped in front of it, giving her a stink eye.

"I'll get you a spoon." He did.

"Thank you."

"Sit at the island."

She obeyed. He was ticked.

Ronan pulled up the stool next to her and sat close, facing her. "Do you want to explain why a man was turned away from seeing you last night?"

It must have been Chubby on the phone. What if Ronan found out she'd been with Gio the whole night? Would Gio be safe? "I don't know. I wasn't running the door." How was she supposed to know that guy had Ronan's number?

"Well, you'll take care of him tonight." Ronan turned and noodled around on his phone while Morgan ate.

Celeste came into the room, looking a little worse for the wear too, and like she just woke up.

Ronan's phone rang. "They won't give up today. How many men did you disappoint last night, Daisy?" He answered the phone.

He was sitting close enough for Morgan to hear someone on the other end asking if he would accept a collect call from the federal prison. He grunted and agreed.

"Why are you calling me directly, you moron?" He stood.

Celeste filled up a pot and turned the switch on the gas stove.

"Wait a sec. Celeste. Take Daisy back to her room and lock her in." He stalked away.

Celeste shot Morgan an irritated expression. "Let's go."

Once she was sure Ronan was out of earshot, and keeping her voice low, Morgan asked, "Do you really want to keep letting him boss you around?" She tossed her spoon in the sink.

"Just go."

Morgan threw the container away and shuffled to the stairs. Could she get through to Celeste before the feds showed up? Or would she cause a problem? "Why'd you even come here? You had a chance to get out when Bobbi got arrested. Why didn't you run?"

"Is that what you keep trying to do?" Celeste shoved Morgan toward the stairs.

She stumbled but turned and faced Celeste. "You aren't even really one of his girls. He hasn't even changed your name yet. Where's your R tattoo?"

"I do better work and earn him more money than you ever could. I don't need to be branded. He loves me for me."

"Ronan doesn't know how to love anyone but himself. Do you really believe he loves you?"

Celeste slapped Morgan. "Go upstairs before I drag you by your hair."

Morgan raised her hands. "I'm going." She went up the stairs. What else could she say that wouldn't get her in more trouble if Celeste ratted on her to Ronan? She couldn't think of anything.

When they reached Morgan's door, she turned to try one last time. "Celeste, come on, we've been friends for a long time—"

"Stop! You selfish pig." The squeal in Celeste's voice was piercing. "Just shut up. Stop trying to poison my mind against Ronan. He's been nothing but good to me."

"You call heroin good?"

"You ain't taking it right if you don't like it. And at least he doesn't hit me like Bobbi did."

"You just haven't made him angry enough yet." Morgan lifted the side of her tank top, revealing the bruising that had turned an intense shade of purple and blue.

"You fell down the stupid stairs after not following the rules. You got what you deserved."

"I deserved to be raped?"

"He's your husband; it's not rape."

"I am *not* married to that lunatic. This is not what marriage is. And rape is not acceptable, ever."

"It's our life, Daisy. If you don't like it, go kill yourself, so I don't have to listen to your whining anymore."

"Celeste."

She pushed Morgan inside, slammed the door shut, and threw the bolt.

Morgan sank onto the bed. Without Celeste on her side this could get dicey. Had she pushed her too far?

God, help. I can't even talk to Iris or Violet or Lily. Are they here? Are they okay?

She pulled Gio's shirt out from under the covers and traced the words with her finger. *"Faith can move mountains." Faith. How do I muster the faith, Lord?*

A distant memory from her childhood sprang from the recesses of her mind. Sunday school with her cousins. Muster—mustard seed. The teacher had passed out the tiniest little seed Morgan had ever seen and said faith only needed to be that big. God would take it and move mountains.

She held the shirt close. "God, that's all I've got right now, the teeniest tiniest faith, but I believe You can do it. Move this mountain."

Crash! A huge ruckus came from downstairs.

Ronan was yelling. What if he was coming up here? What if one of the other girls was near him while he was raging?

Oh, dear God, help.

The bolt rattled. She backed up to the headboard, clutching the shirt.

The door burst open, and Lily ran in, slamming the door behind her. "Ronan knows what you did!"

"What do you mean?"

"Talking to the FBI!"

Her lungs deflated as they did the time she'd hit the ground after falling off the highest point of the playground swing.

Lily crawled onto the bed. "What do we do?"

She regained use of her lungs. "We get out. Are you with me?"

"Yes."

Morgan slipped Gio's shirt on, then pulled his phone out from under the mattress. She texted him and hit send before Ronan burst into the room.

Morgan and Lily both screamed.

Chapter Twenty-One

GIO WAS GROWING FRUSTRATED. Hours had passed, and they still didn't have the warrant. Matt hadn't found anything about Ronan. And bureaucracy was getting in the way of them having a full team to go in and take Ronan down.

They did not have enough evidence to bring him in as a suspect in Jamie DeRozan's murder, so that was off the table, even though Gio was certain Ronan killed her. Person of interest was even a stretch since they had nothing, absolutely nothing, on who this guy was. He really seemed to be a ghost.

If they had more time, he'd see if Morgan could get a DNA sample. But they didn't have time for anything like that. Those girls, including Morgan, were at risk of being out on the street or locked in a hotel room again tonight. The selling of flesh had to stop.

His phone dinged. A text message from his other phone. Morgan.

"Jacq." He held up his phone.

He opened the text. *911 – Ronan knows I ratted to the feds.*

The phone clattered on the desk. They couldn't wait any longer. "We have to go, *now!*"

He picked up the phone and texted back. *Coming!*

Warren came out of his office. "What's going on?"

"Witness in eminent danger."

"Go. I'll send back up."

Gio jumped to his feet and the team followed suit. They all made it to the Bureau's SUVs with Kevlar vests in record time.

Gio took the front passenger seat while Dylan drove.

What if they didn't make it in time? Gio had promised Morgan he'd rescue her. What if he couldn't? What if it was all for naught, and they were too late?

He fervently prayed as hard as he could, even though words failed him.

Morgan reached out to Lily and pulled her close to her side.

Ronan's ears were bright red and his jaw set. "I just got off the phone with Bobbi. You remember him—the bozo who let the feds interfere. I always thought it was one of his girls that ratted on him."

He strode toward the bed. "Then Trent got mixed up in it. I thought it was because of his proximity to the cops. He had a good play planned, so I really couldn't figure out how the feds got wind about how he was grooming the Harris girl. Well, turns out Bobbi has been able to dig up who the dirty little rat is. Do you know how surprised he was when the feds tried to flip Ezra on me? Not near as surprised as I was when I learned my best girl was the one ruining everyone's lives."

Morgan moved herself in front of Lily.

Ronan came over and stroked Morgan's cheek. "My best girl. A lousy piece of garbage it turns out. No wonder you've been sneaking around." He shook his head, anger mounting. Fire raged in his eyes.

"This is your one moment to defend yourself. I want it to all be a lie. I want what Bobbi suggested to be wrong, dead wrong. Maybe Duke's wanting to get you hooking for him, and he's trying to take you from me. I could handle that kind of betrayal, but snitching? Oh, that, my pretty, has an entirely different level of punishment."

He grabbed a chunk of hair at the base of her skull. "What do you have to say for yourself, Daisy?"

She swallowed. She was done playing. But she needed to get out. She needed to stall so Gio could arrive. Getting herself or Lily shot would *not* help.

The doorbell rang.

Gio!

Ronan dragged her by the hair.

She struggled to keep her feet beneath her as Ronan flew down the stairs to the front door. Halfway to the first floor the smell of natural gas assaulted her nose, but Ronan didn't slow. Thankfully, she managed not to fall again.

Ronan peeked out the door and opened it.

Not Gio?

Scissors appeared on the other side. He shot Morgan a fraction of a smile before giving Ronan his full attention.

Ronan told him to come inside. "I thought I made it clear you were to get as many guys through her room as possible last night."

"Yes, sir. And we made a ton of money."

"Then why did I get a call from an unsatisfied man saying you and another guy pushed him away and wouldn't let him see this piece of flesh?"

Morgan's head ached more and more. He wasn't holding her at her natural height so the contortion her body was forced into made her already sore muscles scream in agony.

"Look, boss, she was busy. There wasn't time for him."

"That's not possible. Was the line a mile long then?"

Scissors didn't answer.

Where was Gio? She knew he got the message because the screen had lit up right before she shoved it under the blankets.

Ronan jerked her head as he put his finger in Scissors' face. "What aren't you telling me?"

Scissors shot her an apologetic look. "One man paid for a longer time, and I let him have it."

Gio.

Ronan grunted and pulled his phone out of his pocket. "Was it this guy?"

Dylan.

Scissors shook his head. "Nope."

"This one?"

The agent who had arrested her. Matt.

Oh God, please don't let him have a picture of Gio.

"What about this guy?"

Gio.

A sob escaped her lips.

"What do you know? The piece of trash actually has feelings for a fed!"

"A fed?" Scissors asked. "That man was no fed."

"Oh really? Do you think a fed is so wholesome he won't pay for sex?" Ronan laughed, then went deadpan. "You're an idiot."

He pulled on Morgan's hair.

She couldn't help crying out in pain.

"Dude, stop hurting her." Scissors pushed Ronan's shoulder.

Ronan shoved his phone in his pocket and yanked Morgan in front of him, letting go of her hair while grasping her arm with the other hand.

He was going for his gun. As soon as his hand moved from his waistband, she ducked and tried to pull her arm away.

The distraction gave Scissors the opportunity to go for the gun. He grabbed Ronan's wrist.

Profanities spewed from Ronan's mouth.

Scissors' size matched Ronan's strength.

Ronan, hand still gripping Morgan's upper arm, shoved her into the wall.

She hit hard and slid to the ground, every part of her body protesting. She couldn't move.

The guys struggled over the gun. Down the hallway toward the kitchen.

Morgan had to get up, had to do something. Scissors had stood up for her. She needed to help him. Ronan's back was now to her as the men ended up in the kitchen.

She pushed herself off the floor and wall. *Just get to Ronan.* She ran and jumped on his back.

The shock gave Scissors the moment he needed. He pulled the gun out of Ronan's hands and backed into the kitchen. "Come on, dude, I don't want to kill you. Let's call it good."

Ronan reached behind his back and seized Morgan and tossed her across the room again.

She slammed into the support beam at the corner of the dining room. Her vision clouded. The men became muddled figures.

Ronan pulled a knife from his ankle. Where had that come from? He threw it.

She couldn't think. The world was gone.

Chapter Twenty-Two

GIO SCANNED THE AREA as Dylan drove down the street where Ronan's house was. Ronan's vehicle sat in the driveway of a house with towering pines out front. They had the right place. As soon as Dylan stopped the SUV at the curb, Gio jumped out.

Jacq was right behind him and squeezed his arm. "Wait for us. We have no idea what's going on in there."

Gio huffed.

Pkew.

Boom.

Gio and Jacq dropped to a squat.

Gio rubbed his ear. "What was that? Other than the gunfire."

Jacq shook her head. "Sounded like a bomb."

They stood, and Dylan came around the car and took charge. "Jacq, Matt, front door."

Gio said, "I spotted a side door by the garage."

"Go. Aliza and I will take the other way toward the back door."

They all ran in their assigned directions. Gio skirted the side of the house where the three-car garage opened to a wide driveway. The side door sat past the garage doors and Ronan's SUV.

Gio scanned the area for trouble and, seeing none, ran to the door.

He reached for the knob in hopes it was unlocked. A mass hit him, slamming him into the narrow strip of brick wall between the side door and garage door. The brick bit through his polo shirt.

A hand pinned his shoulder back against the wall. Ronan. This was the man who had raped and sold Morgan. Gio balled his hand into a fist, but Ronan beat him to the punch.

His head jerked to the side, vision blurring for a moment. "What are *you* doing here?"

Gio ignored the question. Before Ronan could get another slug in, Gio undercut Ronan in the ribs. Gio's hand screamed. At least one of the cuts from yesterday split open again.

Ronan jabbed his fist into Gio's side.

Breath nearly knocked out, Gio gasped for breath.

Gio had to get off the wall. With a one-two punch to Ronan's gut and cheek, he gained half a step. Far enough for Gio to get his back off the wall and gain his footing.

He lunged at Ronan and slammed him into the grill of the SUV with a thud.

"Where is she? Where's M—Daisy?"

Not waiting for an answer, Gio punched him in the face, this time connecting with his jaw.

Ronan shoved him back.

Gio slid on his feet to keep his balance, exposing his side. He needed to temper the fury building inside of him. He just wanted to put his hands—

With rage in his eyes, Ronan kicked the side of Gio's knee.

Knee buckling, Gio stumbled and reached for the wall for support. With space between them, Gio drew his Glock.

The side door opened, and a girl came out along with a poof of smoke.

Ronan grabbed the girl and wrapped his arm tightly around her neck. "Don't even think about it. Drop it, or I'll snap her neck."

Gio swallowed. Based on the man's strength, Gio didn't doubt he had the physical power to do so.

Gio squatted and set the gun on the ground. He stood palms toward Ronan. "Don't hurt her."

Ronan thrust the girl forward and into Gio.

He caught the girl. By the time he looked for Ronan, he was gone, probably into the tree line.

Gio eased the girl off his chest. "Are you all right?" He'd send her to the front and chase after Ronan.

"I'm fine, but the fire is everywhere. Daisy was on the ground inside, and I couldn't get her. I don't know if she's alive. What if she's dead? Did Ronan kill her?"

The words slammed into Gio's gut harder than Ronan's fists. Morgan!

"Go out front. There are other agents. Tell them where Ronan ran."

She nodded and took off.

Sirens sounded in the distance.

Gio spun and went inside, through the garage. At the opposite end, a door into the house hung wide open, smoke billowing out. He wished he had put his t-shirt back on under his polo so he could pull it up over his nose.

He took the deepest breath he could and, holding it, entered the house.

Flames licked the walls, coming from what seemed like the kitchen.

He dropped to his hands and knees and crawled forward. Why hadn't he asked the girl where Morgan was? What if he was too late? He wasn't sure he could handle finding another person he cared for dead.

"Morgan!" Yelling was pointless; now he had lungs full of smoke. He spotted a mass on the floor a few feet away.

He crawled toward it. Morgan! "Morgan, can you hear me?"

The roar of the fire swallowed his words. She didn't respond. He scooped her into his arms, but she was limp and didn't react. Getting her out was first priority.

A light shone to his left. The front door was open.

Holding Morgan tight, he ran outside.

Once to the grass, he dropped to his knees and laid her down. "Morgan, wake up."

He checked her pulse. It was strong. She was just unconscious.

He leaned close and stroked her face. "Morgan. Please wake up."

Her hand gripped his arm, and her eyes fluttered open. "Gio?" Her eyes squeezed shut as if she was in pain.

He slid his arms under her again and drew her to his chest. Relief washed over him. She was safe.

But Ronan was still on the loose.

Paramedics arrived and took Morgan to an ambulance, away from the house and away from Gio.

Jacq pulled Gio over to Dylan, who stood near another ambulance with four girls from the house. Firefighters surrounded the house. The team needed to get out of the way until the firefighters were done.

Gio gripped Dylan's arm and took him aside. "Ronan ran that way." He pointed toward the trees. "We need to go after him."

"Aliza and Matt ran that way when Iris came around and told us what you said. We need to take care of everything here."

"I *need* to go after him."

"No. That's not your job right now."

"Dylan!" The rage screaming inside Gio's mind made him want to go in a kitchen and toss every last glass against the wall.

Jacq stepped over and gripped his elbow. "Someone needs you." She pointed to where Morgan sat in the back of an ambulance. "And she needs you to drop your thirst for vengeance and be the tender, compassionate man we all know you are."

Gio deflated and surrendered his anger. *God help me.*

Dylan nodded his agreement with Jacq. "Go be with Morgan. We'll take care of these girls."

"They will likely go into withdrawal."

Jacq nodded. "We'll get them the help they need. You do the same for Morgan. She looks like she's in rough shape. Take care of my friend, please."

Gio drew Jacq into a side hug. "I will. But Ronan is going to be hunting her. We must keep her, all of them, safe from him."

"The girls will probably need longer care, but as soon as Morgan is released, take her to the mountain house. At least we got that donated furniture there on Saturday."

"Perfect."

Jacq gave him the key, and they parted ways.

Gio walked up to the back of the bus where the EMTs were checking Morgan, who sat on the edge of the gurney facing the paramedic.

She smiled at him, and for the first time he noticed she was wearing his t-shirt.

"Nice shirt."

"It helped me find the faith I needed to know you would show up."

He coughed, expelling some of the smoke he had inhaled.

"Are you okay?" she asked.

"Just a little smoke. I'll be fine."

"Good, but your cheek is really red."

He lifted his hand to where it had collided with Ronan's fist. "A gift from Ronan."

Her shoulders dropped. "He knows you were with me last night. Has your picture too. And Dylan's, and, I think it's Matt?"

"Well, we have a clear picture of him now too. Got one at the hotel this morning."

She nodded.

The EMT said, "Sir, we're going to take her to the hospital for observation."

Gio pulled out his badge. “I’ll be accompanying her.”

“Then get in.”

Gio did and sat beside Morgan on the stretcher.

She lay her head on his shoulder. He slid his arm around her, resting his hand on her elbow. She grabbed his hand with hers and wrapped it snuggly against her waist.

He kissed her head. She was out. And safe with him.

Gio leaned back in the chair beside the hospital bed Morgan sat on in the little alcove of the emergency room. The nurse had left with a promise the doctor would be in soon and x-rays would be ordered.

Once the door closed behind the nurse, Morgan said, “I really don’t need x-rays.”

“It’s just to be sure. Hopefully, we can get out of here within the hour.”

“You think they’ll let me leave with a concussion?”

“As long as someone is with you. And I don’t plan on going anywhere.”

“Thank you, Gio.”

He nodded. He hoped he didn’t come across as clingy or obsessive, but he needed to know she was safe. Sure, it was his job at this point, but it was so much more than that.

“I’m sorry you didn’t get Ronan.”

Gio shrugged and laced his fingers across his abs. “Me too.” His blood pressure increased. Why hadn’t he gotten control of the situation? Why had he let him get away?

“Tell me what happened.”

He recounted the scene to her. “What I want to know is, how on earth did the house catch on fire? And who fired that shot?”

"I can only guess." She told him about smelling the gas, and the fight between Scissors and Ronan. "Scissors had the gun. As I blacked out, Ronan threw a knife at Scissors. I think he fired the gun."

"And the gas ignited. It would only take a spark."

She shrugged. "I wonder if when Celeste turned the stove on it didn't light right, or the flame went out or something. Was anyone else hurt? Is Scissors dead?"

"I don't know. I think the girls were all fine. Just the five of you, right?"

She nodded.

The x-ray tech came in and ushered them to the x-ray room. Gio leaned against the wall as she went with the tech.

Why was the rage so quick to rear its ugly head? He hated it. He didn't want to be a monster like Ronan, whaling on people, even ones he claimed to care about, when he got upset. But he'd had to check himself when fighting with Ronan earlier. Maybe if he hadn't, Ronan wouldn't be an issue anymore.

No. He couldn't think like that. *God, forgive me. Help me be the man You want me to be.*

Do not fear.

Gio rubbed his bruised cheek. Do not fear? Where did that come from? Was he being fearful?

I mean, I guess so. I'm afraid of losing Morgan. Of Ronan continuing to hurt her, or worse, killing her. Aren't those legit fears?

But how many times in Scripture was the command not to fear given? A lot. Wasn't it enough to cover one a day for a year?

I just want him to pay for what he's done. Justice. His comeuppance, if You will, right, Lord? How is that fear? Is my anger not righteous?

The verse from Romans chapter twelve came to mind. *"Vengeance is mine, I will repay," says the Lord.*

Gio let out a gush of air. *It's in Your hands, Lord. Help me surrender, to have faith and not fear.*

Peace filled his soul. Peace that passes all understanding. He was still on-guard; this wasn't the kind of peace that made one let loose. This was the kind of peace that, despite the boat looking like it would capsize at any moment, one could sleep on. In due time, God would command the wind and waves to be still. And in time, Ronan would face the penalty for his sin.

But it wasn't in Gio's hands. It was in God's, and God would guide him. Deep in his gut, he knew all things work together for the good of those who love God and, ultimately, for God's glory. It was Gio's job to trust. To follow the Lord's leading. And to stand by Morgan whatever was tossed their way.

Chapter Twenty-Three

After several hours of waiting, Morgan walked beside Gio through the hospital hallways. She'd been released with only bruises and a mild concussion. Smoke inhalation was not an issue, thankfully. She'd insisted they check on the other girls, especially Lily, before they left.

Gio's presence was, as always, strong and protective, not overbearing and domineering.

They turned down another hallway. At least he knew where they were going, and she trusted him. She would have no idea how to get out of here at this point. Why were hospital halls so confusing?

They strolled past a nurse's station where a tall man leaned on the counter speaking with the nurses.

The man said, "Who else do I need to see before I head out?"

She knew that voice. Was it him? Did he work in the hospital? It would explain his ability to get the drugs he'd given her.

Her insides quaked. It couldn't be him.

He said something else. It was him.

Duke.

She reached over and slid her hand into Gio's. She desperately wanted to get a glimpse of the man and confirm his identity.

Turning her head slightly, she caught his reflection in a large mirror. His head was down as he signed a paper, but she saw enough. It was actually him.

Gio gave her hand two quick squeezes. "You all right?"

"Yeah, sure. I'm fine." For Gio's sake she didn't want Duke to see her with him.

Duke asked the nurse, "What room is she in?"

"1156."

"I'm going to head out after I see her. I have a date tonight."

"Have fun." The nurse's voice was flirtatious.

Morgan wanted to throw up. A date? Hardly.

Fresh fear washed over her. She was going to stand Duke up. How would he react to that?

She squeezed Gio's hand tighter and refocused on the hallway ahead.

Room 1156 was ahead.

Quick, heavy footsteps came from behind. He was headed toward them.

Why couldn't the floor open up and swallow her and Gio? Why wasn't Gio walking faster? Where was the next hall for them to turn down?

She could sense Duke coming closer.

What was she supposed to do?

Gio started to turn his head toward Duke. No!

She pulled Gio to a stop and toward herself. Letting go of his hand and using hers to block their faces, she cupped his face and planted her lips on his. She tugged him to the wall.

Duke chuckled but passed by.

Gio kissed her back, but tension consumed his body. Like he was fighting it, but enjoying it at the same time.

She broke the bond between their lips. But their faces lingered close.

Kissing Gio was exhilarating. She leaned back in, but he turned his face a millimeter away.

"No." The word came out breathlessly.

"I'm sorry."

The door shut down the hallway. Duke was gone.

"Why?" He breathed deeply and his warm breath tickled her cheek.

"I ... I just. I'm sorry. I shouldn't have done that." She hated making him uncomfortable, but she wanted to kiss him again with every fiber of her being.

"Don't get me wrong. That was delightful." He moved his face farther from hers and met her gaze. His cheeks were as red as last night.

She traced his face and dropped her hands to his chest.

He shifted his grip slightly, making her aware of how he held her waist. "I still want to know why. Why here, right now?" His eyes held a bit of sorrow. Had she stolen something from him? Had she used him the way she was used to being used? How could such a yucky feeling follow so quickly behind the bliss of that kiss?

"I'm really sorry."

A smile played with the corner of his mouth. "I can't say I am."

She released a nervous laugh.

"I saw someone and was scared he'd see us."

"The man who walked by?"

She nodded.

"Then we should keep moving before he comes back out of that room." He stepped away from her, taking her hand.

They continued down the hall in silence and turned away from where Duke had disappeared into the patient room.

Around one more corner, Jacq and Dylan stood in the hallway.

Morgan pulled Gio back before they were spotted. "I owe you one."

"How so?"

"You take the lead on the next kiss."

"If you insist." He raked his hand into her hair and leaned in.

She giggled and pushed him back a smidge. "No, I mean, the next one is what you imagined our first kiss would be like."

"I can live with that. For a moment I thought I was going to have to give you CPR earlier. Also not my dream first-kiss with you."

"That would not have been very romantic."

He winked at her.

"Well, you have my permission when you think we're ready."

His cheeks reddened yet again.

"I really am sorry. I didn't think about anything other than hiding."

"No need to hide. If he were to give you grief, I'd punch him in the face."

She wanted to laugh, but Duke's intensity flashed in her memory. "Not with that one. He's ... " She didn't know what word to use.

Gio wrapped his arms around her and held her to his chest. "I will do what I can to protect you. But God's got you even better than I could. I know it probably doesn't feel like He's protected you over the years, but—"

"But He has. So many times I could have died. Somehow I know He's been with me even when I couldn't see or feel Him. I can't explain it."

"You don't have to explain. We'll praise Him for it."

She nodded and stepped out of the embrace.

"Let's go see Lily. Then go somewhere safe."

"Thought you said I didn't have to hide."

Gio dropped his head back and laughed. "Touché. But I'd rather find Ronan on my own time not his, and as far from you as possible."

"I can appreciate that."

Without holding hands, they went back around the corner and talked briefly with Jacqui and Dylan before Morgan went in to see Lily.

The clock in Gio's SUV read five minutes after nine by the time he'd turned off the main highway headed toward Jacq's mountain house. They'd stayed at the hospital for a few hours as Morgan helped Lily settle. She'd been so shaken and nervous to trust Jacq, especially if Morgan wasn't going to be there.

They'd met up with Aliza and Matt, who had brought some groceries and other things they would need. They'd then gotten dinner before leaving Knoxville. It had only taken Morgan about ten minutes to fall asleep, curled up in the passenger seat.

Gio was so grateful she trusted him. Had he really earned her trust so thoroughly yet? Would she try to turn tail and run soon?

The memory of her lips entangled with his surfaced, stirring fresh desire inside him. But it also left him frustrated on so many levels. He wanted to pull her close and deepen the kiss. He hadn't kissed a woman like that in many years. So many years. His last attempt at a relationship hadn't even made it to the second date, let alone a kiss. The girl he'd been dating when Eddie took his life had moved on, while Gio wrestled with finding hope again. He'd become too focused on his career and getting traffickers off the streets to take a relationship seriously since then.

"Gio?" Morgan stirred in her seat.

"Yeah?"

"What are you thinking?"

He chuckled. "Nothing you want to know."

"If it's about your life, I do want to know."

"I was thinking about how much I really did like that kiss."

She turned toward him. "Oh really? It's been a while?"

"A long while. You'd laugh if you knew."

"You embarrassed by it?"

"I guess not. Maybe a little."

"No need. I'm a little embarrassed by how many different men ... No, not embarrassed." A heaviness fell over her.

He offered her his hand. "There's freedom in Christ from all our guilt, shame. All of it."

She slipped her hand in his. "But it's so deep. I know the Sunday school answers, but it seems like it's too much. I mean, I know it's not too much for Jesus, but what about you? Why would you want to hold my hand? You just told me you haven't even been with a woman in years."

"I haven't *kissed* a woman in years."

"You've never ...?"

"Nope."

"All the more reason." She pulled her hand away. "Gio, you deserve a woman who has saved herself for you. Not a whore like me."

"That's not how this works." More words were lost. This was exactly why he hadn't wanted to tell her. How did he communicate to her what was on his heart? He left his hand out to her, refusing to be done.

The trees thickened on both sides of the country road.

"It's so dark." Morgan stared out the window.

"It is." *God, give me the right words, please.* "And not just here on this mountain road. But there's hope. The night can only last so long. Morning is coming. You're closer than you think to seeing God's goodness evident in your life. And listen to me"—he pulled the car off to the side of the narrow road—"your past doesn't define you. You are not a whore."

He turned in his seat, hand still extended and open to her. "You are a beautiful woman created in the image of God. Yes, you are a sinner, we all are. But you were abused and taken advantage of. There is forgiveness for your sins, and healing for your wounds. In Christ you can be a new creation.

"I can't promise you the world. Oh, how I want to. However, I know I'm a fallen, sinful man who, try as I might, can't love you like Christ does. But I sure will try, if you'll let me. God placed you on my heart years ago." He snapped his mouth shut. How much did he tell her? He didn't want to scare her.

She turned, questions in her eyes.

"Promise not to freak out?"

"Does your hair have magical qualities?"

"You and Jacq have no ability to stay serious, do you?"

"Part of why we got along so well."

He chuckled, grateful for a slight break in the intensity of the conversation.

"I promise not to freak out, as long as you're not a serial killer."

"I am many things, but not that." He shot her a wink, and she bit her lip.

"Let me get something."

He got out of the SUV and grabbed his sketchbook from the trunk. Once back inside, he opened it to the image he'd been drawing when Jacq recognized Morgan in it.

"I drew this a little over a week before I ran into you at Walmart."

She took the pad and stared. "Had you seen one of Jacqui's pictures of me?"

"Nope." He reached over and turned a page back. "I drew this one before I even met Jacq."

She gasped. She flipped backward in the book and saw the other sketches he'd done. "When did you draw these?"

"The dates are on the bottom."

She tapped on the date of the first one and looked off to the side as if she were calculating something. "I think that's the year I moved to Tennessee. That part of my life is a little blurry. I'd gotten clean somehow, but there's a big blank in part of that time. I remember that was the year I came up here."

"Where were you before that?"

"Miami." She continued to stare at the sketches, flipping back and forth through them. "I can't believe this." She was on the second one where she looked severely underweight. "This is almost like looking at pictures from my past. This one wasn't long before Ronan found me. I'd been starving myself because my pimp at the time had us weigh in every day. If we were too heavy—let's just say it wasn't good. Where'd you come up with this? You haven't been stalking me, have you?"

"Definitely not. You're going to think I'm totally weird if I tell you."

"Could it really be any weirder than you having sketches of me from the last six years?"

"Got me there."

Her playful smile toyed with his heartstrings.

"Dreams."

She turned to the fifth one. "I don't remember ever looking or feeling like this."

"That one was different. Someday I'll tell you about it, but not now." Telling her it was a vision he'd had of their wedding day before he even met her was too much right now.

"I will ask again."

"Please do, but not yet."

She narrowed her eyes and considered him. "Fine." She handed him the sketchbook. "Thanks for sharing that with me."

"Not too creeped out?"

"For some reason, no."

While he loved that answer and was confident it was because the Lord was behind all of this, he still worried about her. She was probably the strongest woman he'd ever met, but she'd been through so much, used and manipulated by so many.

He put the car in drive and continued down the road. Once again he offered his hand.

She laced her fingers through his.

His heart danced. *Help me, Lord. May I be a true representation of Your love. Help me to love her the way You do. And ultimately help her to truly comprehend how much she matters to You.*

Chapter Twenty-Four

Morgan let go of Gio's hand when they pulled up to the gate that led to Jacqui's house. He jumped out and the headlights illuminated him as he swung the gate open to let them onto the property.

He climbed back in the car, drove a tiny bit, then repeated the actions to close the gate. As he drove up in front of the cute house, he said, "Welcome to the Smoky Mountains. Jacq has some clever name forming for this place but hasn't settled on anything yet."

"It's amazing."

In typical Gio fashion, he came around and opened the door for her. "Thanks." She got out and took a few steps toward the house, then redirected to the clearing to her right.

Fireflies dotted the field of tall, waving grass. They sparkled like glitter dumped in a bowl of water.

She stared. She hadn't seen anything like this since she was a little girl. The air was fresh and unburdened by the smog of the city.

Gio followed but stopped behind her. He leaned close, voice soft. "You are free."

The truth of those words hit her like an earthquake and shook her shackles away. She was no longer subject to any man's evil desires. No longer a slave to Ronan. Free.

Gio walked away and let her have her moment.

She wandered into the clearing. Opening her hands out to her sides, she twirled. *God? You did it. You really did it. Am I really out? For real? For good?*

She strolled a touch farther and dropped to her knees.

Jesus, can I really have freedom in You too? Would You forgive me for all my sins? The way I've manipulated people, my unfaithfulness to You, the way I've abused my body. I know in my head what was done to me isn't my fault, but I can't help but wonder if I hadn't fallen into sin back in college, maybe none of this would have happened. Please forgive me.

In her mind's eye, she saw herself coming into the throne room, dirty, naked, beaten. She fell to her knees at the foot of the King of Kings.

In the middle of the clearing she lowered her face to the ground, grass poking her arms as she stretched them out in front of her. The grief of all she'd endured over the last thirteen years flowed from the depths of her soul. Her shoulders heaved, and she tried to catch her breath.

The image of the woman who washed Jesus's feet with her tears meshed with the image of Morgan in the throne room. Jesus reached down and took her face in His hands. ***My beloved.***

Jesus really did love her. He died for her. His blood had been poured out for her and washed her clean. Healing would take time, but she could feel it beginning.

Be my Lord, my Savior, my Redeemer.

The brightest sunrise always came after the darkest night, and no matter how late it was now, the Son was rising in her.

Footsteps crunched the grass behind her. She pushed herself up and reached out to Gio.

He closed the space and dropped to the ground beside her.

She fell against his chest. He didn't ask anything or try to fill the space with words. He didn't do anything other than hold her and occasionally stroke her hair.

By the time the tap in her eyes stopped flowing, the front of his polo shirt was soaked, and she sat up. "As if you didn't already need to change your shirt."

He chuckled but said nothing.

"Gio?"

"Talk to me." His voice was soft and gentle.

"When I was eight, my cousin and I went to church camp for a week. I met Jesus for the first time. It was amazing, I knew He saved my soul. But a year later my stepdad ..."

"Say it however you need to."

"He raped me."

Gio took in a sharp breath.

"God saved me from him, though, and as far as I know he's still rotting in jail. But life was always off-kilter after that. Always a struggle, in and out of trouble. And I ran right into sin in college, despite having great friends like Jacqui, who pushed me to Christ."

She took Gio's hand and fidgeted with his fingers.

"I don't want to live like that anymore. I know what it's like to be a slave to sin. I want Jesus to be the *only* Lord in my life."

She jumped to her feet, raised her arms in the air, and danced around. At the top of her lungs, she yelled, "Jesus, You are Lord. I worship You!"

The joy in Gio's heart at seeing Morgan dance for the Lord in the middle of the moonlit field was uncontainable. *Thank You, Jesus!*

He waited until she reached for his hand.

She tugged him to his feet and met his gaze with the sparkle of the fireflies twinkling in her eyes. "Thank you."

"Me?"

"Of course. Thanks for getting me out of there. For keeping me from having to endure all I could have last night."

She pulled him close and wrapped her arms around his neck. "And for pointing me to Jesus."

"That I will always do."

"Please." She kissed his cheek.

The temptation to kiss her raged within him. "Let me show you the house." He took her hand and led the way. He'd taken all their things in and turned on the lights. The fresh gray paint, new light fixtures, and sporadic boxes and furniture made the place feel welcoming.

They settled in and took showers.

He used the master bath, while Morgan showered upstairs. When he'd finished, he could still hear the water running from the other bathroom, so he organized the groceries they had, grateful Aliza and Matt thought to buy paper and plasticware along with the food. There were still bound to be important things they didn't have since no one had lived here yet, but at least it was clean and there were a couple of beds and a couch.

Gio took the sleeping bags and pillows Matt had packed for them and placed them in the upstairs bedrooms. When Gio came out of the second bedroom, Morgan stood in the bathroom doorway toweling her hair.

"Feel better?"

She nodded and crossed the hall to him. Reaching up, she tousled his hair. "You?"

He took her hand and removed it from his head. "Indeed, but you are going to drive me mad, Morgan."

She stepped back. "Sorry." There was no trace of regret in her smiling eyes. "I don't really think about it."

"I know. But I've waited this long, so I can wait until marriage. But every time you get close, it's tempting to throw that to the wayside."

"I wasn't even thinking that far."

"I know, but you are a beautiful woman, and you are worthy of respect, and my throwing my conviction aside would do you a disservice." He stepped toward her and cupped the side of her face. "I desire *you*, not your body. I want to *know* you, what you think and feel. Your dreams and passions. I want to give you time to heal from the abuses you've experienced. I also want to prayerfully consider what the future holds for each of us individually. It's not up to me. It's all God's."

"But Gio, I don't have any dreams or passions."

"We'll get to know you together then. You need space from all that's happened to find yourself again, and not it in the worldly, new-age meaning of that. You get to discover who God created you to be."

"But you'll stick around?"

He nodded. "Absolutely. I'm only going anywhere if God takes our lives in different directions, and He'll have to make it abundantly clear it's from Him. For now, let's make some popcorn and watch a movie on my laptop."

She giggled, and they went downstairs. They found a funny movie neither of them had seen, but one he'd heard good reviews on.

When the movie was over, Gio checked the doors were locked, and they went upstairs.

At the top of the stairs, he turned to Morgan. "Let me know if you need anything. Don't hesitate to wake me."

She grabbed his hand. "You have to sleep in a separate room?"

"It really is best. We don't have chaperones in my ear tonight."

With sleepy eyes, she smiled. "Fine."

He kissed her forehead and left before he was tempted to pull her close. He went to bed and lay there, staring out the window at the stars, praying for Morgan until sleep overcame him.

Hours later a scream woke him.

Chapter Twenty-Five

JACQ RAN BACK DOWN the hall toward the hospital rooms where the girls were. What had she been thinking, going down to the vending machines? She should never have left. She had just pushed the buttons for her Snickers bar when Dylan texted her: *911. Ronan spotted.*

They had to get that guy and, more than anything, not let him hurt any of these women again.

She bolted around another corner and nearly knocked a nurse off her feet. Down the hallway, she could barely stop herself before she ran into Dylan, who stood in the hallway, gun drawn. Jacq drew hers as well and, like Dylan, kept it trained on the tile floor. "Where?"

"Hospital security spotted someone matching his appearance coming in the emergency entrance. When he noticed security was following him, he ran."

"Matt and Aliza?"

"Joined the search. Can you check on the girls?"

"Of course." She slid her Glock back in its holster and entered the rooms. First, she went in Celeste's. She was asleep, or at least pretending to be, so Jacq backed out quietly. Then she slipped into the room where Iris, Violet, and Lily were. The three of them had refused to be separated, and with a bit of effort, the hospital accommodated them.

They were all three awake.

"How are you girls doing?"

Each of them half-nodded, half-shrugged. They looked tired, sweaty, and beaten by the withdrawals.

Jacq went to Lily's side. "I know it can be rough. But you'll get through. Did you all know Natalie, Sydney, and Lexi?"

Blank faces stared back at her.

"Of course you didn't know them by those names. Nova, Stella, and, what was Lexi's name?"

"Luna. Bobbi's girls. We kind of knew them," Iris said. "Daisy knew them a little better because Ronan took her over there sometimes."

"Was Celeste one of Bobbi's girls before everything happened with him?"

They nodded. Pieces were coming together.

Jacq ran her finger along the siderail of Lily's bed. "I talked to Natalie, Nova, earlier. I didn't name you, but I spoke vaguely about your situation. She ended up on heroin and wanted to encourage you ladies to stick to the detox. It's worth it."

Lily folded and unfolded the edge of the sheet between her fingers. "Doesn't seem worth it right now."

"I know. But the doctors here have some good protocols to help."

Lily smiled. "I hope they're as good as whatever Duke gave Daisy. She was clean by the time she came home. It was crazy."

Jacq squeezed Lily's shoulder. "I hope so too. I have a tough question for you all."

They appeared intrigued.

"Is there any reason to believe Ronan would come after any of you girls? And I mean, beyond trying to get you to go back to him."

Lily's hands stopped fidgeting. "Me. It's all my fault. Daisy would have been out if she hadn't come back for me. He hurt her so badly. He's going to try and kill her, I'm sure. And he might use me to get to her."

"Oh, Lily. Morgan—Daisy is safe, and we will keep you safe too. Here's the next hard question."

Lily nodded.

"When we catch Ronan, are you willing to testify against him?"

Iris said, "Don't you mean *if*?"

"No, I don't. I'm staying confident we will get him and bring him to justice. He won't get away with how he's treated you all."

Lily nodded. "If you're sure you can keep me safe, I will."

The other two shook their heads.

While Jacq was disappointed, she wouldn't push them. Lily's and Morgan's testimonies should be enough to lock him away for a long time.

She chatted with the girls a little more then went back to the hallway. "Anything?"

Dylan shook his head. "No sign of him."

She told him what Lily had said. "We'll have to stay vigilant."

"And call the marshals in."

"But I want them to stay close; the house is safe."

"Maybe the marshals will use it, if we offer."

"I hope so. And you know Gio isn't going to want them carting Morgan off to some secret WITSEC location."

Dylan laughed. "So true. But it's our job to call them, so they can do theirs."

"I know. I can do that now."

"Jacq, it's two in the morning."

"If Ronan is stalking the hospital, we can't wait."

Gio jumped from bed and snatched his phone from the floor and his Glock from under his pillow. He darted out the door, down the hall, and into Morgan's room.

She was alone, still lying in bed. She groaned and fought the air.

He set his gun down and went to the side of the bed, careful to avoid her swinging arms. He put a steady hand on her shoulder. "Morgan. Wake up. It's only a dream."

Her writhing stopped. Her eyes fluttered open. "Gio?"

She sat bolt upright and threw her arms around his neck. Surrounding her with his arms, he held her close. "It's all right. You're safe."

She trembled.

He stroked her hair. "You are safe."

"It was only a dream."

"Yep. Need to talk about it?"

"Ronan was coming after me. Then Duke. I couldn't run. They attacked."

"I'm not going to let them get you." *Who's Duke?* With the state she was in, he couldn't bring himself to ask.

They sat in silence for a long time before she finally said, "Are you sure you can't just hold me tonight?"

Her question made his soul ache. "I wish I could. But we aren't married. I can't."

She sat back and met his gaze with longing eyes. "Then maybe we should get married. I don't want to be away from you. Tomorrow morning, go to a judge and get a piece of paper? Then you can hold me forever."

He ran his hands up and down her arms. "I love your suggestion, but I care too much about you to jump in like that. I want us to learn to love each other outside of this situation. We can't make decisions based on how we're feeling in this moment. You need to learn to be on your own, depending on Christ alone, not me. I'm a broken, sinful man. Christ has to be your source of strength. I can't be around every moment of every day. He has to be your go-to, not me."

"I don't know how, Gio."

He loved the way she said his name. "Morgan, I've been walking with the Lord consistently, for the most part, for the last twenty-three years, and I'm still learning. You aren't going to figure it out overnight."

"I'm scared though. There's so much uncertainty."

"You're one of the bravest people I know. And remember bravery doesn't come when you aren't scared of anything. It's the opposite. But God tells us over and over we are to 'fear not' for He's with us."

His words were like a two-by-four upside his own head. He chuckled. "And so you know, I'm preaching to myself. I struggle with fear too. Fear I won't be able to help people, you especially. Fear I'll become like the monsters I'm fighting."

"You could never be like them."

He looked down at the cuts on his hand that he probably should have bandaged again after his shower.

She took his hand and gently touched the wounds. "Trust me. That monster is nowhere in here." She tapped his sternum.

"It's here that the problem lies." He pointed to his temple. "Trust me, Ronan doesn't want to come anywhere near you ever again."

She smiled and a yawn escaped.

"You're tired. Sleep. I can't hold you, but I can sit here until you fall asleep."

"Even if it takes a while?"

"Of course."

"Read to me again?"

"I can do that." He grabbed his phone and read to her from the book of John.

When Morgan woke the sun was high in the sky, illuminating the mountains all around. She padded to the window in the little alcove, leaned against the wall, and looked out across the Smoky Mountains. Was she really free? Wasn't someone going to expect something of her? She probably shouldn't linger too long.

No. She could. There was nothing pressing, no one wanting their way with her, no demands. Just freedom. She didn't know what to do with it.

"Knock, knock."

She turned at the sound of Gio's voice.

He lifted a wax-coated paper cup that steamed a little. "Coffee. I think I remembered how you had it two mornings ago."

"I could get used to this you-being-around-in-the-morning thing."

He brought her the cup.

She encircled it with her hands and blew on liquid the perfect shade of light brown. Once it had cooled a bit, she sipped a little.

He stayed at the entrance to the dormer, leaning on his hand on the corner of the wall. His t-shirt pulled snug across his body. He was so strong. But it wasn't just the physical. The strength of this man's character was incomparable.

A tiny bit of her was embarrassed by her rash question last night, but at the same time, she didn't regret it one bit. Yet she recognized his wisdom. She needed time, but she prayed God would let her and Gio have a future. Maybe she was hero-struck, but she was certain there was something more.

Movement outside caught her eye. A car pulled up the driveway. "Who's that?"

Gio stepped beside her, placing his hand on her back. "That's Jacq. She has a new car."

Careful not to slosh her coffee, she planted a kiss on Gio's cheek and darted from the room, down the stairs, and out the front door. She set her coffee on the porch railing and ran toward Jacqui. Another vehicle pulled in behind her.

Morgan skidded to a stop, acutely aware of the gravel beneath her feet.

Jacqui emerged from her car. "They're U.S. Marshals here to help protect you. Two are also staying with Lily."

She pulled her gaze away from the man and woman exiting the large, black SUV and met Jacqui's eyes. "What about Violet and Iris, and even Celeste?"

"None of them want to testify, so we can't offer them the same protection. But sounds like the two of you need it most anyway."

Morgan nodded and finally did what she'd raced outside to do in the first place and pulled Jacqui into a hug. The friends held each other for a long time. Until Gio's voice tore Morgan's attention away.

She turned. Gio was shaking the hand of an equally tall man. The marshal's light brown hair blew in the breeze, and his suitcoat barely fit over his broad shoulders. He couldn't be a day over twenty-eight. The woman, probably in her early forties, extended a hand to Gio.

Jacq introduced Morgan. "This is Morgan Zalman, although the target refers to her as Daisy. Morgan, these are U.S. Marshals Liam Hoffman and Tiffany Umber."

They both extended their hands to her. She shook them but was not impressed. Couldn't Jacqui and Gio keep her safe enough? Especially up here. What if these marshals wanted to haul her off to some undisclosed location away from the only friends she'd ever had?

She swallowed hard and fought the urge to throw herself against Gio's chest.

Jacqui squeezed her arm. "For now the marshals have agreed for you to stay here as long as it fits their standards, so let's go in and show them around."

She followed but tried to catch Gio's eye. That didn't happen until they were inside. He attempted to smile at her, but it wasn't his normal smile. Why was he worried about this?

Marshal Umber came up to her. "I hear you've been through a lot in the last two days."

Morgan prickled. What did this lady know?

Marshal Umber continued, "We're here not only to keep you safe, but to help you too. Let me know if you need anything."

Morgan wanted to laugh, but that would be rude. Gio and Jacqui could provide everything Morgan needed. It wasn't like she was going to talk to this random lady about her past life.

They showed the marshals around, but as they were headed upstairs, Gio's phone rang, and he slipped away. If Marshal Umber hadn't kept trying to talk to her, Morgan would have followed him.

When they finally went back downstairs, Morgan managed to slip out the front door. She found Gio on the porch, leaning against a post and talking on the phone. He lifted his free arm and invited her close.

She tucked herself against his chest.

He spoke into his phone. "Yes, sir. I understand. Goodbye." He let out a shaky breath and slid his phone into his pocket.

"What's wrong?"

He wrapped his other arm around her. "Boss says I have to go back to Knoxville."

She tightened her grip around his waist.

"I know, but maybe this is your chance to be okay without me. A practice in having faith in God alone. But I'll be back. And you've got Jacq and two marshals."

"I don't trust those two as far as I can throw an elephant. How can I?"

"They're professional protectors. We have to trust God foremost."

"I know. I just really like having you around."

"At least they aren't whisking you away to a place I'm not allowed."

She pushed back from him only far enough to see his face. "And for that I'm grateful."

"I'll be back as soon as I can. We still have to find evidence to connect Ronan to Jamie DeRozan's murder."

"Rose?"

He nodded. "That reminds me, do you know of a girl named Amber Erickson, otherwise known as Aster?"

"Aster? Yeah, she was one of Ronan's girls. She was in prison when Ronan brought me in. She had a baby in prison; that's why she let herself get arrested. As far as I understand, she gave the baby up, but she was only home for a week before Ronan put her in her own place, or at least that's what he said. Said the same about Rose, and, well, we know how that turned out."

"Interesting."

"How did you know about her?"

"Her tattoo came up in our search."

"When do you have to leave?"

Gio looked at his watch. "Probably should leave within the hour. Would you like to go for a walk, assuming the marshals approve?"

"I'd like that. Hopefully Jacq has a pair of shoes I can borrow. I'm guessing flip flops aren't great for walking around here."

He chuckled. "Probably not."

Armed with a pair of tennis shoes and permission from the marshals, Morgan set out on a walk with Gio.

Once they were about twenty yards from the house, Gio asked, "May I hold your hand?"

With no attempt to suppress it, a giggle escaped her lips. "I was afraid to ask."

"Why? It's not like we haven't held hands before."

Weaving her fingers with his, she said, "I'm afraid you're going to push me away so I'll trust God."

"Nope. I'm not going to manipulate the situation at all. I'm only going away because I still have a duty to find Ronan and bring him to justice."

"Even if you want to execute vengeance?" She bit her lip, hoping the teasing came across in her voice like she had intended.

"I'm not sure I like how well you already know me."

They both laughed.

"Execute is definitely the right word." Gio laughed harder.

He tugged her hand and led her out of the clearing and down a narrow path that revealed a creek.

It was beautiful. Wildflowers grew along the sides, and the water cascaded over piles of stones as it flowed downhill.

"Gonna give me a sermon?" She tossed him a teasing smile.

"I'm all preached out for now. Just want to soak in God's gorgeous creation before I head back into the fray."

She leaned her head against his arm and squeezed his hand tighter. *God, help Gio to do Your work. Help him find Ronan, so we can sleep soundly at night. And help me to trust You without him here to push me toward You.*

Chapter Twenty-Six

Back at the office, Gio struggled to get his head back in gear. He'd been there for an hour but still wasn't focused.

A wad of paper fell on his keyboard. He followed its trajectory back to Dylan, who was staring at him with his arms crossed. A quick glance at Matt confirmed he had the same countenance. Aliza just laughed.

"Shut up. You three aren't helping any."

Aliza said, "What are you even trying to do, Gio? Because I'm pretty sure it's hard to get anything done staring out the window."

"I'm trying to figure out who Ronan is, so we can figure out where he's hiding."

Matt chuckled. "Do you see him in the parking lot?"

It was Dylan's turn from his spot closest to the window. "*I* can't even see the parking lot from my desk."

"You guys have anything? We need leads."

Matt pointed at his computer. "Well, I found this interesting tidbit. Looks like Ezra, after nearly two months waiting for a trial, finally made bail this morning."

"Ronan." Heat rushed through Gio's body.

Matt said, "Probably. But why? And how'd he not get caught? His face has been plastered everywhere."

"Well, find out. We need to know anyone else who might be connected to them."

Matt nodded. "On it."

Gio tried to refocus on his computer screen. How was this guy so completely off the radar? He rubbed his still-sore cheek. At least he was not chasing a ghost.

About ten minutes later Dylan said, "I got a message from the ME. He has an ID on the body from yesterday's fire." Dylan put the photo up on the large screen.

"Scissors."

Warren burst out of his office. "The officer watching Ronan's house just called in a shots fired at the house. Victim DOA. He's in pursuit of a possible suspect. Go!"

Everyone jumped to their feet, except Matt, who said, "Shouldn't someone keep looking for who let Ezra out, boss?"

"Agreed."

Gio, Dylan, and Aliza left in a Bureau SUV.

They arrived on scene in less than ten minutes. Local LEOs and paramedics were already there. A uniformed officer pointed them to the back of the house that had been destroyed by yesterday's fire.

They met up with Aliza's fiancée, Gabe, around the corner. Aliza squeezed his arm. "Do we have an ID?"

"Ezra—"

"No!" Gio didn't believe it. He rushed toward where the body lay on the patio. This kid wouldn't have come back to this house. He was scared to death of Ronan. But if he didn't know about the fire and the girls getting out from Ronan's grasp, perhaps he came looking for one of them.

With tight lungs he stared down at Ezra's lifeless face. Two gunshot wounds. One to his left knee and the other to his chest—right through the heart. This was not the first time Gio had seen those injuries.

Jamie "Rose" DeRozan.

By four o'clock in the afternoon, Morgan was bored out of her mind. There was pretty much nothing to do, and the longer she sat around, the crazier places her mind wanted to take her. She needed to not think about Gio or Ronan or Duke or the past in any way, shape, or form.

She'd spent a lot of time talking to Jacqui, and it had been wonderful to connect with her long-lost friend. Morgan had even convinced Jacqui to start really thinking about a wedding date. Dylan would be happy. He could thank her later.

Morgan wandered around the house and found Jacqui in the master bedroom. "Hey."

"Bored?"

Morgan let her body dramatically droop. "Out of my mind. Please give me something to do to help you around here. I've never painted a wall, but I bet I could figure it out. Clean something? Anything."

Jacqui chuckled and pulled her bright red hair back in a ponytail. "Actually, I have just the thing you could help with. And if you're the same Morgan I remember, you'll love it."

Morgan clapped her hands. "You've got me intrigued."

Jacqui's countenance shifted. "First, I need to tell you something. Dylan called." She told her about Ezra.

Morgan's hand flew to her mouth.

"Do you know who would possibly have helped Ronan bail him out?"

Morgan shook her head. "Not really. Not if Celeste is still at the hospital. I think she'd do anything for Ronan."

"Sorry for such the downer."

"It's life right now it seems. I'm sure Ronan did it."

"We are too. Or at least Gio's pretty certain the same person killed Jamie DeRozan and Ezra."

Morgan nodded.

"But anyway, on to better things. We have a bunch of boxes of books—"

"Books?" Morgan shoved all thoughts of Ezra and Ronan out of her mind. She hadn't read a book in more than thirteen years.

"Yes, books. They were donated from a friend's church that was closing down their library."

"Closing a library? Who does that? It's straight-up tragic."

Jacqui's face distorted as she tried to contain her laughter. "Anyway. Could you sort them out? See what's worth keeping and what's not, what type of book they are, and such. Think you can handle that?"

"As long as you don't want it done in a decent amount of time."

"Seriously, whenever. Feel free to read as you go! The boxes are in the loft. You can sort them up there. Bookshelves are coming one of these days."

"Yay, books. Thanks, Jacqui." She gave her friend a big hug and darted up the stairs to the loft.

She hadn't thought about possibly needing something to cut tape with, but her nails were long enough to pick at the tape and rip it away from the cardboard.

The first box held commentaries on many of the books of the Bible. The next box had a Bible and the rest of the books in the set of commentaries. She stacked them against the wall, arranging them in order with the help of the table of contents in the Bible. She would love to dive into them. The thirst for biblical knowledge was almost palpable.

A third box had an array of books that addressed particular life issues. She set a few aside that seemed to have no place in a house for rescued women. Most women wouldn't be interested in reading a book about men's struggles. *Although* ... She picked it back up. What kinds of struggles did men like Gio face?

She flipped it open, then slammed it shut. *Nope. Not going to think about Gio.*

She sorted through a few more boxes before she found one full of fiction. "Eeek!"

Now she wasn't going to be able to make any more progress.

The books she pulled out were ones she remembered from high school. Dee Henderson. Lori Wick. She loved these authors.

But the next book stopped her. *Redeeming Love* by Francine Rivers.

Her hands trembled. She'd read this book once upon a time. She'd never forgotten it. But while so much of the storyline was a mystery since it had been so long, she did remember enough to know it would be nearly impossible to handle today. Still, something deep in her soul ached to read it again, no matter how hard it would be.

Should I?

She opened it. The dedication caught her eye. "To those who hurt and hunger."

Closing the book, she brought it to her chest and held it tight. This was exactly what she needed at the moment, wasn't it?

She stood and, abandoning the boxes, went to her bed to curl up and read.

Gio was frustrated. It was already Thursday morning, and he hadn't been able to visit Morgan, but he knew she needed space away from him. And frankly, he needed the space too. Emotions were running too hot between them, and Gio could only take so many cold showers. He was glad Jacq was able to stay with her and the marshals.

"Gio?" Aliza's voice pulled him back into the FBI field office.

"Yep?" He leaned back into his chair.

"Find anything interesting in outer space?"

He rolled his eyes and focused on his computer. He'd been combing through other murder cases looking for a matching MO. They had two murders with the same pattern. The chances that Ronan had murdered before were growing.

He glanced over at Aliza. "Nothing yet." He lifted his coffee mug to his mouth, then was sorely disappointed when nothing but a single drop hit his lips.

Setting it back down with a thump, he said, "Guess I need more coffee."

"Got it." Dylan appeared beside him and set a fresh cup next to the two already on his desk. "Sleep might go a long way too."

"That's for the weak."

"Another dream?"

Gio nodded. Last night's had left him unable to go back to sleep for nearly two hours. Not that he remembered it, but he'd stayed up praying for Morgan the entire time, and, of course, sketching a new picture of the woman he was falling hard for.

"I take it you don't want to talk about it."

"Nothing to say. I don't remember the dream."

"But you always remember a sense of something from them."

Gio lowered his voice so Matt couldn't hear. "I prayed for her for about two hours after, if that tells you anything."

"A battle for her soul?"

"No, her soul is securely in the hands of the Father, where it can't be snatched away, but for her life."

"Gotcha. So let's find that—what do you call him?"

Gio shook his head.

"Let's find that bad word before he finds her."

Gio once again turned his attention to the screen in front of him. He flipped to the next case file that had come up in his search for murders with a gunshot wound to the knee and chest. A man in his mid-twenties with a gunshot wound to his left knee, then one directly to his chest. Both point-blank, maybe even as close as only a foot away as there was gunshot residue on the victim. Just like Ezra. Caliber was also a .45 ACP. Those two details were impossible to know about Jamie DeRozan as her chest wound was through-and-through so no bullet was recovered.

The firearm found in Monday's fire was also chambered in .45 ACP. Ronan had a favorite caliber it would seem.

Gio kept reading the report. Number one suspect was the man's brother, Keenan Robins. Age at the time of the murder was twenty-six. Those interviewed said Keenan and his brother had a falling out over a woman.

The murder took place fourteen years ago in a suburb of Austin, Texas.

"This one looks promising. Morgan said she thinks Ronan is around forty. The guy who was suspected for the murder, but never caught, would be forty now." He told them what he had found and clicked on the attached file of the suspect's photograph.

Ronan. He was fourteen years younger, had longer hair and a thinner build, but it was definitely the man who had been selling Morgan as a commodity. Gio's blood ran hotter than lava straight from the mouth of a volcano. He cast the picture up on the team's screen.

Aliza gasped.

Matt said, "We got him."

Gio shook his head. "Not hardly. They haven't been able to catch up to him in fourteen years. How is knowing his identity going to give us what we need?"

Dylan stood and, staring at the photo of the young Ronan, folded his arms. "It's something, even if we don't know how it'll help yet."

Gio sighed and sat back in his chair. Ronan was officially a serial killer. But they had no evidence linking him to Jamie's murder yet, other than the similarities. If only they had a bullet, some hair, even a crime scene. Something more. Anything.

Chapter Twenty-Seven

Gio tapped his hand furiously against the door handle as Dylan drove up the mountain road. Gio couldn't say no when Dylan asked him if he wanted to go along to deliver Harper, who dozed in the backseat, plus a ton of things Jacq had ordered for the house that had been delivered to Dylan's apartment to keep the number of people who knew they were there to a minimum. But per the marshals' orders, the team had switched from their normal vehicles to make the trip. So Dylan was driving his dad's car.

The trip seemed incredibly long tonight. He didn't want to admit it, but he was nervous about seeing Morgan. It had only been fifty-four hours. Not that he was counting. But what if the space she'd needed had actually squelched her feelings for him?

He was frustrated with himself. If the time had done that for her, then fine. But it hadn't for him.

They arrived right around five-thirty. Gio fought the urge to run inside, and instead assisted Dylan in hauling armfuls of online orders into the house. Harper even helped carry a package until she saw Jacq, then she dropped it and ran to her mom.

Jacq greeted them on the porch. After giving Dylan a kiss, she said, "Please tell me you thanked your mom profusely? It really was better to help get Morgan settled and security established before Harper was here."

"How's Morgan doing?" Dylan asked.

"Really good. Can't get her nose out of a book though. She started sorting them, but after finding a particular one, she's barely done anything but read. And sleep. She has done plenty of that."

"No surprise after all she's been through." Gio tried to sneak a peek into the house.

"She's not in there. Went off to her special spot to read."

"Special spot?"

Jacq's smile grew. "Apparently you two found a good location on your walk the other day."

"I hope she's got bug spray."

Jacq laughed. "She wouldn't dare forget after the mosquito bites she got yesterday. Go find her. She'll be happy to see you."

Without hesitating, he dumped the packages he held into Jacq's arms and bounded down the stairs.

He found the path off the clearing that led down to the creek and wound his way to where he discovered Morgan sitting on a rock outcropping by the water.

Her index finger rose, telling him to wait. But she hadn't looked up to see it was him.

"Hey." His voice almost didn't work.

Her head jerked up. "Gio." Her eyes widened as did her smile. "Welcome back."

"Thanks. What are you reading?"

She held up the book. The title was *Redeeming Love*. "Only the second best book in the world."

He stepped closer to her.

Her cheeks were moist, and the tip of her nose was an adorable shade of pink.

"Do books normally make you cry?"

"Just ones like this that jump right into your soul and cleanse you from the inside out. Well, it's God doing the cleansing, but

He's using this book all right." She marked her spot near the back of the novel and patted the rock next to her.

He hopped the creek and joined her. "The marshals don't mind you coming out here?"

"Liam's probably not too far off. He circles around and gets his steps in apparently."

Gio sat close but not quite touching her. "Liam?"

"What else am I going to call him? Marshal Hoffman every time?" She snickered.

"Are they treating you all right?"

"They are. Mostly letting me be and keeping a watchful eye out."

"Good. What's the book about?"

"A girl who was sold into trafficking."

His breath caught between his lungs and the forest around them. "That's not too close to home?"

"It's perfectly close to home. You know what happens though?"

"I haven't read it. Or seen the movie."

"There's a movie?"

He nodded.

"Will you watch it with me?"

"Of course." Although he had no idea what he was actually agreeing to. He only knew he recognized the title. "What happens?"

"Angel learns what it really means to be loved unconditionally. Michael Hosea showed her what God's love truly looked like in her everyday life."

"Hosea?"

"It's based on the book of Hosea."

He had to swallow, but it had become incredibly difficult.

"Gio?" She turned to face him, crossing her legs like a preschooler.

He met her eyes and waited for her words to fill the space when she was ready.

"Are you *my* Hosea?"

He couldn't breathe. "I'd like to be."

"Good. Because you've already shown me God's love, and for that I thank you."

Holding back was no longer an option. He lifted his arm, inviting her close.

She shifted on the rock and, tucking herself into his embrace, leaned her head on his shoulder and her knees against his leg.

Gio held her close and kissed the top of her head. All his fears from twenty minutes ago flew off the mountain. This was not the same woman who had clung to him the other night. Tonight her countenance radiated faith and courage; her affection was filled with hope and love, not desperation.

"Seems like a lot's happened in two days." He rested his cheek against her hair.

"Yes and no. I have a long path of healing, Gio, I know that. But God is doing the work, and I'm ready to walk down whatever path He has for me."

"I get the feeling this isn't the only book you've been reading."

She giggled. "Been reading the Bible a lot too and talking to Jacq. Her faith has grown so much since we were college students. I can't wait to keep learning from her."

An idea sparked in his mind. He'd have to check with Jacq first, but if she hadn't taken care of it, he would get Morgan her own Bible.

After dinner, Morgan picked up her novel and went to the couch, which had found a more appropriate place in the living room. While Jacq had roped Gio and Dylan into a project in the yard, she settled in to read.

Reading about a character named Angel was strange, when she kept hearing Duke's voice in her mind ... Duke ... she shuddered. That was also the name of the bad guy in the book she was reading. What were the chances?

The memory of her first meeting with Duke came to her mind. She'd given him that nickname. Why? And she wished she knew why Duke expected her to know why he'd called her Angel. Maybe it was connected. But how? Had they run into one another before? Her memory was blank. A giant piece of the puzzle was missing, but she didn't want to care about it. She shook the whole train of thought free from her mind and dove back into the story in her hands.

About a half hour later, Gio came into the room. Without thinking she snapped her book shut and sat up.

His eyes narrowed, and he tilted his head. "Keep reading." He held up a book. "I brought mine too." He sat next to her and opened his paperback.

Morgan stared at him for a moment.

He looked at her sideways, a silly grin on his face. "Seriously, just read."

"This is so weird and amazing and ... I don't even know."

He chuckled and pulled a box closer to prop his feet on. Sitting back again he resumed his reading posture.

"Okay." She leaned back, half against the couch and half against Gio, with her legs draped over the armrest. She read for a moment, but soon all the tears she'd cried as she read Michael and Angel's story had made her thirsty. "I'm going to get a glass of water. Want anything?"

"That sounds great, but I'll get it. You keep reading."

"What? No, I can get it. That's fine."

"Morgan. It's all right." He tapped the tip of her nose. "I'd love to serve you."

"Umm, all right."

He winked at her, sending blood rushing to her cheeks.

She sat in awe, unable to read while he was in the kitchen. He came back with two Solo cups and handed her one.

"You were supposed to keep reading."

"I'm not used to people getting things for me."

"Get used to it." He sat closer to her this time, and kissed her temple before grabbing his book and settling in. "Read."

"Are you guys staying tonight?"

He rested the book in his lap. "No. We're leaving once Dylan helps Jacq get Harper tucked in. But they needed a little family time first."

"I love that."

"We'll be back on Saturday, Lord willing." He shifted slightly. "Do you want to do something other than read? Talk? Play a game?"

"I'm not sure. I simply like being with you. Reading or not. Talking or not. Quiet is good too. It's yet another thing I'm not accustomed to. I've never had the opportunity for my mind to be quiet. I was always on alert, not knowing what kind of mood Ronan would be in, what kind of trick I'd end up with that night. Sorry, you don't want me to talk about that."

"I've told you before, and I'll say it again and again because it's not going to change: If you need to talk about anything, I'm your guy. Might make me uncomfortable, I'm not going to lie about that, but I'm here for you. It's not about me."

"I still don't get you."

He chuckled. "No one does."

She lifted his arm and slid up against him. He draped it around her, resting his hand respectfully on her hip. No groping, no caressing, just simple touch. "Tell me something else you've missed that you're looking forward to again in this new free life you have."

"This."

A question played with his facial muscles.

"I've always loved physical touch. I was the kid constantly in my mom or dad's lap. My brother even snuggled with me while we watched movies as kids. I can't help but give people hugs. But that part of me has been lost. When you live with guy after guy who sees your body as an asset, you lose a lot of yourself, and that's part of me that was lost until you found me. That first time we ran into each other at Walmart, I wanted to hug you, and I didn't even know why. I love that you just hold me and don't try anything or expect anything."

When he didn't respond, she looked up into his face.

His lips were pressed together, and his hand grew heavier on her hip. Taking her hand in his free one, he kissed her knuckles. "I'm sorry. Then hold you I will. It's an honor. And I pray I will always honor you when all you need is a good cuddle."

This man's honesty once again caught her off-guard. He was only a man and had to pray he'd honor her, but what man would want to honor her? It didn't make any sense.

"Will I ever get used to your awesomeness?"

"I'm not sure if that would be a good thing or a bad thing."

She giggled. "Me neither."

She curled in a little tighter to Gio and picked up her book.

On Saturday, the clock in Gio's SUV read five twenty-two in the morning when he pulled up to the address he had been given by dispatch. A crime scene. Murder. Related to their cases. That was all he knew.

He'd been tempted to contact Jacq directly but had called Dylan instead. Gio had picked him up on the way to the scene. Dylan had been on the phone with Jacq when Gio arrived. Morgan was safe and sound in her bed.

But Gio wasn't feeling at ease knowing that. Something was still off. And he just wanted to punch someone.

He cut the engine and took a breath. Fear was rearing its ugly head again. He was scared. Had someone else lost their life in Ronan's quest for power, vengeance, or whatever he was looking for?

God, help me to trust You and not fear. I'm walking with You through this.

Gio, with Dylan by his side, ducked under the police tape, which was wrapped from one tree to another near a playground. His stomach knotted itself as if it were a skilled sailor. A murder near a playground? He really hoped this was not related to their cases.

"Hey, guys." Gabe walked up to them.

Gio asked, "You're the one who told them to call us in?"

"Guilty. Sorry to wake y'all, but you're gonna want to see this and take the case."

"Why?" The dread in Gio's gut tightened.

"Come see for yourselves." Gabe's voice was somber, and he motioned for them to follow.

Bright floodlights had been set up, illuminating a woman's naked body in a grave of sorts. Bile rose from Gio's empty stomach. It was one of the girls from Morgan's house. Celeste. Her cloudy, unseeing eyes stared into the lights. Gio wiped his face. He couldn't bring himself to look at her.

"Gio?" Dylan's hand gripped his arm. "You have to see this."

After swallowing hard, Gio took in the scene. Gunshot wounds to left knee and left-center of chest. On her abdomen was a small bouquet of assorted wildflowers, including daisies.

His hands trembled.

What was Ronan trying to say with this choice of flower?

Dylan knelt beside the body and poked at the disturbed earth. "This is weird. Why only dig a six-inch grave?"

Gio went around the body, paying attention to the grave in particular. "I have no idea. All he did was pull up the sod."

"Maybe he ran out of time? Got spooked?"

"Agents!" A uniformed officer shouted from the other side of a large oak tree.

Dylan stood, and they strode to the officer.

Gio asked, "What—"

Another shallow grave had been dug. This one was empty except for a full bouquet of daisies.

Gio's whole body shook. He clenched his hands out in front of him as if he were going to choke someone. Oh the things he would do if Ronan showed his face.

"Hey." Dylan smacked his arm. "We'll get him."

Gio glared at his friend. "Dylan."

Dylan raised his index finger. "Stop. Focus on what's possible for us to do here. We have to gather what we can so we can get him, within the parameters of the law."

Gio nodded and sucked in a huge breath before releasing it slowly. "You know what he's saying with this, don't you?"

"Pretend I don't." The pallor of Dylan's face told Gio he did indeed.

"Please tell me those marshals are worth their no-nonsense salt."

The same officer called to them again. "Agents. There's another one."

Gio's knees buckled. "Flowers?"

He and Dylan walked over.

"Yes, sir. Daylilies."

Lily.

At least the grave was empty.

Gio said, "I hope the marshals with Lily are keeping her safe."

"They moved her to a secure rehab facility yesterday," Dylan said. "She should be out of reach."

"So why did he kill Celeste?" Gio turned back toward where her body lay.

"Maybe she crossed him or ran out of usefulness?" Dylan shrugged.

"Do you suppose she went and found him?"

"Two days was all she lasted in rehab, so I'm guessing so."

"Or he found her."

"I'm not sure we'll ever know."

Gio ran his hand through his hair. "What we know is Morgan's and Lily's lives are in danger."

Chapter Twenty-Eight

Morgan shoved the eggs around in the pan and checked the clock yet again. Ten. Gio had said he'd be here by nine to have breakfast with her. But he wasn't, and she couldn't wait any longer to eat.

Jacqui had been on the phone a lot since Morgan had gotten up, but she hadn't said anything about it. And both Liam and Tiffany seemed more on edge than their normal teetering.

Harper wandered into the room with her bunny tucked securely under her arm.

"Hey, cutie."

"Hi, Auntie Morgan."

She smiled at the little girl, grateful she'd adopted her as aunt and no longer called her "pretty lady."

"I hungry."

"I've got plenty of eggs here." Morgan lifted the pan.

Harper's nose crinkled.

"Don't like eggs?"

She shook her head.

"Did you eat breakfast?"

Again her head indicated the negative. Whatever was going on really had Jacqui distracted if she hadn't gotten Harper breakfast. "Well, let's get you something to eat." Morgan lifted Harper and plopped her in her booster seat with little sound effects.

Harper giggled.

Morgan found a bowl and spoon and Harper's favorite cereal. After sliding her own eggs onto a plate, she poured Harper's cereal and milk and sat across from the three-year-old. "Just you and me for breakfast this morning, I guess. Thanks for the company, Harper."

The girl gave her a toothy, milky, cereal-filled grin.

Being a mom would be amazing. Too bad she was pretty sure that could never happen for her. To have lived in the game for so long—and to only have gotten pregnant once—didn't bode well. Not that she hadn't taken the morning-after pill plenty of times.

How many babies could have been? And how old would the child she did know of be today?? Eight maybe?

"More?"

Morgan met Harper's eyes. "More cereal?"

Harper nodded.

Morgan fixed her a second bowl. Maybe she could love on Harper and whatever other children Jacqui ended up having. Be the best auntie they could ever have. She could do that.

The question remained: How was she supposed to tell Gio? Would that be a deal-breaker for him? But more than anything she wanted to know where he was and if he was still planning on coming.

The bright glow of afternoon had dropped to blinding beams streaming into the office window. It was after five, and they were still in Knoxville.

Gio banged his fist on his desk. Thankfully, the cuts from Sunday were mostly healed. "We have to get out of here, Dylan."

"I know."

Warren exited his office. "Give me a rundown, guys. What do we know?"

The whole team looked at Gio. Who made him point on this one? Whatever.

"Cynthia Bigney, known as Celeste, was murdered in the exact same method as Ezra Wayman, Jamie DeRozan, and the brother of Keenan Robins. Robins was the number-one suspect in his brother's murder because of DNA found at the scene. They were also reported to have had a major falling out. We've contacted the local LEOs who worked that case.

"The flowers left at this morning's scene were all bought at a local florist shop. They don't have any security cameras but were able to identify Ronan from an array of photos. The florist said he now has a bit of a scruffy beard and was wearing a baseball cap. He was in the store yesterday morning and didn't talk much."

Aliza added, "I heard from the crime lab. DNA was found on the body, so they're processing that."

Dylan said, "The ME reported Celeste had similar injuries to Jamie, although not as prolonged. The size of the bruising and scrapes on her ankle were the same as the damage to Jamie's bone."

Warren stroked his narrow beard. "So he held her for a few days?"

Dylan nodded.

Gio asked, "But where? We need to find where he killed both Jamie and Celeste. He might be hanging out there."

Dylan said, "Yep. And the ME said he was having soil samples analyzed to help with that. Might be able to narrow down to a smaller region at least."

"So what else needs to be done right now?"

Matt sat back in his chair. "Sir, we need to keep searching for possible aliases and potential properties, but Aliza has that covered. Can we let Dylan and Gio go to help keep Morgan safe? While Lily is also under threat, the marshals have her so far removed she should be fine. But Morgan, while the house is secure it's connected to Jacq, and that poses a risk. The more people we have protecting her the better." Matt shot Gio a "you're welcome" nod.

"Seems reasonable to me," Warren said. "Morgan's court date has been set for Tuesday. The marshals and I both tried to get it dropped. But while Matt was the arresting agent, the PD processed her, so the ball was already careening. We need a plan to keep her safe getting to the courthouse. Those records are public, so Ronan could know where she'll be."

Dread dropped into Gio's stomach. How could he have been stupid enough to forget she'd have to appear before the judge for her arrest?

Warren continued, "Get out of here, you two, but keep me in the loop for Tuesday's plan. And Olsen, Blake, let me know if you need more hands. It might be a holiday weekend, but justice doesn't care about barbeques. Find this guy!"

Gio snapped his laptop shut, stuffed it in his bag, and was on his feet ready to go before Dylan could say, "Yes, sir." Gio stayed about twenty steps ahead of Dylan all the way to the elevator.

After depressing the elevator button at least a dozen times, the doors finally opened. Dylan stepped in Gio's way and hit the floor number. "Chill. We'll be there soon enough. Breaking the elevator won't get us there any faster."

Gio grunted at his friend. “I won’t be satisfied she’s safe until we get there.”

“You really think Jacq’s going to let anything happen to her?”

Gio chuckled. “Point taken.” He forced himself to lean back against the wall of the elevator and relax. But the urgency in his spirit didn’t let up. He needed to get to Morgan now.

Chapter Twenty-Nine

Morgan helped Jacqui pull the chicken and rice out for dinner. Her friend had been quiet and serious all day. Something was wrong, but when Morgan pressed, all Jacqui said was yes, something was up, but she needed to wait until Gio and Dylan got there to explain. Nothing more.

At least she finally knew Gio was, in fact, coming today.

Morgan had spent most of her day playing with Harper inside, where she was told she had to stay, and sorting more books while Harper napped. In the process, Morgan had picked out another book to read, since she'd finished *Redeeming Love* after Gio left on Thursday.

Morgan set the rice on the counter next to where Jacqui was measuring water.

"I probably should have just told you what's going on, and I'm sorry to keep it from you, but—"

Morgan put her hand on her friend's shoulder. "It's okay. You have your reasons, and I promise to try and not be mad at you once I know."

"Try?"

"Yeah, I know Yoda wouldn't be impressed, but that's the best I can do."

Jacqui laughed. "I can appreciate that." She wrapped her arm around Morgan. "Thanks for trusting me."

"Of course. But only if you promise Gio will be here soon."

"Oh girl, you've got it bad."

"I feel so stupid about it. I need to not be attached to a man for once in my life. Shouldn't I be free and single for at least a year or two?"

"God's timing is always what it needs to be. And I will tell you this, He's doing something with you and Gio. Sit back and appreciate God's process."

"Will do."

Jacqui's phone indicated there was motion at the camera she'd set up on the gate.

"Is it them?"

Jacqui checked. "Yep. Dinner can wait."

They abandoned the food preparations and dashed out the front door and down the steps.

A large, black SUV pulled in. It must be one of the Bureau's. Both guys jumped out. Jacqui ran to Dylan and the couple embraced.

Gio strode to Morgan and stopped just shy of her.

"Jacqui wouldn't tell me anything. What's going on?"

"She didn't?" His eyes narrowed, bringing deep creases to his forehead.

"Nothing. Only that something was going on, and you would tell me when you got here."

Gio wrapped his arm across her shoulders and scanned the area before turning her toward the house. "Let's go inside and find a private space to talk."

They walked in. Liam sat on the couch and Tiffany was at the dining room table, so he led Morgan upstairs to her room. They sat on the edge of her bed.

Her insides felt like they weighed a billion pounds. What was so serious that he wanted this much privacy?

"There's no easy way to say this, but Celeste is dead."

Morgan's insides bottomed out. "Ronan?"

He told her about the consistencies, including Ronan's brother.

All these years she'd lived with a killer. She'd known he had a darker side than his normal midnight, but premeditated murder?

"There's one—well, technically, two—more things." He described the graves and the flowers.

She remained quiet as she processed the obvious threat to her and Lily.

"Are you all right?" Gio's hand rested on her back.

"Sorry. Yeah, I think so. Celeste is dead?"

He nodded. "Were you two close?"

She shook her head. "She wasn't exactly the nicest person. It's hard to be close to someone who's constantly vying for the man-of-the-house's attention. She was still fighting for her position among Ronan's girls. Stupid thing is she fought me mostly, but I didn't actually care. I didn't want to be bottom."

"No? Wasn't there some privilege, so to speak, in being bottom?"

She shrugged. "Supposedly, and I guess I saw some benefits, if you can call richer guys a privilege. I just wanted out."

"And you are now."

"Yeah, but Ronan's hunting me. I may be out, but can I ever actually be free?"

"We will get him and lock him up, where he can't hurt you ever again."

She leaned her head on his shoulder. He tightened his arm around her. She trusted Gio would do everything to protect her, but at the same moment, she wasn't sure it could ever be enough to keep from Ronan's sneaky tentacles. He was ruthless, and his moral compass only directed him to what was best for him. He'd already proved he'd kill anyone who got in his way or didn't do what he said.

Morgan traced an imaginary line on his knee. "Maybe Celeste was right."

"About what?"

"Being selfish. If I hadn't wanted out so bad and gotten myself involved with talking to you guys, Ezra and Celeste would still be alive."

"But Natalie might not be. And what about Marissa? Anna? Sydney and Lexi? They're all free because of you. We heard from Sydney the other day; she found out she's having a baby boy. Helping those girls at the risk of your own life was anything but selfish."

She pulled up her legs onto the bed and curled in tighter to Gio. "Don't let go."

"I wouldn't dream of it."

The tears she'd been convinced were all poured out showed up and, once again, soaked Gio's shirt.

Gio rubbed his neck. After an hour of sitting at the dining room table Sunday afternoon, they were still struggling to come up with a plan to keep Morgan safe while at the courthouse. "This shouldn't be so difficult. Have you guys never protected a witness before?"

Morgan came up behind him, handed him a cold can of soda, and settled her hands on his shoulders.

He squeezed her fingers in thanks, then opened the can. How'd she known this was exactly what he wanted?

Liam, obviously growing more exasperated by the moment, huffed. "Yes, we have. But the most secure area of the courthouse, where we normally bring witnesses in, is under construction. That leaves us with very few options."

Morgan's thumbs worked their way through Gio's tense muscles. He couldn't help but relax a bit. It wasn't Liam's or Tiffany's fault this was tricky.

Morgan said, "I really don't think he'll try anything that brazen. He doesn't have a rifle that I know of, so the sniper idea isn't an issue. Plus, everything is personal with him. Want me to speculate why he shoots the knee first?"

No one said a word.

"He likes to watch people suffer, especially if they've wronged him in any way. Trust me, I know." Her grip grew tighter on his shoulders. "He wants to look his victim in the eye and tell them exactly what he thinks of them. He's not going to try and shoot me in a crowd. It's not his style. He'll separate me from you all. That's what he'll do. And he'll either shoot me in a quiet place or take me to some hidden location, where he can get as much money as possible by selling me before he puts a bullet in my chest. He won't do it in public."

Gio shifted slightly so he could turn and look up at her. He took one of her hands in his. "We aren't going to let that happen."

"I know. But y'all don't understand. No amount of planning and brute force is going to protect me. His game always starts with the psychological, and how do you even safeguard against that?"

"Stay with me. Talk to me about everything. I can't even fathom how he could get to you psychologically at this point."

She nodded.

Liam said, "Based on what Morgan said, we need to worry less about entrances and exits, and focus on keeping Morgan close and inaccessible. We need formation and contingency plans. If-this-then-that scenarios."

Gio led Morgan aside. He leaned close to her ear. "You don't have to be a part of this. You can go read if you'd like."

"I know, but it is about me. I kind of like being part of it. I do know how Ronan thinks, after all."

"Sure. How about we grab you a chair then?"

"I could share one with you." The teasing glint in her eye made him want to whisk her into another room and kiss her tender lips.

"No."

She giggled.

They went back to the table. Gio tapped on Dylan's shoulder and motioned for him to move over. He obliged, and Morgan took a seat next to Gio. Within an hour they had a decent plan for Tuesday. Now it was a matter of executing that plan without a single departure from it, so they could keep Morgan safe.

Afterward, Gio and Morgan wandered to the front porch.

She slipped her hand in his. "I'm still afraid he'll pull something we haven't anticipated."

"That's why we tried to anticipate every possible scenario."

"But you guys don't think like he does."

"True. And most of the time that's a good thing."

She chuckled. "Ain't that the truth."

The front door opened, and Morgan pulled away from Gio. He wanted to laugh at how one moment she didn't care about touching him in front of others and the next moment she did.

Dylan approached. "I heard from my brother. Do you remember Chad?"

Morgan shrugged. "Vaguely."

"He hasn't always represented the best clients, but he is an excellent defense attorney. He's offered to represent you."

"I have zero money. I can't afford anything more than the state-provided lawyer."

Dylan smiled. "He's going to do it pro bono."

Gio wanted to keep his mouth shut, but his filter had turned off. "Is he doing penance?"

Dylan laughed. "It's about time."

Morgan's brow furrowed.

"Let's just say the clients my brother—"

Morgan held up her hand, cutting Dylan off. "No need to explain. I really appreciate his willingness to help out. Glad he's come around."

Dylan said, "He also mentioned it was the least he could do for you after you warned us about what was happening to Anna."

Dylan left, and Gio faced Morgan. "How about we pretend for a moment none of this was going on. What would you like to do today?"

Her eyes widened as she gazed off into the distance. "I'm not sure. I really can't fathom what it's like to actually be able to do something I want to do."

"Well, it's Independence Day for you today."

With a smile and a contented sigh, she turned toward the railing, and leaned her forearms on it. "There are too many things. Let's go to the beach, to the movies, rock climbing—no, jet skiing!"

"Adventurous, huh?"

"Not really. A movie isn't too adventurous."

"Depends on the movie we see."

"I guess. Which of those would you like to do? A movie would be my first choice."

"Can I take a book to the beach?"

"Duh. But only if you promise to go snorkeling too."

"That I can do. So you really want to get away from here?" He propped himself up against the porch's post and considered her.

"Nah. I love it here. I could stay forever. Actually, Jacqui and I were talking. She suggested I make this my home too. I still have a lot to figure out about living outside the game, but maybe once I do, I can help other girls find their feet and their faith."

"I love that. I've seen the way you care for Lily and the others. You would be wonderful at helping women find their new life."

"New life. I can't believe I actually have one of those; well, will have once Ronan's locked up."

"You do."

"It's not entirely my own with two marshals grounding me to the house. But I know what you mean. I have faith that it'll all work out sooner or later."

Silence fell between them as they both simply let the warm July breeze swirl around them.

"Gio? I want to get baptized."

"That was random."

"Not really. This morning I was reading about Philip and the guy studying the scroll in Acts. He put his faith in Christ and wanted to be baptized right then and there."

Gio nodded.

"I never did get baptized when I was younger, and even if I had, I want to proclaim my new life to the world."

"That would be fantastic. Let's see what we can set up when all this is over."

"Not right now?"

"Even if there was a pastor here, the creek isn't deep enough."

"Surely it drops off into something deeper somewhere, maybe even becomes a river."

"Perhaps, although I don't think those overbearing marshals will let us."

"Fine. But one of these days."

"Absolutely."

This woman amazed him. Only a week ago she had run off on him for the third time. Her bruises from Ronan's beating were healing, and she was no longer holding her ribs if she laughed too hard or turned too far.

However, the emotional and spiritual sides—most often the hardest part—were also healing quickly. He wasn't a fool, though; this was only the tip of a monstrous, life-changing iceberg, but she was doing the work and so was God.

Chapter Thirty

MORGAN SNATCHED ANOTHER SLICE of watermelon from the counter between Liam and Dylan and went in search for Gio. He'd disappeared a while ago and hadn't reappeared. Everyone was hanging around after a good ol' fashioned Fourth of July barbeque with grilled hamburgers, potato chips, corn on the cob, and, of course, watermelon.

The sun was dipping low in the sky, and while Dylan and Liam had described all the fireworks they would set off, that was not going to happen tonight. The last thing they needed to do was alert anyone to their presence here on the mountain. The country music Jacqui had playing on the front porch, where she and Tiffany were teaching Harper to jump rope, was enough noise.

But where was Gio?

Morgan wandered out onto the porch. "Have you guys seen Gio?"

Jacqui smushed her lips together as if suppressing a laugh.

"What? Are you really surprised?"

Jacqui shook her head.

"There you are." From behind her, Gio's deep voice held a touch of laughter.

"I wasn't the one who disappeared." She put her hands on her hips.

His smile grew. "Come here." He nodded to the side.

She looked at him sideways but took a few steps closer.

"I thought you trusted me."

"I do." She stretched out the *oo* as long as possible.

Gio chuckled and held out his hand. She placed hers in his, and he tugged her inside and up the stairs. He turned into her room.

She tugged back. "What are we doing?"

"Trust me."

She once again allowed him to pull her forward and to the open window.

"Ready for some adventuring?" He made a sweeping gesture toward the window.

"You aren't afraid of heights?"

"Eh. Not my favorite, but I'll be fine. You?"

She shook her head.

He led her onto the roof. They climbed to the top, above the dormer, where Gio had laid out a couple of blankets.

"You did this for me?"

"I didn't do it for anyone else." He winked.

The slope of the roof was just gradual enough to keep them from sliding right off. "Good thing the incline isn't any sharper."

He sat. "Wouldn't have brought us up here if it was."

She settled next to him.

"Look." He pointed to the west.

The sunset lit the sky in a beautiful array of yellows, pinks, reds, and purples, the mountains taking on an amazing shade of blue. Morgan could see forever up here.

The sun sank lower and lower until it finally vanished beneath the edge of the horizon, changing the mountains from blue peaks to black shadows to nothing.

Gio chuckled.

"What?"

"As I had hoped. Look there and there."

She followed where he pointed. In the distance they could see multiple fireworks displays.

"That's probably Knoxville, and there—Gatlinburg." He named a few more cities. She scooted closer to him and once they'd figured out the best angle to see as many shows as possible, Gio wrapped his arm around her, drawing her close. Together they watched tiny bursts of fire light the sky with all the colors of the rainbow.

He leaned his head close to hers and whispered, "Happy Independence Day."

She drank in the truth of his words. After so many years of living in slavery, she was free. She would be able to sleep tonight without a man touching her, raping her, or forcing her to do whatever pleased him. *Thank You, Jesus.*

Gio leaned on the porch railing the next morning, cradling his cup of coffee. Last night on the rooftop was exactly what he had needed. It had been perfect. But during the middle of the night, he had been woken up by a terrifying dream. He couldn't remember the details; still he was left with an image of Morgan holding a gun. But she didn't know how to use it. Even though he didn't remember what happened in the dream, it wasn't good.

But he had a solution. He would teach her how to use the gun, and, hopefully, should any situation arise that required her to use a firearm, she'd be prepared.

She hadn't emerged from her bedroom yet, so he waited.

Dylan came out, mug in hand. "I thought I heard someone up."

Gio nodded a good morning but didn't move. Dylan sat on the steps.

"Have you found a good place on the property to shoot?" Gio asked.

"That's random."

"Not if you had the dream I had last night."

"Dream?" Dylan asked. "Oh, that's not good. Not if it's leading to shoot your gun."

"I need to be sure Morgan knows how to use one."

"Let me finish my coffee, and then we can hunt for a range."

Gio raised his cup in agreement.

The two friends finished their coffee in silence, then hiked into the woods after telling Jacq what they were up to. It took an hour of traipsing across ten acres before they found an area with a high backdrop a good distance from the house, yet far enough within the property not to disturb any neighbors. But it was Tennessee and gunfire out in the woods was of much less concern to folks in these parts than in any city.

When they walked into the dining room, the marshals, along with Jacq and Harper, were eating breakfast. Still no sign of Morgan. They had stayed up late on the roof, so Gio wasn't too surprised, but the urgency he felt in the dream made him impatient.

He had barely sat down and poured milk on his cereal when delicate hands ran across his shoulders. He caught her fingers and brought them to his lips. "Morning, sleepyhead."

Morgan giggled. She reached down and snagged a marshmallow from his bowl. "Healthy choice, I see."

"Every once in a great while, everyone should be allowed a bowl of Marshmallow Matey's."

Morgan put a hand on her hip. "I thought that was Harper's cereal?"

Dylan stopped with the spoon halfway to his mouth. "She likes to share with me and Gio."

Morgan laughed. "Can I have some too, Harper?"

With a mouth full of cereal and milk, Harper nodded. Gio poured the cereal for Morgan when she came back to the table with a bowl. They all enjoyed their sugary breakfast, but everyone else was done before Morgan. Soon the two of them were the only ones left at the table.

Gio twirled his spoon around his empty bowl. "I have a plan for our morning. I hope you're up for it."

She looked at him out of the corner of her eye. "Tell me more."

"Have you ever shot a gun?"

Her spoon clanged in her bowl.

His throat tightened. What if she was against the idea of learning?

"Not that I remember."

"I would like to teach you how to handle one and practice some, so you feel comfortable with it—should the need ever present itself."

With eyebrows drawn together, Morgan slowly nodded.

Twenty minutes later they were out at the spot Gio and Dylan had found with a bag full of empty cans and bottles to shoot at.

A stump served as a table. He set his range bag down and unholstered his Glock and set it beside the bag.

They set up the targets along the top of a fallen tree.

Morgan's normal chipper self was MIA. She wasn't teasing him or joking around. No flirting either. He appreciated that she understood the gravity of the situation, but he missed the goofy side of her. And he was afraid he'd scared her off with the idea of shooting practice.

Before proceeding with the lesson, he took her hands and cautiously drew her to himself. She came to him readily, dispelling his fear.

"Are you scared?" he asked.

"I don't know. You'd think I'd been around enough of those"—she eyed his Glock—"in my life. But most of the time they've been waggled in my face or someone else's with a threat behind it."

"Whose hands it's in matters most. In the right hands, it can be a powerful tool for protection. But we have to know how to handle it properly, so we aren't a danger to ourselves or those we're trying to protect."

She nodded and placed her hands on his chest. A slight smile curled one side of her mouth up. "I trust you. And if it came down to it, I'd like to be able to protect you. Even if the chances are so much greater you'll be the one protecting me, as always."

He moved his hands to her hips. "Then let's do this." He leaned forward and touched his forehead to hers. The desire to kiss her came on fast and strong. But now wasn't the time. He kissed her forehead and turned away as quickly as he could.

She giggled; apparently, she hadn't missed it. "Later."

He closed his eyes. *You have no idea.*

Dropping the desire like a flaming potato, he redirected their focus. "Before you even pick up a firearm, there are four rules you *must* follow."

"Teach me." She came up beside him.

He half expected her to grab his arm, but her serious mode was back on, thus flirty Morgan was not present.

"First rule: Always treat every gun as if it's loaded."

"That's a lot of superlatives." Her snark hadn't gone anywhere, though.

"But it gets the point across, does it not?"

She chuckled. "Always loaded. Got it. Rule two?"

"Keep your finger off the trigger until you're ready to fire."

"Is that the one that drives you most crazy when watching movies?"

"You better believe it." He held up three fingers. "Rule three is to always be sure of your target *and* what's behind what you're shooting at."

She nodded.

"That's why Dylan and I found this spot where the hill goes up behind where we're shooting. Bullets don't automatically stop when they hit their target. They are moving at high velocities and keep on going."

"Be certain of your intended target along with what's beyond it."

"Rule four is the most important one. Always point the muzzle in a safe direction. Be sure you're willing to destroy anything you point the firearm at."

"So don't point it at you, ever."

"Exactly." He picked up his Glock, dropped the magazine, and cleared the chamber. He showed her how to check the gun was clear. "Even if you see someone clear a weapon, check it yourself."

"Rule one."

He nodded and handed her the Glock. She checked it. He showed her how to hold the firearm and how to aim. They tried a few dry-fire exercises.

"Time for the real thing." Gio handed her a pair of earmuffs and safety glasses. With eye and ear protection on, Gio instructed her on how to load the weapon.

"Start at the left and shoot at each can until you hit it."

She lifted the gun and aimed. The first can took three shots, then she took a little breather before aiming at the second.

Before she shot the second, he tapped her shoulder. "When you need to rest, rather than dropping your aim, practice bringing the gun close to your chest like this." He showed her. "Then you can press it out and get back on target more quickly."

She nodded and copied his action. She shot the second can, then the third, and the fourth, each with only one bullet.

"You sure you haven't done this before?"

"Yes. Is it bad that I'm imagining Ronan is each can I shoot?"

"I plead the fifth."

Her head dropped back as she laughed. But there was a hint of something else in her laughter. He took the gun from her hands and set it on the stump before drawing her to his chest.

She laid her head against him for a moment, then looked up into his eyes. "I know we're just joking about it, but what if I really had to shoot him? I'm so conflicted. I'd hate to kill someone, I really would, but at the same time, part of me feels he deserves it for all he's done to me."

"That's the hard part. Vengeance belongs to God, not us. We can't act on our own accord. Deadly force should only be used when there is no other option. If your life or the life of someone else is in jeopardy, pull the trigger without hesitation. Otherwise, it's murder."

She nodded and hugged him tight. "Thank you for teaching me, but I really hope I never have to use it."

He stroked her back and held her close. "Me too."

Morgan held Gio's hand as they strolled back to the house. Despite how somber she was feeling, she appreciated Gio taking the time to teach her how to use a firearm. It was equal parts thrilling and terrifying.

They walked into the clearing by the house and spotted Liam sitting on the steps. He jumped up when he saw them. "How'd it go?"

"Ronan won't stand a chance if he turns into an aluminum can," she said.

The guys laughed.

Liam stuffed his thumbs in his pockets. "I found you a spot."

"Really? Here on the property?" she asked.

"Honestly, it may not actually be on Jacq's land, but close enough. As long as we don't linger, I think it will be fine."

Joy bubbled inside of her.

"Someone want to clue me in?" Gio tugged on her hand.

"Not yet." She snickered at the suspicion in his eyes. Oh, how she loved the way he looked at her sideways. "It's your turn to trust me."

"I can do that."

"Then put some running shorts on; we're going for a hike." She asked Liam, "Is it far?"

"Nope. But it's down a ways. Hiking back up will be the biggest challenge."

An hour later, and after they had lunch, they set off through the woods following Liam. Gio was the only one who didn't know what was going on, but he was being a good sport, not asking too many questions.

At an especially steep part of the hike, Gio went down first and turned to Morgan, holding out his hands to her. She put hers on his shoulders, and he took her hips. She loved his touch, so tender and respectful.

He set her on the ground but didn't let go. He had that look in his eyes again, the look of wanting to kiss her. But he wouldn't with everyone else around.

They continued on hand-in-hand, and, five minutes later, came upon the stream that flowed down from near Jacq's house, but it was more than a stream here. It was easily five feet across and probably three to four feet deep in places.

Morgan tugged on Gio's hand. "Suppose we can call it a river now?"

He wabbled his head.

Jacq came up beside them. "If by river you mean like the Tennessee, no, but cute attempt."

Gio said, "Hard to still call it a creek though."

They followed the river past a waterfall and ended up beside a lovely pool. The water was a beautiful blue and barely murky at all.

Liam swept his arm toward the pool. "As you requested. Thanks to a few beavers, you have a nice little pond, or swimming hole, if you'd like. I tested it out too. The bottom is smooth rock, not gross at all. And thanks to the waterfall, no unwelcome guests should be around."

She turned to Gio and leaned close. "Gio, baptize me."

"Me? I'm no pastor."

"Who said a pastor was needed? Didn't Jesus tell the disciples to go and baptize? He didn't ordain them first."

He chuckled. "I'd be honored. I'm not sure exactly how my church—"

"I mean right now. Right here in the middle of some random wannabe river in Tennessee."

"Right now?" His gaze drifted to the people gathered around them.

"Yes, right now." She touched the side of his face, bringing his focus back to her. "Jesus is Lord of my life, and I want to live for Him. I want to declare that to the world, even if that's only you. Oh, and them too."

His face lit up, the worries of Ronan and the case fled from his countenance. "Then I don't even have to ask you the customary questions since you just answered them."

They took off their shoes and waded into the pool.

When the water was past her knees, her foot slipped. As the water splashed around her, her lungs closed up, and she squeezed Gio's arm with a vise grip.

Gio pulled her to her feet. "Are you all right?" His eyebrows were tightly knit.

"Yeah. Water freaks me out some because I can't really swim." She turned to the others. "I'm fine."

They continued into the pool until it was to their waists.

He moved her into position, placing one hand on her back and the other on the hand she used to pinch her nose shut. "I baptize you in the name of the Father, Son, and Holy Spirit." He dunked her.

The water covered her face. Death to her old life. Buried, drowned beneath the flowing river. Washed away, no longer a part of her.

Gio raised her up again.

Risen with Christ. The old was gone, and new life was hers in Christ. She was a new creation.

Gio beamed at her, and everyone clapped. She threw her arms around his neck. And wet as she was, he embraced her.

Close to his ear, she whispered, "Thank you."

"You are welcome." He held her.

Clean. New. Alive. Restored to right relationship with Christ.

Thank You, Jesus. Help me to live for You all the days of my life. We can face whatever is coming because I know You're with me.

Regardless of what the judge said tomorrow morning, her past had been washed away in God's eyes.

Chapter Thirty-One

GIO SAT IN THE backseat of the marshals' SUV with a quiet Morgan. She was dressed in one of Jacq's sharpest pantsuits, the sides of her curly hair pinned back and flowing down her back. She was the picture of sophistication, but he could see past the exterior. He'd caught the look in her eyes when she'd come down the stairs this morning. They both felt it. Something was off.

As they entered Knoxville, Morgan reached for his hand. He took it and laced his fingers with hers. So much tension was held within their hands.

He couldn't stop praying. Not only was this a vulnerable position to put her in physically, but it was also vulnerable in every other way. While guilt or innocence for her prostitution would not be determined today, it was the next step in the process. Chad's plan was to get the charges dismissed, expunged even, but there was no guarantee. She could be looking at up to six months in jail.

Where was the justice in punishing women who were truly victims of trafficking? The guys buying sex should be strung up. Let alone the men holding these women captive and throwing them at the highest bidder.

He leaned closer to Morgan. The sides of their heads touched. With a voice barely loud enough for her to hear, he prayed. "Dear Heavenly Father, we know You hold us in Your hands. Be with Morgan today. Calm her nerves as she stands before the judge. Give her favor in the eyes of the court. And above all, keep her safe. Help us both to not fear but trust You above all."

"And peace too, Lord. We need peace." Morgan's voice was soft yet tight. "Amen."

Liam pulled the SUV up to the curb outside the courthouse, where Matt and Aliza waited. Liam got out, and Matt took his place. He came around and, once Tiffany was out, opened Morgan's door. She slid out with Gio right behind her.

He offered her his arm, and she wrapped her hand snuggly around his elbow. He still had plenty of access to his firearm. Aliza took up rank on Morgan's other side, while Liam led and Tiffany took Morgan's six. As soon as they moved toward the building, Matt drove away to park the SUV. Dylan and Jacq, who had taken Harper to Dylan's mom, joined them before they even entered the building.

Once inside, they met Chad in an attorney-client conference room. Gio relaxed a bit in the small room, and Morgan let him go. Chad stepped forward and extended his hand. "Morgan, I'm so grateful to be able to finally thank you in person for saving Anna."

"I'm glad I could make a difference."

"And today, we're going to make a difference for you."

Chad, Morgan, Dylan, and Jacq all sat. Gio stayed on his feet and stood behind Morgan.

She and Chad discussed her case, how the preliminary hearing should go, and all the possible outcomes for today.

Gio was hopeful about the hearing, but something was nagging him, though he didn't know what.

Morgan stood beside Chad as the judge entered the courtroom. Gio and the others were all directly behind them in the sitting area.

The hearing began, and the judge confirmed everyone's identities, including Morgan.

She responded, "Yes, your honor, I have been known as Daisy Smith, but my legal name is Morgan Zalman."

The judge made a note and the hearing continued. The prosecution explained the joint task force sting operation that had resulted in Morgan's arrest.

When given the opportunity, Chad stood with Morgan. "Your honor, we are requesting that this case against Miss Zalman be dismissed."

"On what grounds?"

"Miss Zalman was soliciting out of compulsion as she was being trafficked by a man known as Ronan, who the FBI suspects in multiple homicides."

"This Ronan isn't on trial today, Mr. Harris. Keep to Miss Zalman's case, please."

"Yes, your honor. Miss Zalman is also currently under Federal Witness Protection and has been a vital asset as an informant in rescuing multiple girls, including my eleven-year-old daughter and Marrissa Highwater, from sex-trafficking situations."

The judge addressed the prosecution. "What do the people say in response?"

The lawyer leaned toward his colleague and spoke in hushed tones. After only a brief moment, he turned to the judge. "We are willing to drop all charges."

Morgan's heart launched from the courtroom floor. This was the best possible outcome they had discussed.

The judge looked her in the eye. "Then I see no reason to continue. Thank you for your assistance to the FBI. You are free to go. All charges against Morgan Zalman, also known as Daisy Smith, are dismissed." The judge rapped the gavel on the desk.

Morgan gave Chad a big hug, then met Gio's eyes. His smile matched how she felt. Too bad he was too far away to hug.

A piercing alarm shattered the celebration.

Morgan jumped. It took her brain a moment to recognize the sound as a fire alarm.

Everyone in the courtroom rushed out, shouting at one another.

Immediately, Gio vaulted the divider and was beside her, wrapping his arm around her. The team of protectors ushered her to the doorway at the front of the courtroom, where the judge had disappeared.

Tiffany went through the door. Gio took Morgan's hand, and she followed him.

A woman, rushing down the hallway, slammed into Morgan and Gio, breaking their hands apart.

She stuffed something in Morgan's jacket pocket and grabbed her hand. "I'm so sorry. There's a real fire, and it's spreading fast. Run!"

The woman continued her sprint down the hallway.

Gio faced Morgan. "Are you all right?"

"Totally. Let's get out of here." What had that woman put in her pocket?

Gio did not retake her hand, giving her the opportunity to at least slip her hand in the pocket. It felt like a folded photograph. What on earth?

She pulled it out but couldn't look at it yet, so she put it back. They kept moving forward, and she stayed as close to Gio as she could without tripping him up. As they turned into a crowded hallway, the team formed a tight wall around her, and they all scanned the crowd. She retrieved the photograph, finally able to take a glance at it.

Gio.

With a giant red X across his face.

She stuffed it back in her pocket, heart pounding with the same intensity as the alarm blaring in her ears.

Chapter Thirty-Two

GIO DIDN'T LIKE THIS stupid fire. The timing was suspicious at best, but he was certain this was Ronan's doing somehow. And they had a plan. Since there was no choice but to exit the building, they would keep her close and leave the area as fast as possible. He stole a glance at Morgan over his shoulder. She was looking at her hands. The adrenaline pumping through his veins amped up out concern.

"What's wrong?"

She jerked her head up at him. "The noise is getting to me." She rubbed her ears.

"We're almost to the door."

He and Tiffany led the way out of the building and into the crowd filling the sidewalk. There were too many people.

He surveyed the area, noting every single face. One caught his attention, but he'd moved his eyes too fast. By the time he swung his gaze back, the face he'd recognized was gone. "Careful everyone, I may have just seen Ronan."

Everyone scanned the crowd.

Liam said, "We need to get her out of here."

Dylan nodded. "Matt ran for the SUV."

Gio turned to tuck Morgan under his arm. She wasn't there.

He whipped around. "Morgan!"

The team, who'd had her surrounded—though half of them with their backs to her—all spun, searched, and yelled.

His heart hit the concrete. Where did she go? How'd Ronan get her?

Tiffany took charge and directed them to head in different directions.

Gio searched frantically. Where did she go?

Every woman in a dark suit had to be considered. Every woman with long, dark hair.

"Morgan!"

He couldn't find her. He couldn't breathe. He couldn't process what to do next.

Weaving between people, he grabbed the arms of women who looked similar. Yet time and time again it wasn't Morgan. She was gone.

He pulled up a selfie he'd taken with her yesterday afternoon and started asking people if they'd seen her.

"Nope."

"No, sir."

"Nah, sorry, man."

An older woman said, "I believe I saw her running that way."

"Thank you so much." Gio ran.

The crowd thinned as he made his way to the corner.

A black cloth object caught his attention. He picked it up. Jacq's jacket—the one Morgan had been wearing. Why did she take it off?

He held it close. It smelled like her hair.

Something was in one of the pockets and gave resistance where the jacket was folded over his arm. He reached in the pocket. A photograph. Of him. A red X covered his face.

His mouth went dry.

A threat to his life. Is that why she ran? Why didn't she say something?

He turned the photograph over.

Get away from the feds or he dies.

Tell them anything and he dies.

Meet me at the north side of the building or he dies.

Now it made sense. But where did this come from?

Morgan's hand shook as she strutted with fake confidence down the center of the sidewalk along the north side of the building. A white SUV drove up beside the curb; the window slowly lowered.

With a baseball cap pulled low over his eyes and a beard, Ronan looked like a different person. "Get in, Daisy."

She froze. She didn't want to be a slave to this man again.

"Get in or lover-boy dies. It's that simple. I've got a guy who will do the job for me in a matter of minutes. Should I call him?"

Ronan could be bluffing, but she doubted it.

She obeyed.

"Good job, Daisy. Where's the picture?"

"I threw it in a garbage can first chance I got." *God, forgive me for lying.* Somehow she was certain God would be okay with that one.

"Good."

"Now what?" She buckled her seatbelt.

"Nope." He reached over and unbuckled the belt. "In the backseat."

She climbed over the console and into the back.

"Put these on." He held out a pair of zip-cuffs.

She did as she was told, and Ronan reached back and pulled them tight. He then drove away from the curb.

Looking out the window, she spotted Gio, her jacket in his hands. *I'm sorry, Gio. I love you.* If only he could hear her. But maybe if he found the photo, he'd understand why she had to leave. His life was worth more than hers. He'd get over her and find a nice girl to marry. That's what he deserved anyway.

She'd get what was coming to her. Penance would have to be paid. She just hoped Ronan would end it quickly and not drag it out with hundreds of men first.

Chapter Thirty-Three

Gio stared at the note. He'd need to wrestle with where it came from later. He looked around to gain his bearings and took off running toward the north side of the building.

He skidded around the corner and continued to run, scanning everything. She had to be here somewhere.

Several cars drove down the street. The crowds were dispersing. Firefighters worked on the west side of the building.

But Morgan was nowhere to be seen. She was already gone.

The weight was too much. He dropped to his knees, and the concrete stung through his dress pants. He'd failed to keep her safe. How was that future picture possible without her?

God, what just happened? Please, protect her! Help me find her!

A black SUV pulled up to the curb in front of him. "Gio, let's go." Matt held the door open for him.

He joined Matt, Liam, and Tiffany in the marshal's SUV. He handed Matt the picture from the jacket. Once he was inside, Liam drove away.

"Ah, man. She legit gave us the slip for you."

Gio nodded. "Let's head back to the field office and figure out where he's going to take her."

"You should see this." Matt handed him an evidence bag with a single daisy inside.

"Where was this?"

"On this SUV in the parking garage."

"I want confirmation that fire was intentionally set."

Matt nodded. "I'll contact the fire chief."

Gio handed the evidence bag back to Matt and dropped his head into his hands. She was gone. Why hadn't he pressed her back in the building to tell him why she looked upset? "That woman who ran into us in the hallway. I bet she's the one who gave Morgan the picture."

Liam hit the steering wheel. "I should have caught that."

Tiffany huffed. "We all should have, but what I don't understand is why she ran off."

Matt had slipped the photograph into an evidence bag, which he handed to Tiffany. "In addition to this, it's what she does, what she knows. She was just learning to trust us all. She also knows Ronan better than any of us, and knows he's capable of following through with his threat."

"But we can protect Gio too. It's our job. We've never had anyone killed under our watch."

Gio shook his head. "That may be true, but her fear overrode the truth."

His heart pounded in his chest. He was barely holding himself together. He couldn't think like an agent right now. All he wanted to do was face off with Ronan and beat the man until—

Gio stopped himself. *God, forgive my wandering mind. Vengeance is Yours, but please, please protect Morgan and direct me to her.*

They arrived at the FBI field office ten minutes later. Gio grabbed his and Morgan's go bags, which they had packed yesterday, and threw them in the back of his SUV. He hoped he'd be able to find her and run, while others dealt with Ronan. Because if he was the one to face off with Ronan ...

Once inside the building, they strode to the elevator. Waiting for it to go up the three stories was agony. He needed his computer, not that he knew what to look for.

Direction? Help? We need it, God!

When they exited the elevator, Jacq and Dylan stood in the hall talking to their former teammate Sabrina.

Gio and Jacq made eye contact. She ran to him, and he wrapped her in a big hug. The tears he hadn't even realized were brimming in his eyes spilled out. This sister of his was in as much anguish as he was.

He hoped Dylan didn't mind him holding Jacq.

Another set of arms surrounded them. Dylan.

After a moment, he stepped back and took both Jacq and Gio by the shoulders. "I promise the two of you, I will do everything in my power to bring her back safely. Let's go see what we can put together."

They all went to the office and crowded into the bullpen. Dylan took charge and assigned tasks.

When he went to give Jacq an assignment, she said, "Yesterday, Morgan and I went through all the different names of Ronan's associates, along with girl's names she knew, including all the aliases she was familiar with. It's not a lot, but I'd like to run those."

Dylan agreed.

Gio was the only one he hadn't given a task. "Boss?"

"Pray. And listen to everyone. Take it in and find the connections."

His best friend knew him well. There was no way he could focus on a single task.

Morgan slid across the backseat and slammed into the car door. Ronan had turned off the interstate and was speeding down a rough, back road. She managed to brace herself before he hit another gigantic bump. Where was he taking her? This seemed to be out in the middle of nowhere. No one would ever find her.

At least if Gio couldn't find her, he wouldn't get hurt. But oh, how she wished he could rescue her again. She longed to be in his arms. Hope had grown in her heart—hope that they could have a future, hope that she could have a life.

Had she done the right thing, running off at the threat? What else could she have done? She couldn't let Gio die because of her.

The road took them farther up a mountain until it finally leveled off slightly.

Ronan stopped the vehicle at the base of an overgrown stone staircase in the side of the hill, leading up to a small, dilapidated cabin with wood panel sides. It looked like the wood at the base was rotting.

Ronan opened the door. "Get out."

Her insides shook, but she fought to keep it from showing as she scooted across the seat and slid to the ground, her heels sinking into the soft dirt. At least she wasn't wearing stilettos.

He grabbed her by the zip-cuffs and yanked her up the stairs, which were slick from the intense humidity hanging in the air. Trees towered above, shielding them from the life-giving sunshine, casting shadows between the brilliant beams of midday.

With Gio it would be a beautiful place, but not with Ronan. A heaviness settled over her, and it wasn't the humidity or the shadows. This was something entirely more sinister. Evil even.

God, I need Your deliverance. I see no way out of this without a miracle from You. Please help.

At the top, Ronan shoved her forward.

She stumbled and fell headlong onto the damp, wooden steps leading up to the cabin's little porch.

Morgan listened. Nothing. No one was anywhere nearby.

"You're such a klutz. Would you get up?"

She scrambled to her feet, grateful to get upright before Ronan could yank her hair or something.

He unlocked the front door and thrust her inside. The smell of rotten wood, mildew, and something metallic—was that blood?

Ronan flicked a switch, and a small amount of light filled the room. Definitely blood. Large dark circles stained the floor. Was this where he'd killed Celeste? Rose?

A lone bed sat in the back right corner of a room no more than ten feet square. In the opposite corner was a cabinet and a small sink, and there was a bucket under the bed. That was it. How long had Rose lived in this place?

Ronan grasped Morgan's arm and tossed her to the bed. He reached beneath it and pulled out a chain with a giant clamp and a lock at the end. He snatched her leg and attached the chain to her ankle. She would not be running away.

He had been quiet, so quiet—an unusual state for Ronan to be in this long. It was unnerving.

"What are you going to do to me?" she asked.

He chuckled. "Not what I want to do. But you will be useful for me one last time." He took her hands and cut the zip-cuffs off her wrists.

She didn't want to know what he wanted to do or how she'd be of use, but she couldn't resist asking. "How's that?"

"You'll have to wait and find out."

The crazy in his eyes sparked a shudder that ran its course through her body. *Oh God, please hear my cry!*

Chapter Thirty-Four

Gio paced back and forth through the bullpen, listening to snippets of conversation as the team researched, letting his mind turn it all over. Morgan had not known of any other places Ronan had, but there had to be somewhere he was hiding out.

They knew he'd murdered two women for sure, but they hadn't found a crime scene.

He stopped midstride. Maybe that was the key. Where had he killed Celeste? Where had he killed Jamie?

They knew where Jamie's body had turned up. That would narrow the search field. Hadn't a team been working on figuring out where she could have come from? Morgan had to be there.

Gio grabbed his keys and backpack and darted out the door.

He was in his car, driving through the FBI gates, when his cellphone rang.

He answered it.

"Where did you go?" Dylan's voice was sharp.

"I was going to call you in a minute. We know where Jamie's body was found. There must be a place up there in the mountains where he kept her. Morgan said she'd been gone for months before she would have been killed."

"Sure, but that doesn't answer where you are."

"I'm driving up there."

"What on earth, man? You can't go up there by yourself."

"I have to. I can't sit still and wait for us to find the link. You guys find it, and I'll be there ready to find *her*."

"You need backup. Didn't what happened to Jacq prove that to you?"

"I will have backup. You find the address, and I'll go scope it out and get eyes on the situation. Then you all will show up along with local LEOs. You aren't going to change my mind, Dylan, and you know it. What would you do if it was Jacq?"

Dylan growled. "Point taken. But be careful. We'll redirect our focus on finding a possible spot."

"Please. Figure out where Jamie's body would have flowed from. Cross reference names of property owners in that area with the girl's names and family names that connect to Ronan's legal identity."

"We know what to do."

"I know, but—"

"I get it. Just be careful, and don't do anything stupid."

Gio didn't respond to that. He was not in a state to promise anything other than that he would find Morgan.

Morgan tried to adjust the chain on her leg. It had only been twenty minutes or so, but it hurt like mad the way it rubbed against her skin. She attempted to pull her pant leg through it, but the cloth came out if she moved at all.

Ronan had disappeared out the door about five minutes ago, giving her an opportunity to inspect her surroundings better. The place was disgusting. Between the mustiness and the body odor coming from the bed she sat on, she thought she'd hurl.

She stood and walked across to the little cabinet. The chain barely reached that far. Anything might work as a weapon right now. Fighting back was her only chance. Packages of dried cereal and crackers. No forks, no knives, just one plastic spoon. What was she going to do with that? Scoop out his eyeballs? Probably not.

She picked the spoon up and considered it. It was a sturdy plastic spoon, not one of those cheap flimsy ones. Why was this stupid little spoon all that was available to her? She gripped it between her hands. All the frustration of having to walk away from Gio flowed down her arms. She snapped the spoon in half.

Great, now she didn't even have a spoon to eat cereal with. But wait ... she tossed the spoon part back in the cabinet and held up the handle. It was quite jagged where it had broken. She touched it. And sharp too. Maybe it would do in a pinch.

Footsteps fell on the wood steps of the cabin. Morgan darted back to the bed and hid the end of the spoon between the mattress and the springs.

Ronan turned the key and entered the little room without locking the door again.

Morgan noticed the lock. It needed a key for both sides, so even if she didn't have a chain around her ankle, she wouldn't be able to get out the door next time he left.

Ronan towered over her and glared.

Fear choked out her ability to breathe. She did not want to endure the "lesson" he'd taught her a little over a week ago. Not again. Her body couldn't; there was no way. She would shut down, and she wasn't sure she could ever come back from a total shutdown. But Gio.

She needed to survive, to get back to Gio. For the first time in her life she had a reason to fight for her life.

"How do you have so much grit left in you? Have I not beat it out of you yet?"

She resisted the urge to spit in his face.

He slapped her. "Unfortunately, I can't"—he ran his hand into her hair and gripped her scalp—"do what I'd like to you." He moved closer and snarled like a rabid dog. "But you're my ticket out of here."

He let go of her head with a jerk.

Her scalp stung.

Ronan dialed his phone and leaned back against the door. "I've got her. And she's all yours if—"

The person on the other end must have interrupted him.

"If she's worth as much to you as you've indicated, I think you'd want her to be yours and not just a weekly fling. Do whatever you want with her, but she's not going to come cheap for you to have her for good."

Ronan paused.

Who on earth was he talking to? Weekly fling? It couldn't be.

"You're an idiot." He removed the phone from his ear and poked it. "There. You're on speaker."

"Angel?"

It was him. "Duke."

"Do you want to come live with me?"

What was she supposed to say to that? It was, in fact, the second to last thing she wanted. Death sounded like the better option.

"Angel?" Duke's voice was firm and steady.

"He's going to kill me if you don't take me."

Ronan nodded.

Duke said, "But I need to know you're choosing me."

Maybe she could get away from Duke. Should she lie? Maybe going with him was better than death if there was a chance she could get back to Gio. "Sure. Beats being with Ronan."

Ronan's lips tightened, and he pointed at her. "Watch yourself." His voice was barely audible.

"All right, then. What's your price, Ronan?"

Morgan felt like puking. Duke wanted to buy her, but only if she was willing to *choose* him? He was more psychotic than she had realized.

Ronan listed his desires. "I want a one-way plane ticket to a nonextradition country, fifty-thousand dollars, and a new ID. Think you can get those things?"

"Not before tomorrow. The ID will take a bit of time."

"Then Daisy gets to work for me for one more night."

"If she's hurt, you're dead."

"We'll keep it easy." Ronan rolled his eyes.

He clearly hadn't seen Duke's expression when he looked at Morgan. She had no doubt he would kill Ronan.

Ronan hung up and stepped toward her. He took her jaw in his hand. "You're welcome. I didn't tell him anything about your stupid FBI boyfriend, but you cross me, and I will."

She clamped her lips shut.

He let go of her. "It's time to get you posted. Well, not you in particular. Wouldn't want your FBI friends to find you. Not making that mistake again. All I need to do is let a few certain circles know the cabin is up and running. Celeste was such a quick run last week. Although Rose was great for such a long period."

"I thought you said Rose moved up in the game, not down."

"Up might have been an option for her if she hadn't started keeping money from me. She could have kept working up here, but she tried to escape."

"Aster?"

"Oh, Aster, well, that was good for a long time after the whole baby nonsense. Too bad I haven't been able to keep this cabin going more over the years, but you"—he ran his hand down her face and neck—"you were much more lucrative in town than up here. And too pretty for the guys that like to come in here. This is a special clientele. But you'll find that out soon enough."

He went on his phone and punched at the screen with his thumbs. "Although I will have to keep you in halfway decent shape for Duke, so there are a few guys I'll have to turn away. They like things a little ... let's just say a little rough." Ronan laughed.

It chilled her insides, despite the suffocating humidity filling the cabin. *God, help. Don't let any more men use me for their own sick pleasure. Please, help.*

Gio had been driving for about an hour and was getting close to the place where Jamie's body had been found. But he hadn't heard from the team. Where had she been buried? Had she been killed in the same place or, at least, near it? Was there a place Ronan could be staying?

I-40 gained altitude, but it felt like his heart sank lower and lower. He'd spent most of the drive pleading with God to protect Morgan. But he was out of words and tears.

He drove on in silence. He couldn't even bring himself to listen to music, the thing that sustained his sanity most of the time. But he couldn't.

His phone rang. Dylan. Gio clicked the answer button.

"Tell me you have something."

"I have something—after talking to the techs who were working the water flow and the soil samples."

"And?"

"I bet you still have ten miles to go, unless you've been driving way too fast, so you can listen to my explanation since you weren't here helping."

Gio grunted.

"As I was saying, given those two pieces of information we were able to narrow down our property search. Lots of campgrounds and recreational, touristy places. But among all that we found a few plots of private property. One went really far back—it hadn't changed possession in about fifty years. It's like the property was completely forgotten about. But in researching the owner we found it connected, however distantly, to Keenan Robins."

"No way."

"The police from his hometown had never looked into it as a hideout. They couldn't find it because it was so obscurely connected."

"But that has to be it. Any more information? What's on the land?"

"It's next to impossible to tell. From satellite photos, it just looks like trees on top of a mountain, but there might be a small structure like a shed. It's not very big, that's for sure."

"It wouldn't take much."

"I'm sending the GPS coordinates. Scope it out and fall back, even if she's there."

"What was that? You're breaking up."

"You can hear me perfectly fine. Be careful."

"Yes, mom." Gio could almost hear Dylan shaking his head.

Gio's phone dinged a text from Dylan. "Got them. I'll be in touch."

"We're getting ready to roll."

They hung up, and Gio pulled off the side of the highway and plugged the coordinates into his GPS.

He was only fifteen minutes away. He whipped back into traffic and pushed the limit on speeding.

Chapter Thirty-Five

GIO TURNED ONTO ANOTHER back road, this one even more *back* than the single-lane one he had just been on. At least that one had been paved. Cavernous ruts cut deep into the earth, making it difficult to traverse. He was grateful to have an SUV.

At every fork for the last few miles, he'd noticed a red rope tied around a tree or a signpost, indicating the direction he needed to go to get to the property. His gut told him that was significant, but why was lost on him. Too often his gut had been right about things, but he knew better. It wasn't simply intuition, not at all. The Spirit of God was speaking to him.

When he saw another red rope closer to the spot, he decided he should go the rest of the way on foot. If Ronan had Morgan on this ridge, Gio didn't need to alert him by driving right up there.

He got out of his SUV and went around to the back. After changing into his sneakers, he ditched his tie and button-up for a t-shirt. He replaced the laptop in his backpack for Morgan's tennis shoes and clothes, since he didn't know what state he would find her in. It had only been a little over two hours, and if they'd driven straight here, she'd have been at this location for an hour already.

Ronan might have taken her clothes ... and worse. Of course that was assuming she was not being driven across the country.

God, You led me here, right? Show me what to do.

Gio checked his magazine and confirmed a round was chambered in his Glock. He made sure he still had a third and fourth loaded magazine in his backpack. He was ready.

Trekking up the mountain through the dense foliage was not Gio's idea of fun, but staying off the main drive would surely pay off.

He was able to find an area where the undergrowth wasn't quite as dense. By checking his phone he confirmed his location on the property.

A white SUV parked ahead indicated someone was here.

Staying behind the trees, Gio spotted a cabin, if he could call it that, at the very top of the ridge.

As he passed the SUV, he snapped a picture of the license plate and sent it to Dylan with the message: *There's a vehicle on the property. Approaching a small shed-like cabin to confirm occupancy.*

Taking a roundabout way through the forest, he inched toward the cabin. He needed eyes *inside*. Was Morgan there? Was Ronan? If Gio could get Morgan out while Ronan wasn't there, that might be best, but Ronan needed to be taken down too.

Gio crept up the hill, moving toward the side of the cabin, where a small window might reveal the inhabitants. He forced himself to keep his breathing steady and his steps soft and intentional. There wasn't any noise coming from the cabin, so the slightest sound could alert Ronan to his presence.

Gio reached a point where he could partially see in the window.

A body moved into view, but all he caught sight of was the side of an arm. Probably Ronan's. Short sleeves revealed defined biceps and triceps. The body turned.

Gio ducked behind a large tree. He waited for three breaths before easing around the side. The person had moved to a different spot in the cabin, so Gio continued his approach. He needed a different vantage point to see if Morgan was, in fact, there.

Step after agonizingly slow step, Gio finally reached a height on the hill where he could spot a head of dark hair. The person was sitting or somehow much lower than the arm he'd glimpsed a moment ago.

A few more steps.

The soft dirt beneath his feet slipped. He caught himself but crunched a twig. He froze for a second before hiding behind another tree. *God, help.*

He didn't hear anything—like someone coming out to check—so he glanced around the tree before moving on. Clear. When he was about fifteen feet away, the window came to eye level.

Morgan.

Despite the rest of her face being pale, her left cheek was pink, as if she'd been slapped.

Gio's insides raged. *Lord, I'm not sure I'll be able to keep myself from taking Ronan's life in my own hands. Please help me.*

Gio grabbed his phone and sent a text to Dylan. *Eyes on Morgan.*

Dylan replied: *Stay put. Calling in local backup. We are on our way. Left two minutes ago.*

He dropped his backpack to the ground. It might kill him, but Gio would stay as long as Morgan wasn't in immediate danger, but if Ronan made one wrong move, Gio wouldn't hesitate to defend her.

Morgan shifted on the bed. Ronan had been quiet for the last five minutes, focusing on his phone. She stared out the window. *God, I need to know what to do. I've never fought back much. What do I do? How do I overcome him? He's so much stronger than me.*

His keys were probably in his front right pocket; that's where he normally kept them. If she could overcome him, she'd have to get his keys and unlock her ankle, assuming that key was on the ring. Then she could take his car. But that would require more than she could manage. If she was free of the ankle chain, she'd just run, but that wasn't the case.

She sank back. It was impossible. Surviving the night might be her best bet. When Ronan passed her to Duke maybe she could find a window to run. But what if Duke didn't take her to Knoxville? If he took her to his house ... the woods were massive. Would she be able to find her way? She knew nothing about surviving in the woods.

Movement outside the window caught her eye.

"It's all set."

She darted her gaze to Ronan. But what had she seen outside? Was that a person or a bear?

Ronan slid his phone into his back pocket. "I was thinking, I've always enjoyed our intimacy, Daisy. I'd love the chance to be with you one last time." He removed his gun from its holster and hung it on a hook in the far corner to the left of the door.

She couldn't reach that corner. Before he turned, she searched the woods for the figure she had seen.

Gio! Their eyes connected for a split-second. He was here. God had answered her prayer for help. She tried desperately to keep all emotion from her face. Ronan did *not* need to know Gio was there.

"You know I'm more interesting than a bunch of stupid trees." He stepped forward, unlatched his belt, and unbuttoned his pants.

Out of the corner of her eye she saw a flash as Gio moved toward the door.

She lay down on the bed and reached around the side of the mattress.

"That's it. You know what to do. You always were one of my favorites." He climbed on top of her.

Her fingers found the spoon handle, but it was with her left hand. Could she get enough force to stab him with her non-dominant one?

He unbuttoned her pants and ran his hands along her body. As he moved down her body, he left the side of his neck exposed.

She swallowed and thrust the spoon handle at him.

It hit his skin but snapped in half.

He swore and slapped her, jerking her head to the side.

His hand went to his neck. He pulled it away. She'd definitely done damage, but not enough.

"I thought we could make love, but that's not what this is going to be now."

She screamed as loud as she could. "Gio!"

Chapter Thirty-Six

GIO FOUGHT THE URGE to run in there, guns blazing. But as soon as he heard her scream for him, he rushed up the stairs and gripped the doorknob. Yes! It was unlocked. He threw it open.

Ronan straddled Morgan. Magma filled Gio's blood vessels.

In two steps he crossed the room, seized Ronan by the shoulders, and threw him to the floor.

Ronan landed on his side. Before he could get to his feet, Gio grabbed his collar and punched the man's face with all the force his body could swing. And again.

Ronan swung his legs and knocked Gio over. He stumbled but caught himself on the bed before he hit the floor.

He connected with Morgan's terror-filled eyes momentarily before he returned his attention to Ronan. He had to take this guy down.

Ronan charged at him. The full force of his body slammed Gio into the wall, narrowly missing a small sink.

Ronan raised his fist. Gio dodged, and it went through the wall. Gio delivered three successive punches to Ronan's left side.

Ronan reached for Gio's head and put him in a hold. Gio kept punching his side, but Ronan returned the motion.

God, help me overcome him.

Using his foot, Gio shoved them both off the wall.

Ronan lost his hold. Gio shoved him backward. Slammed him into the opposite wall. The force shook the whole shed. An object fell to the floor.

Gio caught sight of it. A gun.

They both rushed for it. Gio slammed Ronan into the wall and kicked the gun backward toward Morgan.

"I got it," she said.

The guys grappled with one another. Gio needed distance, but Ronan wasn't stupid enough to give it to him.

How long could they go on before one of them finally got the upper hand? Gio wouldn't give up though. For Morgan he'd fight until he won. Letting Ronan get the high ground wasn't an option.

Ronan pinned him against the doorjamb. Gio shoved him.

Ronan hurled Gio backward and bolted.

Gio stumbled. Once he regained his footing, he pursued.

Ronan was running down the porch stairs.

Gio drew his Glock and took aim right at Ronan's back. If he pulled the trigger this could all be over.

He shouldn't.

When Ronan reached the SUV, he turned.

Gio moved to the top of the stairs, keeping Ronan in his sights. Gio's finger twitched, wanting to go to the trigger.

He couldn't.

"Do it." Ronan dared him.

He was unarmed and not a direct threat at the moment. Gio didn't want to be a monster. He wouldn't.

Ronan jumped in the vehicle and flew down the drive in reverse.

Gio kicked the dirt and swore. Why didn't he at least shoot out one of the tires?

"Gio!"

He holstered his gun, spun, and ran to Morgan.

She stood in the center of the tiny cabin. He swept her into his arms. His heart thundered as he held her tight against his chest.

"I'm so sorry." Her words were muffled against him.

He pulled back and wiped tears from her cheeks. "I know. I found the picture he sent you." He cupped the sides of her face and searched her eyes. He loved her so much. "I was terrified I had lost you."

"But here we are."

The intense urge to kiss her overwhelmed him. But this isn't what he'd envisioned. They were supposed to be at peace, not in a life-and-death, adrenaline-pumping, stress-induced, heart-pounding moment.

Her lips turned up, and she giggled.

The enticement was too much. He leaned down but her mouth captured his first. Their lips moved together, although barely, holding the intensity of the moment suspended in time. Each movement might break the intimacy between them.

Her arms slid across his back, and he entangled his fingers in her hair.

The kiss deepened with slow, intentional motions.

His phone vibrated in his pocket. He tried to ignore it, not wanting to break the spell between them.

But it was broken.

She ended the kiss and slid his phone from his pocket.

He reeled, heart pounding like a jackhammer. Despite deep breaths, he couldn't breathe.

Locking his gaze with hers, she traced his face with her fingers. Her cheeks were flushed and breathing intense too. She held up his phone. "Who so rudely interrupted us?"

Finally able to get a satisfactory amount of air in, he chuckled and took the phone.

Dylan. *Status check.*

Gio replied, letting him know he was with Morgan and Ronan had run, but left out how much his hand hurt from repeatedly punching Ronan.

Gio slid his phone into his pocket, dashed outside, grabbed his pack, then raced back into the cabin.

Morgan, arms crossed, sat on the edge of the bed. "You're doing it again."

"What?"

"Not telling me what you're thinking."

He chuckled. "You aren't alone in that problem."

"But what are we going to do with *this* problem?" She raised her right foot.

He hadn't noticed the chain before. Opening his backpack, he found his lock-picking tools. The lock on the ankle clasp was an easy pick, and within two minutes he had her free.

He pulled her clothes from the pack and stepped out of the cabin while she changed and put the tennis shoes on.

She opened the door. "Now what?"

He came back in. "My car is just down the hill. We go there and either get out of here or wait for the local LEOs. My team isn't too far away now, either." He put her dress clothes in the pack and stood, offering her his hand. She took it.

They left the little cabin and walked quietly down the drive to his car.

"Gio."

He spotted it too. His tires had been slashed. They went around the SUV. All four tires were useless. He opened the hatch. "I guess we'll have to wait."

Gio found a universal holster he kept in his car and slid Ronan's gun in it before securing it in his backpack.

He pulled his shorts out of his duffel and changed. It was entirely too warm for suit pants. Morgan sat on the end of the car eating a protein bar, a comical smirk on her face. He hadn't thought twice about changing in front of her. Heat filled his cheeks.

"Well, that escalated quickly." She winked at him.

He tossed his pants at her head.

A shotgun racked in the distance.

Gio froze. Had he really heard that?

Pkow!

Chapter Thirty-Seven

Gio dove toward Morgan and pulled her away from the window. Pellets barraged the downhill-facing side of the car.

"What was that?"

"A shotgun."

He threw his pack on. "If that's Ronan, we can't stay here."

She nodded and hopped out of the SUV. They ran up the hill.

Another shot fired. Pellets of birdshot pierced the trees around them. They dropped to the ground.

Gio drew his gun and fired in the general direction the shots were coming from. "Run!"

While they ran back toward the cabin, he pulled his phone out of his pocket. He needed backup.

The pain from punching Ronan made it difficult to hold the phone firmly. Another round of birdshot littered the woods around them. A piece of bark flew and smacked Gio's hand. He dropped his phone. It slid down the hill.

Glancing up, Gio spotted Ronan lifting the shotgun again.

"Keep moving." Abandoning his phone, they crested the hill and dropped feet first down the steep incline on the other side.

He yanked Morgan to the ground. "Stay low." Gio found Ronan in the iron sights of his Glock.

He was too far.

Ronan shot again.

Gio ducked his head close to Morgan's.

There was a pause. Must be reload time.

Gio raised his head and fired. But Ronan had gone behind the tree. Keeping his sights on where he believed Ronan was, Gio waited.

He was a decent shot, but it was far. Still, he'd trained for this.

Sirens echoed off the mountains.

Ronan shouted. "Oh good, backup's here."

"That helps me not you."

"I don't think so. Looks like I'm Gio Crespi today." Ronan held out Gio's badge from around the tree. "And thanks to the swelling in my face, I can even pull off your picture."

Gio couldn't believe it. When had he dropped his wallet and badge?

Ronan said, "Come on out, *Ronan*." The end of the shotgun came around the corner of the tree.

Gio's team was still about thirty minutes out. He slid lower down the hill and set his gun down. He tried to use his watch to call Dylan, but his phone was just out of range or wasn't syncing properly.

He punched the dirt with the side of his fist. Pain shot through his hand and up his arm.

He grunted.

Morgan rested her hand on his back. "Don't hurt yourself. What do we do?"

"Hide. Run. We need to buy time for my team to get here. If Ronan convinces the locals he's me, we're going to have a difficult time proving him wrong. They probably won't have enough information to sort it out."

"Where do we go?"

Gio observed their surroundings. Through the trees, he spotted water. Was that the Pigeon River? It curved around everywhere, but I-40 ran along the other side.

"That way. To the river. We can walk along the side until we find a bridge. Then we find a phone and connect with Dylan."

She nodded.

They descended the ridge. Thankfully, the incline did not remain steep, but the closer to the water they got, the thicker the undergrowth became. They struggled to get through. Gio took his knife out and tried to cut at some of it to help, but he needed a machete, not a pocketknife.

Once through the brush, they found themselves at the top of another steep embankment. There was a bit of shore at the bottom, but it didn't stretch very far. Walking along the river might not work the way he'd hoped. What were they supposed to do now?

As Morgan slid down the embankment, roots and branches bit her legs and arms. Frankly, it almost felt good against the mosquito bites that now littered her ankles.

Gio reached the bottom before her. He turned and caught her by the hips. The river rushed in front of them, winding around the curve. "We'll have to cross it." He took off his backpack and removed a plastic bag holding a few granola bars.

"But how deep is it?" Hadn't she told him she wasn't a strong swimmer? What if she couldn't touch? But what choice did they have?

He put the granola bars in a different pocket of the backpack. "I don't think it's over our heads here. We can walk through it, and if it gets too deep we can wander downstream until we find a shallower path." He put both his and Ronan's guns, along with extra magazines, in the Ziploc bag.

"But Ronan could see us."

"If the cops are with him, he can't shoot at us. Plus, it'd be good if the LEOs spot us; we need the team to know where we are. As long as Ronan stays with them posing as me, we're actually safer, but only if we have distance." He shrugged into his backpack and buckled the chest strap.

"Okay." She took Gio's hand.

He turned to her. "Your hand is shaking."

"I told you before, I can't swim."

"I don't think you'll need to. We'll look for the shallowest crossing." His grip on her hand tightened. "I gotcha."

She gave him a tiny nod. She trusted him.

They stepped into the water, and it wasn't as cold as she'd expected, but it wasn't bathwater either.

Her tennis shoes quickly became soaked and heavy, but the bottom of the river was rocky, so barefoot would have been worse.

Within three feet, the water was above their knees, and the current was strong. She held onto Gio with the tightest grip possible.

He moved forward into deeper water that only went up to his hips, but it felt significantly deeper to her as it hit her mid-torso. Any deeper, and she'd end up getting baptized again.

Hand-in-hand, they continued their trek, the water getting deeper with each step. It was now up to her armpits.

A few more steps, and her foot slipped. She almost went under. She threw her other arm toward Gio. The current pulled her, threatening to take her down.

Gio heaved her up and wrapped his arm around her waist. "Only one baptism is necessary."

She tried to laugh around the hyper breaths of panic. "It's too deep."

"Let's see if down here is shallower. Over there might be a better place to go ashore anyway."

They moved downstream, the water pushing them along. Gio kept looking over his shoulder at where they'd come from.

"Do you see them?"

"No. I'm not sure if that's a good thing or not."

"At least no one is shooting at us."

"I'll give you that one." His eyes sparkled. She wished she could kiss him again like they had in the cabin. It was the sweetest, most tender kiss she had ever experienced. True. Pure. Innocent. It felt more intimate than any of the times she had supposedly made love. It completely redefined her understanding of intimacy and love.

Morgan held onto Gio as they continued through the deep waters.

"Careful here, the rocks are sharp and slick." He helped her across the rough spot.

She followed Gio, trying to trust him even though panic welled up inside her. The water was now up to her shoulders, propelling her forward and making it incredibly difficult to keep her footing.

The rushing water knocked her off her feet. She went under. The current swept her downriver.

Her hand slipped from Gio's.

Chapter Thirty-Eight

JACQ LOOKED OVER AT Dylan's phone, which was mounted to the dashboard of his Charger. Still twenty-five minutes out. Even though Dylan was driving extra fast, it was taking forever. And Gio wasn't answering his phone. What had gone down? Why had he said he was with Morgan? What had happened? Were they all right?

She tried Gio's phone again. No answer.

Setting the phone back in her lap, she prayed for her friends. The last few hours had been more than she could stand. The elation of the hearing going well, followed by the panic of the fire alarm. Then the devastation of losing Morgan.

Even hearing Morgan was with Gio now wasn't enough to pull Jacq out of the turmoil of what had happened. It couldn't possibly be gone until her arms were firmly wrapped around her friend.

Her phone rang. Gio? No. A number she didn't recognize but with an eastern Tennessee area code. She answered, "Special Agent Jacq Sheppard."

"Hi, this is Deputy Quinn. We responded to a call for y'all. Two others arrived before me, I just got here. But there's an agent on scene claiming to be Gio Crespi. Now my memory ain't great, but he doesn't look like the guy I met a while back."

"Can you send me a picture of him?"

"I thought you might ask that so I took one as best I could. It ain't great but, well, you'll see. Sending now."

"Got it." Jacq pulled the phone away from her ear and opened the image file Quinn had sent.

"That is not Gio Crespi. Please take that man into custody. He goes by Ronan, also known as Keenan Robins. He is a murder suspect in multiple homicides, dating back fourteen years."

"Will do. Going to head back over to the others now. How long until you all arrive?"

"Twenty minutes. Be careful. This guy is ruthless."

She hung up, turned to Aliza and Matt in the back seat, and explained what she'd been told, adding, "Dylan, drive faster. Those deputies are going to need backup!"

Morgan reached for Gio, but the river swallowed her.

No! How had she survived Ronan just to die in a stupid river? She thrashed desperately, trying to shove the water aside in a semi-front stroke. She needed air. She needed Gio.

A strong hand gripped her arm. Another one made it beneath her and thrust her above the water. She gasped for air, but she was still moving downstream, Gio along with her.

The water roared in her ears, but Gio's voice made it above the thunder. "Hold onto me."

He pulled her hand toward him, and she managed to clutch the straps of his pack and clenched it tight. He moved her hand to the far strap and flipped her on her back, pulling her close. He angled them toward the shore and the current took them there in quick order.

As they approached the other bank, the river grew shallower and Gio put his feet down. He gripped a low branch hanging over the water.

Gio lifted her to where she could grab the limb.

"Quick, this water probably isn't the safest."

She scurried into the tree. "What do you mean?"

He climbed up next to her. "Dark still waters are ideal for water moccasins."

She pulled her leg higher. "Now you tell me?"

He chuckled. "Let's keep moving. I hope this brush isn't too thick before we get to the highway or at least another road."

He climbed out of the tree and offered her a hand.

She took it, and, once again, they found themselves fighting through trees, shrubs, and vines.

Over. Under. Around.

Gio cut back some of the vines that were impossible to push through. Trees towered above them, hiding the sun, but also trapping the humidity around them like a wet blanket.

Her soggy shoes made each step weigh twice as much as it should.

Gio put his arm out and stopped her. "Good thing our shoes are already wet."

"What now?" She looked around him. Another stream of water. "Probably can jump it."

"Do you think you can?"

She nodded.

He jumped first and caught her when she hit the other side.

One more obstacle overcome. How many more must they face, though? She was tired of fighting. She wanted to go home with Gio and watch a movie. A funny romantic comedy. Nothing emotional or angsty, though. Just funny and carefree. One where the prince rescues the princess, maybe.

She brushed against a branch, and something tickled her skin. The ugliest red and yellow, triangle-shaped spider crawled along her arm. She screamed.

Gio whipped around and whacked the spider off, then tugged her faster through the overgrowth and up the hill.

They burst through the other side and jumped a guardrail. Morgan flailed about, swiping at every inch of her body. She grabbed the bottom of her wet shirt to rip it off.

"Morgan!" Gio snatched her hands, stopping her from removing it.

"Are there bugs all over me?"

"Stop flailing, and I'll check."

He pulled her wet hair together and laid it over her shoulder. He ran his hand along her back and arms. "You're good."

"But maybe one went in my shirt."

"Lift the back of your shirt, and I'll check, but *you* can check the front."

"What fun is that?"

"Morgan!"

"Sorry, new creation in progress."

He laughed so hard his head dropped back. Once he regained his composure, he examined her back. He leaned close to her ear. "You're all clear."

She looked down her shirt then turned to him.

"Am I good?"

"So good!"

She bit her lip, then inspected him for bugs. "Now what?"

Gio took his gun out of the backpack and put his holster on his belt. "We walk. I wish I had my phone, then I could be sure where we're headed. We need to find some civilization, so we can call the team." He turned from side to side, looking down the road.

She did too. Nothing indicated which would be the best way to go.

He pointed to the right of where they'd come out. "Let's head this direction, I guess."

She slid her hand in his and walked beside him.

Gio wiped the sweat from his brow with the collar of his t-shirt, his still rather wet t-shirt. They'd only been walking for about five minutes, but they were both so beat from hiking and climbing, fighting the current, and running for their lives, that trekking anywhere felt impossible. Of course, he had totally missed that this direction would take them uphill, otherwise he would probably have chosen the other way, but the incline had been so gradual, it was hard to notice. Yet it was still painful on already exhausted legs.

Morgan's grip was loose on his hand but constant. As hot and sticky as it was, he wasn't about to let go. He couldn't explain the bond they had, but he looked forward to things settling down and to spending more time with her outside of traumatic experiences. He wanted to explore their connection.

"Gio." Morgan tugged on his hand and pointed ahead of them. "Driveway."

"Good. Let's hope they're friendly."

"Having your badge really would be helpful, but you had to give it to Ronan."

If it hadn't been for the teasing glint in her eye, he'd have been annoyed. "Because I did that on purpose."

She giggled.

After another hundred yards, they came to a driveway, but it didn't lead to a home. A sign stood beside it and read: River Adventures Outpost. Beneath that: Exit Only.

"Hope that only applies to vehicles."

Morgan chuckled. "One way to find out." She tugged him toward the drive, not that he required the tug.

They needed his team to find them before Ronan did. It wasn't lost on Gio that Ronan was out there. Maybe he was just leading the police on a wild chase, but it was also possible he had followed them. Gio hadn't seen any evidence of it, but he didn't want to take any chances.

The engine of a car coming around the curve quickened his pace down the tree-lined driveway. He was now the one pulling Morgan along.

That ever-present sense of urgency ratcheted up a notch or ten.

"Gio?"

"Let's move."

They all but ran down the curved drive that led to a parking area in front of two large buildings. One had a large sign welcoming visitors and indicated that was the place to check-in.

"I bet there's a phone in there."

"And hopefully helpful people."

There were no cars anywhere to be seen. "I'm not sure there is anyone at all."

They walked to the building and up the two steps.

Gio grabbed the handle. Much to his surprise, it turned. "Guess we aren't in the city anymore."

"Apparently." She went through the doorway.

Gio carefully closed it behind them and discovered why it wasn't locked. The deadbolt was broken.

They had entered a large room with a vaulted and rafted ceiling. Rows of benches lined the side as if to instruct large groups. Another circle of benches seemed set up for smaller-group training. Giant photographs of happy people kayaking, canoeing, and white-water rafting decorated the space.

Gio pointed to the door labeled "office." "That's where we'll find a phone."

Morgan sprinted toward it. He followed quickly. That door was also unlocked.

Once they entered, Gio closed the door behind them.

Inside were four desks. One was to the left of the door, another straight ahead, both facing the door for checking groups in. Two more sat along the far wall. A sunbeam came through a single window along the back wall and illuminated the top of a bookshelf beneath it. Best of all, each desk had a phone.

“Excellent.” From the desk at his left, he picked up a receiver but froze, the dial tone echoing in his ear. Gio didn’t know anyone’s phone number by heart. He’d tried to memorize Dylan’s at one point, but he always mixed up the numbers because it was too similar to his ex-girlfriend’s.

Morgan came over and put her hand on his back. “I have Jacqui’s memorized.”

She punched in the number.

It half rang, then went dead.

Chapter Thirty-Nine

Jacq slammed the car door shut and ran up the hill toward the deputies, going straight for the one she recognized. "Deputy Quinn!"

"Agent Sheppard? That was fast."

She nodded. "Tell me you have him in custody."

"I wish I could."

"What do you mean? Where is he?"

"That's just it, we don't know. I came back over after calling y'all. He'd been searching that area with Howard. But I couldn't find either of them at first." Quinn indicated a deputy coming toward them. "Then I found Howard down by the river."

Howard gave them a sloppy salute. "You still convinced the guy I was searching with wasn't the agent?"

Dylan turned his phone toward Howard. "Is this the guy who claimed to be Gio Crespi?"

"Hard to say. His face was swollen like he'd gotten a few punches."

Dylan pulled up another photo. "What about this picture?"

"Oh. That's more likely the guy."

"That's Keenan Robins or Ronan. Where is he?"

Jacq drummed her thumb against her thigh. Where were her friends? That was the more important question.

Howard said, "After leading us away from the river, he wanted to check that way. I think he saw something because he was looking out over the water and all of a sudden took off."

"How long ago?" Jacq asked.

"Ten or fifteen minutes."

She couldn't hold back the burning question any longer. "But what about the other two people? The real Agent Crespi and the woman with him? Have you seen any evidence of them?"

Quinn answered, "Only the SUV y'all had to pass on the way here."

They'd noticed Gio's vehicle, hatch open, littered with birdshot, and tires slashed.

"Hey, I found something," another deputy called from the highest point on the ridge.

They all went to him, but Jacq ran, arriving first.

Gio's phone was on the ground.

She knelt beside it. "That's why he didn't answer."

Dylan squatted next to her. "Guess we can be glad Ronan didn't find it and lead us astray too."

Where were they? Had they gone into the river and been swept downstream? Morgan hadn't known how to swim in college. What were the chances she knew now? Could Gio swim?

Dylan grabbed her shaking hand. "We'll find them." He couldn't hide the worry in his eyes.

"We have to. But where do we even begin to look?"

Gio punched the receiver button with his fingers to reset the call, but the dial tone would not return. What on earth?

Morgan gripped his arm. "What's wrong?"

"The dial tone is gone."

"It was there before you dialed?"

"I'm certain it was."

Her eyes grew wide. He pulled her to his chest. "We'll be fine. Let's check the desks. Maybe there's a cellphone or a radio."

"But why did the phone stop working?"

"I don't know. And I don't want to speculate. Let's just find something." He searched the desk he was at, and Morgan went to the desks along the wall.

Not finding anything there, Gio searched the desk near the door. He found nothing but office supplies, staples, pens, paper clips, and other miscellaneous items.

"Find anything?"

"Nope. I have a bad feeling, though," she said. "Maybe he found us and cut the phone."

That was exactly what Gio was afraid was going on, but he didn't want to vocalize it.

"You were thinking the same thing." She turned and put her hands on her hips.

Through the long glass window in the door, movement caught his attention.

"I'm afraid we're both correct." He skirted the desk, went to the door, and drew his gun.

A figure slid into the shadows near the front of the meeting room.

Ronan.

Gio checked for a lock. There wasn't one. Why was this place so insecure?

He needed a plan. Glancing around the room didn't help much. "Morgan, open the window."

She ran to it.

Gio rounded the desk he'd just searched and shoved it against the door. But it moved way too easily. It wouldn't hold a raccoon back for long, let alone an angry Ronan. He pushed another desk up to it, then turned to Morgan. She'd gotten the window open.

He rushed toward her with quick deliberate steps. He cupped the side of her face and without a second of hesitation met his lips to hers. He kissed her like his life depended on it.

"No matter what happens, I love you. Now, out the window."

"Gio."

"Go."

He set his Glock on the bookshelf beneath the window and laced his fingers together. Morgan used his hands as a step. She straddled the sill before getting both legs outside. He held his hand on the bottom of the window, so she wouldn't hit her head as she ducked beneath it. She jumped to the ground and pivoted back to him.

He handed her the backpack.

The door behind him banged into the desk. He was out of time.

"Run." His heart screamed at him to get out there with her, but that wouldn't save either of them. He needed to buy her more time to get away. He gripped the windowsill.

"But Gio." She grabbed his hand.

He flipped his over and grasped hers. "I love you." He hoped she understood how much he truly did. "Run as fast as you can and don't look back."

The door smacked into the desk over and over.

"Gio!" The panic in her voice matched her eyes.

"Go!"

Her hand slipped from his as she finally turned and ran.

The desks scraped across the floor.

Gio wrapped his hand around his Glock and spun around.

"Drop it." Ronan stood inside the door, pointing a pistol straight at him. How many weapons did this man have?

Gio set the gun back on the bookshelf.

"Move away." Ronan strode around the desks, never taking the gun off Gio. His sneer curled with menacing satisfaction.

Gio stepped toward the center of the room. *God, I'm going to need a miracle to live through this. But if I don't, please get Morgan to safety.*

Gio swallowed. "What do you want, Ronan?"

He stopped out of reach for any defensive maneuvers and swept his gaze over Gio as if deciding on where to shoot.

"I want you dead. Nice attempt at saving her, but you failed. And as a result, Morgan's all mine, and you'll be dead." Ronan dropped his aim and fired.

Chapter Forty

MORGAN RACED AROUND THE side of the building. Maybe Ronan left his keys and she could take his car. But Gio. How could she just leave him?

Pkew.

The sound, while muffled from the walls of the building, knocked her to the ground. Gio! She couldn't run this time.

She got up and bolted to the front of the building but stopped. What could she do? How many times had Ronan overpowered her? But she'd never before wanted to defend the life of the man she loved.

Ronan's gun.

She whipped off the backpack and pulled out the pistol. It wasn't too different from the one Gio had shown her how to use yesterday. Was that really yesterday?

She racked the slide with ease. No safety, so it was ready to go. But her hands shook. Could she do this?

She had to.

God, help.

She pushed the front door open. Banking on Ronan's ears ringing, she ran across the gathering room until she was five feet from the office door.

Ronan stood over Gio. His mouth was running, describing the horrible things he would do, presumably to her.

Gio was on the ground, knee bleeding.

She took a sharp breath.

Gio's gaze came her way. He gave one slow nod.

Ronan's monologue continued.

She'd have to do this right. Quick, sure-footed, no hesitation. As soon as she stepped into that office, Ronan would know she was there, and she'd have less than three seconds to pull the trigger. Gio was safe on the ground, but she'd go in the room along the wall and shoot toward the back wall.

She stepped to the right to see her path in. The gun would have to come closer to her body to go through the door. But they'd practiced that movement.

One more prayer. *God, save us.*

Two deep breaths. She moved.

Three steps to the door. Gun pulled in at the ready.

Four side steps through the doorway and into the room. Pressed the gun out. Aim.

Five shots.

The first one struck Ronan's right shoulder, the second close by it.

Ronan jerked but didn't fall. He raised his gun and shot at her.

She didn't wait for the pain. Before he could fire again, she released three more shots, each hitting Ronan in the center of his chest.

Ronan dropped. His gun fell to the ground beside him.

She ran to Gio.

"Kick ... his gun ... away."

She did so and fell to her knees beside Gio. He pushed up on his elbow. Deep creases in his face declared he was in immense pain.

She set the gun on the ground and stroked his face. "What do I do? You need a doctor."

"See if you can find a phone in Ronan's pockets. He's for sure dead?"

She looked over at his unmoving body. His chest did not rise or fall. "For sure."

"Phone."

She moved to Ronan's body and started her search. "We need to stop that bleeding."

"Find the phone. And then something to hold against my knee—a towel, blanket." He dropped back to the ground.

"Gio?"

"Pain."

The tightness in his voice scared her. "Just stay with me." She found Ronan's phone in his back pocket, where he normally kept it. She retrieved a t-shirt she'd seen in one of the desks.

"Call Jacq first. Then—"

"Okay." She dialed Jacq's number and pressed the shirt against Gio's knee.

He yelped, then fell limp.

"Gio! Stay with me."

She hit send and put it on speaker so she had both hands free for Gio.

"Agent Sheppard."

"Jacqui!"

"Morgan! Dylan, it's Morgan. Are you okay?"

"Yes, but Gio's not. We're across the river from where Ronan took us, at some adventure outpost place. I have to call 911."

"On our way."

They hung up, and Morgan patted Gio's face. "Come on, stay with me."

His eyes flitted open again.

"Oh, thank you, God!" She dialed 911.

"911. Please state the nature of your emergency."

"My ... my ... Gio's been shot!"

"Someone has been shot?"

"Yes, we need an ambulance. He's FBI, and his team is on their way."

The dispatcher instructed her on how to care for Gio.

He was going in and out of consciousness. While there was blood everywhere, he wasn't bleeding profusely. But during his waking moments, his face showed the intensity of his pain.

The sound of footsteps by the front door caught her attention.

Gio looked up at her. "Go get them."

She kissed his forehead and jumped to her feet. The dispatcher talked to Gio to keep him alert. Morgan wiped her face and flew out of the office.

Jacqui, Dylan, and the team.

The women ran to each other, but instead of embracing Morgan, Jacqui's mouth hung open as she stared at Morgan's blood-covered hands. "Are you hurt?"

Had Ronan hit her? She checked. "No, it's Gio's." Her breath got caught on its way in.

Dylan grabbed her shoulder. "Where is he?"

Morgan led the way to Gio as Dylan and Jacqui followed.

Dylan rushed to Gio and pressed the t-shirt to his wounded knee while Morgan lifted his head onto her lap. He smiled at her.

"Stay with me."

He took her hand. "I'm not going anywhere."

"Nowhere but the hospital anyway."

His eyes closed again with a grin on his face.

She stroked his hair. "Open your eyes."

EMTs rushed in and took over, asking her to step away. Dylan motioned for her to join him, as he moved back too. He put his hand on her shoulder. "How are you?"

"My ears are ringing, but I'm fine." She evaluated herself to see if that was indeed true. Her clothes were still quite wet. "Other than being drenched."

The team and a few local deputies joined them. Morgan recounted the first shootout, the trip across the river, and the final showdown.

"So you shot him?" Matt pointed at Ronan.

She nodded. And for the first moment she actually faced what she had done. She'd killed a man. *God forgive me.*

Jacqui stepped into her line of sight. "You did the right thing."

"How can you be sure?"

"Do you have any doubts he was going to kill Gio?"

Morgan shook her head.

"Then you had no alternative. I'm so glad you saved Gio's life." Jacqui took Dylan's arm. "This guy would have been a bear without his best friend."

"Me too." She rotated until she could see Gio again. "Me too."

Almost two hours later, Morgan paced across the waiting room. Almost immediately after they arrived at the trauma center in Knoxville, they'd taken Gio into surgery. They let her ride in the ambulance with him, and as long as he was conscious, he'd held her hand tight.

Now she waited to hear news about him. What if he lost his leg because of the gunshot wound?

Don't jump to the worst-case scenario. He'll be fine.

But would he? She tried to convince herself, but the longer he wasn't with her, the worse her fears became. Being alone in the waiting room didn't help. What if Duke came in here?

She heard footsteps in the hallway and shrank into a corner. She had no out. If Duke walked through that door she'd have nowhere to go, no one to call out to. She was alone.

The footsteps grew closer, and the door opened.

Dylan entered, then Jacq.

All the tension building in her let go, and she rushed to Jacq. The friends embraced. Jacq asked, “Any word on Gio?”

“Not since they took him to surgery.”

“Let’s sit.” Jacq tried to direct Morgan to a chair.

But Morgan stood, unmoving. “I can’t sit. I tried. I can’t shake the memory of the look in Gio’s eyes when he told me to run. He chose to face Ronan, knowing what Ronan would do, but I just ran. Sure I did what he told me to do, but I left him there to face that monster. How could I do that? Gio deserves better.”

Jacq took hold of Morgan’s arms. “But Morgan, you didn’t run away; you did the opposite. You ran back in there and saved Gio’s life.”

“I guess so. But he still got hurt.”

“But he’s alive.”

The door opened again. Morgan jumped.

Jacq threw her a questioning look, but Gio’s doctor entered the room. Morgan released a grateful sigh—she did not want to explain why she’d jumped.

“Mr. Crespi is out of surgery and doing well. We had to repair his patella and the tendons surrounding the knee, but he’ll be fine. Nothing was damaged beyond repair.”

Morgan let out a gust of air. “When can I see him?”

“Once he wakes up. We’ll let you know.”

The doctor left, and Jacq turned to Morgan. “See? He’s fine.”

Morgan nodded.

The rest of the FBI team arrived, and Jacq finally convinced Morgan to sit. Dylan called Gio’s parents to update them. Though Morgan wished they could be with him, she was also secretly relieved they couldn’t. She would like to meet them, but terrified wasn’t a strong enough word to express how she felt about the idea. At least she wouldn’t have to share him yet.

Gio woke, more groggy than he'd ever been in his life. What was going on? He didn't know where he was or why he was in pain, yet he felt numb at the same time. He forced his eyes open. The tiled ceiling looked like that of a hospital. The beeping machines confirmed that assessment.

His leg was the source of pain, but meds were keeping it at bay. His leg was bandaged and stabilized.

It all came back. Ronan. Morgan.

Was she all right?

He took in the curtained-off cubby of a recovery room.

His gaze drifted to the end of the bed. To the right of his feet, Morgan had pulled a chair over and was curled up half in the chair, half on the bed, her head resting on her arms.

If only he could reach her and stroke her hair, but she was too far away. She'd saved his life, and he would never be able to thank her enough.

She stirred and turned her head toward him. Her eyes opened and a grin lifted her lips. "Gio." Her voice was soft and gentle.

"Hey."

She sat up.

The hospital bed was fairly wide, so he shifted himself to the left as much as possible, which wasn't much. He patted the bed. There was barely enough space for her between him and the siderail.

"Are you sure? I don't want to hurt you."

"I think it hurts more having you so far away."

She bit her lip and slid in next him. She tucked herself under his arm and laid her head on his chest.

He held her tight and stroked her face, trying not to whack her with his IV tubes. "I'm sorry you had to shoot him."

"I wish I hadn't left you in there. I'm so sorry."

"Oh, Morgan. I was ready to die to protect you."

"Why would you do that? I don't deserve it."

"Christ thought you did."

She let out a humph. "I guess so. But why, Gio?"

"Why did I? Because I love you. Maybe it's too soon to say that, but it's true. It's fine if you don't feel the same way. And I'm sorry if it makes you uncomfortable."

She pushed herself up on her elbow. "You silly man." She sighed. "I'm still trying to sort out what love actually is. And while I've had plenty of men tell me they love me, you're the first one I believe. I know you love me without you even having to say the words. You've proven it over and over again, and not just when you were willing to give up your life for me, but in all the little things too. Even in the simple ways you hold me. There's a sense of protection and comfort, never possession or control. And above all, you have shown me what God's love looks like. And I can't thank you enough for being a representation of Christ to me."

"Do you understand why Christ died for you?"

"I do, as much as my feeble mind can. I'm made in His image, and for whatever reason He thought I was worth spending eternity with."

He cupped the side of her face.

"And Gio ..."

"Yes?" His breath caught as desire rose in his heart.

"I love you too." She leaned close and met his lips with hers.

The beeping machine faded away. Their lips gently moved together. It was the sweetest, most tender kiss he could imagine. But passion swelled up within him. He restrained himself, yet their kiss deepened.

She released his lips and touched his forehead with hers.

They both breathed heavily, and she lay back down at his side.

No more words were needed.

They both dozed off.

A little while later a nurse came in and checked on him. She kept her voice low while she took his vitals and peeked at his stitches since Morgan still slept against his chest. "A couple of people are waiting to see you. Should I let them in?"

"Only if it's Dylan and Jacq."

"I'll make sure." The nurse left.

Gio kissed Morgan's head. "Wake up, sleepyhead. We have company coming."

She stirred. "Company? Tell them to go away. I don't want to share you."

He laughed. "It's only Dylan and Jacq. I told the nurse to turn everyone else away."

"I guess that's acceptable." She snuggled into him, giving the clear indication she wasn't going to move for the two of them.

He chuckled and tightened his arm around her.

Two minutes later, Dylan and Jacq appeared around the curtain. Dylan said, "You know Matt's a little sore you only let the two of us in?"

"He'll get over it."

Dylan laughed.

Morgan sat up and gave Jacq a long hug.

Gio found the button and raised the bed to a more seated position. The nurse came back and handed Gio a Sprite in a Styrofoam cup with a straw and gave him instructions to drink up.

Dylan leaned against the wall and folded his arms. "I heard from the team at Ronan's property. They found the spot where they most likely think Jamie DeRozan was buried and also found another body."

"Aster." Morgan's voice was soft. She explained what Ronan had said about Aster, Rose, and Celeste, but then quickly turned the subject to her desire to watch a movie marathon, now that the crazy was over.

The four of them continued to chat while Gio discovered if he could keep things down or not. In record time, the nurse told him he was being discharged. Gone were the days when the hospital kept someone after surgery.

Morgan's countenance shifted from happy to reticent.

Gio stroked her back. "What's wrong?"

"Now what? I can't just live off of you guys. What do I do? Where do I go?" She looked at Jacq. "It was great to dream about the future and helping with the rescue home, but it's not ready. I'm not ready."

Gio's soul ached. He wished he could take her home and give her everything she needed, but it wasn't time yet.

Jacq took Morgan's shoulders. "One step at a time. First, we get Gio settled at home. Stick with me, and we will figure out all the details, even if it is day-by-day at this point. But we"—she circled her finger around from herself to Gio and Dylan—"are your home, your family. You can live with me rent-free, whether at my apartment or the house. But I don't even know all those details for my own life yet, so we'll figure it out together."

Morgan nodded and reached for Gio's hand. "And you'll be around."

"I'm not going anywhere. Literally, I'm not sure I'm going to be doing much moving at all anytime soon."

They all laughed.

Gio hoped and prayed Morgan would find her place in the regular world and that she would depend on Christ above all in the process, no matter how long it took.

Morgan poured a cup of coffee in Gio's kitchen. After they'd gotten him settled last night, she'd gone home with Jacqui, and Dylan had stayed with Gio. She and Dylan had switched places this morning as Jacq and Dylan had to go to work. Morgan hadn't argued at all at the idea of taking care of Gio today.

It was difficult to believe it had only been twenty-four hours since she'd appeared in court. And only eighteen hours since she'd pulled the trigger and killed Ronan. Her sleep had been haunted with dreams of him. But he really was gone.

Morgan had also talked to Lily this morning. She was indeed pregnant and thanked Morgan for saving her and the baby. God deserved all the glory for their freedom. Morgan couldn't have done anything without Jesus giving her strength.

She turned and leaned back against the counter. When she'd checked on Gio right after Dylan and Jacqui left, he was still sleeping. While she wanted to let him sleep as long as he needed, it was a little too quiet for comfort.

A clatter in the hallway shattered that quiet.

She pushed off the counter and peeked down the hall. Gio was headed her way on his crutches.

"What are you doing? Get back in bed." She set her coffee down and pointed to the back of the apartment.

He stopped. "I can't stay cooped up in there. I'll go freedom-craving mad."

She laughed. "I'll come back there with you."

"That won't help prevent the going mad; it would only accelerate it. I say we binge-watch all your favorite movies."

"I can't argue with that."

"But first I have something for you." He pointed to the dining room.

Her heart tensed. "Gio, I don't like gifts."

Leaning heavy on his crutches, he gripped her arm. "I think this one will be different enough. Trust me?"

"You know I do." She went with him to the table.

He grabbed a box wrapped in brown paper off the bookshelf and handed it to her.

Her name was written on the paper in his simple lettering. Carefully, she tore the paper away. A study Bible. "Oh, Gio."

"Take it out."

She set the box on the table and lifted the lid to reveal a black leather-bound book. Gold letters were embossed in the corner. *Morgan Zalman.*

"Gio! Thank you." She drew the book out of the box and held it to her chest. Stepping close to him, she kissed his cheek. "This is perfect."

Despite the joy that made his eyes beam, pain streaked his expression.

"To the couch."

Morgan helped him settle into a comfortable position by piling pillows on the coffee table for his leg. She brought in a tray with coffee and breakfast, they settled close, and started the original Star Wars trilogy.

They were halfway through *The Empire Strikes Back* when Dylan and Jacqui arrived.

Dylan lifted a bag from a sandwich shop. "Are y'all hungry yet?"

Gio said, "Yes, I'm starving."

Morgan put her hand to her chest in exaggerated shock. "What, my breakfast wasn't enough for you?"

"It was lovely, but it was one and a half movies ago."

They all chuckled, and Dylan passed out sandwiches and individual bags of chips.

Morgan devoured hers, dabbing the corners of her mouth with a napkin.

Gio's eyebrows rose.

She balled up the napkin. "What? I was hungry."

He handed her his bag of chips. "Then eat my chips too. I'm not near as hungry as I thought I'd be."

She tilted her head and narrowed her gaze. "Really?"

"Yeah, probably the pain meds. They're messing with my stomach."

“Not that. That doesn’t surprise me.” She shook her head. “It’s just … I’m so used to being told to stop eating. I can’t remember the last time I was encouraged to eat *more*. It’s another one of those random things I won’t even realize I need to work through until it pops up.”

“Take them as they come. One thing at a time. But for now, eat up.” Gio winked at her.

She thought she’d melt. She pulled apart the top of the bag and popped another chip in her mouth, then turned to Jacqui. “Now when is this wedding going to happen?”

Chapter Forty-One

One Month Later – Mid-August

Morgan jogged across the church's fellowship hall in her teal flats to hug another guest goodbye. Jacqui's bridal shower had gone off without a hitch. It had been perfect in every way, exactly as Morgan and Aliza had planned. Dylan's mom, sister, and sister-in-law had all been great help in pulling it off in such a short amount of time.

Soon only Jacqui's family and closest friends remained. Dylan, Chad, their dad, Gabe, and Gio then joined them in the fellowship hall, but Morgan's eyes locked on Gio. She wanted to rush over and envelope him in a big bear hug, but he was still using a single crutch to get around, and she didn't want to knock him over.

Gabe's mom came up beside Morgan, pulling her attention away from Gio. "How are you doing? And I mean beyond the surface level. I'm sure planning the shower was a nice distraction."

Morgan gave Bonnie a smile. The older woman had been intentional at reaching out to her and being available, should she need anything.

"I'm doing well, but you're right, planning the shower has been good. Although I don't know if I'd call it a distraction. My counselor has encouraged me to find things to get involved in as I've been working through the last thirteen years of craziness. I can only dwell on the past for so long. This was just one way I can move forward with life in the real world."

"I'm glad to hear it, and you all did a beautiful job with the shower."

"I can't wait to plan Aliza's with Jacqui and Chloe," Morgan said.

Bonnie squeezed her arm. "It will be great."

"Are you up to baking your deliciousnesses for her shower too?"

"Of course! I'm so excited to gain another daughter." Bonnie's voice softened as her tone grew more serious. "Have you seen your brother yet?"

Morgan shook her head. "Not yet, but I talked to him on the phone again a couple of nights ago. It was good, and he's really looking forward to introducing me to his family, but I'm still nervous."

Bonnie put her hand on Morgan's shoulder. "He's family. And if he loves you half as much as we do, you'll be just fine."

"It's hard to get past what my traffickers drilled into my head for so long. How many times did I hear 'your family doesn't want you'? Way too many. But I'm working through it."

"I'm so proud of you. Keep at it. God's truth can always overcome the lies of the enemy."

"Thank you." Morgan embraced her.

"Anytime. Now go get that gentleman of yours."

Heat rushed to Morgan's cheeks. Bonnie snickered and left. Morgan strolled over to Gio and slipped under his free arm. "Do you need to sit?"

He kissed her temple. "I'm fine."

"Physical therapy went all right?"

"Kicked my butt again. I'm not making the progress we expected. I'm frustrated."

"You got this." Her heart hurt for him. Being on desk-duty was a slow death for him, but he was being pulled in to do more sketches throughout the bureau, and he enjoyed that. Not being able to lose the crutch, though, was an automatic desk assignment.

"With you by my side, I'll manage." He winked at her.

She squeezed his middle, and they both directed their attention to their friends.

Aliza's hands were on her hips. "I still don't think it's fair. Gabe and I have been dating longer, been engaged longer, but here we still have to wait another four and a half months to get married."

Jacq chuckled. "Sorry, but you picked the date. Plus I'm going to play the I'm-older and the this-is-my-second-wedding cards."

The entire group laughed.

Morgan bit her tongue. All she wanted to say was that she hoped she and Gio didn't have to wait that long either. But she kept her mouth shut. For now.

Almost a month later – early September

Gio hobbled around the corner from the kitchen of the mountain house, chasing Harper while leaning on his cane. This game was not as easy as it used to be. He lost her around the far corner. A flash of a future day played in his mind. One day he'd be chasing oodles of little Crespis around.

"Come on, Gio." Morgan's voice danced with laughter from where she sat on the couch. "You're gonna let a three-year-old beat you?"

He stopped and pointed the cane at her. "Watch it. Or I'll get you next."

"I dare you."

Harper slammed into his good leg.

He got the cane to the floor just before his knee gave out.

"Gotcha, Uncwa Gio!" She tried to tickle him.

"Oh no. You got me." He stabilized himself and scooped her up. He crossed the room, dropped onto the couch beside Morgan, and tickled Harper.

She squirmed and ran off.

Gio leaned back. "Phew. That kid wears me out." He glanced at Morgan. She stared off into the distance.

He took her hand. "You all right?"

"Sure. Let's wrap the gift before Jacqui and Dylan get back."

"Let's do it." He pushed himself off the couch and retrieved the wedding gift from where he'd left it by the door. They met back in the dining room.

Morgan pulled the wrapping paper out of the bag and laid it out on the table. "All right, I have no idea how to do this. It's been too long."

He showed her what he knew about wrapping, and they figured it out together. He handed the ribbon from the bag to Morgan. "I hope you can figure out how to do this part because ..."

She stared at the ribbon, hand quivering.

"What's wrong?"

"Nothing." She bolted.

Harper bounded into the dining room.

He froze. Something was definitely wrong with Morgan. And when something hit her like that, she needed him almost immediately, even if she acted like she didn't want him there. Maybe especially if she acted that way. But Harper needed attention too, and he didn't know how intense this processing moment would be.

"Hey, Harps. Remember that show I said we could watch later? It's later now."

"Yay!" She clapped and jumped up and down.

He got his computer and set her up in Jacq's room.

"Now, remember don't touch anything else. If you need to pause it to go potty push this long button here. Got it?"

Harper nodded enthusiastically.

He patted her head and returned to the living room, where Morgan was curled up on the couch running the ribbon between her fingers. Tears streamed down her cheeks, accompanied by a tiny sob every once in a while.

He sat down near her. "Talk to me."

She licked her lips and continued to play with the ribbon. "Do you know what the tradition is with ribbons at a wedding shower?"

"Should I?"

She shrugged. "Well, the deal is, for every ribbon the bride breaks as she's opening her gifts, that's supposed to be how many children she'll have."

He smiled, but he wasn't sure what the correct response would be right now, so he waited.

"Dylan's mom kept egging Jacqui on to break them all." She let out a rueful snort.

"How many did Jacq break?"

"Four."

He wanted to ask her if she planned to break eight, because he'd love a big family, but this ribbon had made her cry. He may not know the right response, but he definitely knew the wrong one.

"I see you with Harper, and I know you'll make such a great dad."

Where was this going?

"So Gio, it kills me to say this to you ..." She sniffed and curled the ribbon around her finger, which immediately started to turn blue.

He tugged the ribbon from her hand.

"I don't know"—a hiccup stole her breath—"I don't know if I can ever have kids."

Her words hit him like a cinderblock thrown at his chest. He tried to breathe, but it didn't seem possible.

"I know you want kids, so I don't know if I can keep on pretending our future could be everything you dream it could be. Maybe a future isn't possible for us."

He wrestled the cinderblock from his chest. "That's not how this works."

"But Gio—"

He touched his finger to her lips. "I don't love my dreams of the future more than I love you." He stroked her hair away from her face. "Why do you believe you can't have children?"

She matched his closeness, leaning her head into his hand. "Of all the times I could have gotten pregnant, I only have once."

A baby? But what happened? He kept his questions to himself.

"My pimp forced me to have an abortion, but it wasn't the quick, easy procedure it was supposed to be. I don't really remember the details, but something didn't go right. And my cycles have never been right since."

He pulled her to his chest. They sat there and quietly grieved together. The visions he'd had of their future faded like a cloud in a strong wind.

Unfortunately, abortion was part of the trafficking life, so he wasn't surprised about that. He *was* surprised to hear she'd only had one. But it didn't make his heart break any less for her.

God, why? I don't want to question You; I just want to understand. Why is it so hard to face the idea of not having children when I was settled on it while I was single? Help us to trust You. What is the truth about this aspect of our lives?

Was her intuition right about this? They would have to get a doctor's input, but they did have to face the possibility God might have different plans. Still, it hurt.

Eventually, she pushed off of him. "I'm so sorry, Gio." She wiped a tear from his face.

"You have nothing to apologize for. God knew this when He brought us together. Nothing surprises Him. We have to trust the Lord, and this is another opportunity for us to grow in Him."

"How are you so wise?"

"I don't know that I'd go that far, but so many times in my life things have felt out of control, yet I know He's got it. When I remember that, I can rest in His will, even if I don't understand."

"But you've always wanted kids. If you find a woman without a past like mine, you can have the big family you dream of."

"If that was the most important thing to me, I would have found someone else along the way. But God led me to you, and we will face any challenge together."

"Haven't we already experienced enough? I'm tired of fighting." She laid her head back on his shoulder.

"I know. Don't worry about the baby issue now. That's not a worry for today. We'll face it in time, and we'll do so with God. And if He says *no*, we'll walk in His will, doing whatever other ministry He has for us."

"Can we go to a city other than Knoxville to find a doctor?"

"Of course, but why?"

"I don't want to run into ..."

He sat up a little bit, so she did too. "Someone in particular?"

"Yes and no. I guess there's always a chance I'll run into a trick in the real world. But there was this one guy. We called him Duke; I don't know his real name. Remember that kiss I stole?" A smile played with her lips.

"I'll never forget it. It was that doctor?"

She nodded. "He's the guy who got me clean. Ronan was terrified of him. I don't know why, but it went further than the fact that he was loaded, and Ronan wanted his money."

Morgan told Gio about Ronan and Duke's deal with her. Gio wished she knew who this Duke was so he could take him down. Even if she did know, though, there wasn't much he could do. For now, he would focus on protecting the woman he loved. And if that meant driving to Asheville for a doctor, he'd do it in a heartbeat.

Whatever came in the future, God would hold them and see them through. Gio drew Morgan closer with protective arms. *Help me keep her safe, Lord.*

Chapter Forty-Two

The second Saturday in September had arrived, and Gio, leaning heavily on his cane, followed Dylan into the church sanctuary from a side door. Jacq had suggested a little ceremony up on the mountain, but Dylan had insisted on a church wedding. He didn't want to cause any ripples in his family, after all. Jacq had laughed but quickly agreed to a church wedding, at the traditional church Dylan's parents attended. It was the perfect location. The afternoon sun streamed through the stained-glass windows, causing rainbows to dance across the wooden pews.

Chad came in behind them, and the three took their places at the front of the church. The music changed, and it was time for the bridesmaids to enter. Aliza strolled down the aisle first.

Gio kept his gaze trained on the doorway, though, waiting for the next one. When Aliza was about halfway up the aisle, Morgan appeared. She was stunning in a deep burgundy dress that flowed to the floor.

Her eyes met his, and her smile grew. She glided down the aisle, her gaze fixed on him. When she got to the front, she hesitated before going to her spot opposite him.

His knee buckled, but the cane kept him upright.

Chad leaned over. "You good?"

He gave a quick nod. How he wished he'd been able to ditch the cane, but his knee still wasn't reliable. His physical therapist said he was getting close, but he'd been saying that for weeks with little improvement.

Harper bounded down the aisle, tossing flower petals in every direction. A wave of giggles rippled through the congregates. That kid was being her usual hilarious self. Gio suppressed a sigh.

It had only been two nights ago when Morgan shared that she didn't think she could have kids. If children were in their future, God would handle it, like He always did. They would just have to trust Him.

And Gio trusted God, but it didn't make his heartache disappear. His heart was for Morgan, with or without a future of children.

Harper reached the front of the aisle with an empty basket and gave Dylan a gigantic hug. He scooped her up.

The pianist changed the music once again. But instead of the wedding march it was an instrumental version of one of Jacq's favorite country love songs. Apparently, the woman could only do so much traditional before her rebellious side had to sneak something else in.

The doors opened and Jacq appeared, but Gio kept his eyes on Dylan instead. His best friend was beaming.

From Dylan's arms, Harper declared in a rather loud voice, "Look! Mommy's so pretty!"

Dylan said, "Yes, she is."

Gio caught Morgan's gaze. They exchanged a smile. He didn't know when, but one of these days this would be them.

The ceremony proceeded, and Dylan and Jacq exchanged their vows. Dylan even said a short promise specifically to Harper, who stood beside her mom and soon-to-be dad. The adoption paperwork was already in process.

Perhaps Morgan would be open to adoption if they truly couldn't have biological children. One day he'd ask, but that question could wait a while.

Before he knew it, Dylan dipped Jacq back in a cheer-inducing kiss.

The pastor presented them. "It is my privilege to introduce you to Mr. and Mrs. Dylan Harris."

The guests all clapped. Gio, standing primarily on his right leg, risked leaning his cane against himself long enough to join in.

Once Dylan and Jacq were back down the aisle, Gio met Morgan at the center and offered her his elbow. She wrapped her hand around his arm and leaned close. "That was beautiful."

Her closeness overwhelmed his senses. Words would not come to his now-dry mouth. It would seem all the moisture had moved to the palms of his hands.

Without a doubt, they'd be walking down an aisle much like this again soon. He only needed to ask her. But when? He didn't have a ring yet, though that wouldn't matter to her. She'd already told him she didn't like special gifts because they made her feel as if she was being manipulated. No, he didn't need to surprise her with a ring, just the question. They could pick out a ring together if she wanted.

She squeezed his arm. "You okay?" she asked without hardly moving her lips.

He nodded and tossed a wink her way.

A few more steps down the aisle, and his knee gave out.

Morgan's hand tightened around his arm. "I see I make you weak in the knees."

The only thing that held his laugh back from roaring through the church was the embarrassment of nearly falling. Yep, this woman was made for him, and he'd have to work up the nerve to ask her to be his wife.

They joined Jacq and Dylan in the receiving line. Morgan tugged on his sleeve. He smiled at her.

"What are you thinking about?"

"Wouldn't you like to know." He bared his teeth in a cheesy grin.

"That is why I asked."

He took a deep breath and let it out slowly, forcing his heart to slow down. "Will you save me a dance tonight?"

She opened her mouth, no doubt a smart remark coming his way, but he held up his finger. She clamped her mouth shut with a pout.

He leaned over and kissed her temple. "I promise you won't regret it."

Gio leaned back in his chair at the long wedding-party table, waiting as Dylan and Jacq had their first dance. The reception location was perfect. Twinkle lights hung from the ceiling with the glow of the setting sun still shining through the sides of the pavilion, which was tucked at the bottom of the mountain. Just as Jacq had declared, the view of the mountains was marvelous.

Gio glanced over at Morgan, three chairs away. Harper sat on her lap, and they were both singing and swaying to the music. His heart swelled to eleven.

Jacq and Dylan pulled others out to the floor. Harper bounded off Morgan's lap and ran to Dylan's waiting arms.

Carefully, Gio stood with his cane. He walked over to Morgan and offered his hand. "Would you like to dance?"

"With you?" A sly smile lit her face.

"I wouldn't want you dancing with anyone else."

Her smile faded. She tilted her head and pressed her lips together.

What had he said wrong? "What is it?" He grabbed Jacq's chair and pulled it up next to Morgan.

She took his offered hand, and her smile returned. "It's another one of those moments where my worlds collide, and truth needs a second to win. How is it possible that someone actually wants me all for himself? Not to share, or pass around, or earn a buck off of. You'd actually be jealous of my affection, in a good way. This is going to sound strange, but that is the most loving thing I can think of right now. You want me to dance with *you* and no one else. And I don't want you to dance with anyone else either. I mean, I *might* let Harper steal you for a hot minute, but that's it."

He couldn't help but laugh, then drew her hands to his lips. "I love it when you have these breakthroughs."

"Especially when they work to your advantage."

He shook his head and laughed more. "Of course."

Her giggle overtook her whole body. "Then let's dance, Mr. Crespi. As long as you think you can with that gimp."

"No holds barred. Good grief, girl. Good thing I love you."

"You wouldn't have me any other way."

"True."

She stood and drew him to his feet. He cupped the side of her face and their lips met. He ended the kiss before unbridled passion could take hold. Yep, marriage would have to happen sooner rather than later.

She stepped away and seemed to try to pull in a deep breath, but it got caught. He wasn't the only one struck with temptation, was he?

They strolled to the dance floor hand-in-hand.

With the cane in his left hand, he placed the other on her hip, and she laced her fingers behind his neck. They swayed to the music, completely disregarding the fast song.

His nerves danced in sync with the beat. He'd wait for just the right moment to pop his question.

During the next song, his knee gave out.

He grunted. He hated it. He wanted to enjoy this moment with Morgan, not get knocked on his backside because of the man who had abused the love of his life. Would they never be free of Ronan's grasp, even though he was long dead and buried?

Morgan asked, "Should we sit?"

"No, I'm fine."

"Here. You've held me up enough. It's my turn." She slid her arm under his left. "Just lean on me."

He held her close and kissed her head. "You're too good to me."

She shrugged and laid her head on his chest. She fit so perfectly against him.

After another song, he'd almost worked his courage up to ask her, but she leaned back to see his face.

"Gio." She bit her lip. "We should get married."

She was thinking the same thing he was. "Are you sure you're ready?"

"I am. I mean, I do."

He chuckled. "I'd get down on one knee, but I'm not sure I could get back up."

She dropped her head back and laughed. Once she gained her composure, she said, "You know those formalities aren't necessary with me."

"I know. And I don't have a ring, but we can get that together if you'd like one. You are the love of my life. God brought you to me in a dream, and I never imagined what falling in love with you would be like. Morgan, you stole my heart."

"Nope. I stole your car, your money, your phone, and a kiss, but not your heart. You freely offered that. And I offer you mine in return. I hope I can love you the way you deserve. I know I don't deserve you, but somehow, by the grace of God, you're willing to love me. Thank you."

He swiped a tear from beneath her eye. "Exactly. God's grace. You deserve way more than the piddly human love I can show you. But I promise to do my best, to love you as Christ loves the Church. Morgan, will you marry me? Would you make me the happiest man on the planet by being my wife?"

"Absolutely!"

He kissed her. The din of the wedding reception swirling around them faded into the distance. It was just the two of them. The hope of a bright future ahead. No matter what came their way, they'd have each other. And God's hand, which had protected them through all they'd faced, would continue to hold them.

Gio leaned his forehead against hers. "I love you."

"I know."

He sighed.

"I love you too." She wrapped her arms tightly around his middle. "Is this for real? Are you really going to love me forever?"

"Yes, forever and always. That's my promise to you. But no more running off on me."

"My days of running are long gone. You couldn't get rid of me now if you tried."

They both laughed.

He toyed with a ringlet that had fallen from her pulled-up hair. "Good. What God brings together, let no man separate, and I truly believe He has brought us together."

Thank You, Lord. Gio had finally found what he didn't even know he was looking for and could hardly wait to experience the blessing of a new life with Morgan as his wife.

Keep in Touch

Be sure to sign up for Liz's newsletter. By signing up you will have a short story delivered to your inbox. You'll also be able to stay up to date on release dates and sales!

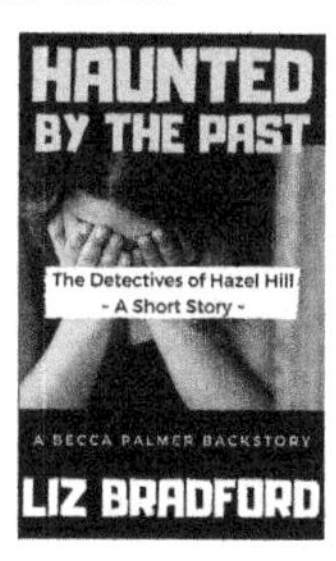

Sign Up for Liz's mailing list by going to:

http://eepurl.com/dGuIjr

You can also find Liz at:

www.facebook.com/lizbradfordwrites

www.pinterest.com/lizbradfordwrites

www.goodreads.com/author/show/18532678.Liz_Bradford

Also By Liz Bradford

The Detectives of Hazel Hill

A FRIGHTFUL NOEL - Prequel - Christmas Novella
NOT ALONE - Book One
PURSUED - Book Two
ON YOUR KNEES- Book Three
A SHOT AT REDEMPTION - Book Four
GIANTS FALL - Book Five
Book Six is in the works

Knoxville FBI
REVENGE IGNITED - Prequel - Christmas Novella
INTO THE FLAMES - Book One
UNDER FIRE - Book Two
SMOKY ESCAPE - Book Three
OUT OF THE ASHES - Book Four - Release to be determined

Tracking Danger – A Search and Rescue Series

TOO LATE - A Novella - Book One - Paperback available now, ebook coming soon
(previously in the Winter Deceptions Collection)
SWEPT AWAY - Book Two - Coming Soon in the Small Town Danger Collection

Acknowledgments

First and foremost, I must thank my Lord and Savior, Jesus! Thank You for the gift of story and allowing me to pen words. I hope and pray that You will use them to touch hearts and draw readers closer to You!

Thank you, Ken for being so supportive as I pursue my dreams and make the voices in my head earn their keep.

Thank you to my daughters for doing your school work without complaint eventually and helping me by not fighting not killing each other while I'm working.

Thank you, Mom for always being just a text or phone call away when I get stuck on a medical issue, a word, or whatnot.

Thank you to my partners in crime and dearest friends, Crystal Caudill, Angela Carlisle, and Voni Harris for your accountability, wording advice, and general mayhem fun.

An extra thank you to Crystal Caudill, you really do deserve at least a tiny byline on this book. How did I ever write books before we were friends?!

Thank you to my new friends on Discord! May your sprints always be productive and GIF filled.

Thank you, Teresa for helping me make my story all that it could be!

Thank you, Sharyn for catching my wording errors (and my readers thank you for your ruthless cutting of the word that)!

Thank you, Alyssa for yet another amazingly beautiful cover!

Thank you, ACFW-Louisville Chapter for being my monthly dose of encouragement and writerly friendship.

About the Author

Liz didn't always know she a writer, but she was. Before she even knew it, God was plotting out this path for her. From her earliest days, stories were a natural part of her imagination. In high school, she toyed around with writing, but it was nothing more than a secret hobby. But one day, when her middle daughter was a little over a year old, a story idea crept in her mind and wouldn't leave her alone. So, she started writing. She would stay up late after everyone else was in bed and frantically write the words that brought her characters to life.

That first novel lives buried deep in her hard drive, and maybe one day it will see the light of day, but that would take a LOT of editing. About the time she couldn't figure out where that first book would end, another idea persisted in her mind. That was Becca and Jared's story, book one in *The Detectives of Hazel Hill* series. Before she knew it, what started as a single novel turned into a trilogy... but wait, there's more. In that series, she now has six stories published (including the prequel novella) and many more percolating. She also has several more ideas for the characters of Hazel Hill, North Carolina. The *Knoxville FBI* series has one more story to go before it is complete. Her *Tracking Danger* series will have two books out later in Spirng 2023. Liz also has numerous other series forming in her mind!

Liz is a member of Faith, Hope, & Love Christian Writers, American Christian Fiction Writers, and ACFW Louisville Chapter. Her heart longs to live in North Carolina (where she was born) or Tennessee and that is why she set her stories there. But, for now, she and her husband live in Southern Indiana where she homeschools their three daughters.

Made in the USA
Middletown, DE
02 May 2023